Already GONE

JOE ROTH

SECOND EDITION 2019

ISBN: 978-0-692-14555-5
Category: FICTION / Coming of Age
Library of Congress Cataloging-in-Publication Data

Written by: Joe Roth | JoeRoth@landofaz.com

Cover Design & Text Formatting by: Eli Blyden Sr.
Formatting Assistant: Jahshua Blyden
www.CrunchTimeGraphics.com

Printed in the USA by:
A&A Printing | www.PrintShopCentral.com

For my best friend...

Already GONE

PROLOGUE

I'd be lying if I told you that I was okay with it—the way it went down and all.

I mean, who would've been? Going from being the windshield to the bug at ninety miles an hour or more. But things happen. They always have.

There are fish that swim upstream, and I never much figured it to be because they liked the challenge. It's survival of the species and nothing more.

You see, things change. It's what they do. And I know that sometimes it takes a good fall for a guy to figure out where he really stands. That is, if he can pull himself up from it.

I oughta know. I've been standing here for quite a while now. Standing here staring at the same old mug in the mirror.

And you wanna know what I figured out after all this time? Yeah, I bet you do. Heck, maybe you don't, I don't know. It doesn't much matter to me either way.

Already
GONE

CHAPTER 1

*W*hat the hell? *Jesus Christ!* It must be eight a.m., I figured.
Where's that goddamn phone? Sure enough. Bastards.

"Hello. Yeah, this is Jack. Last four are 8599. Yeah, yeah. I know the drill. Listen, I hate to cut you off partner. . . . Of course, I know why you're calling, and I'm gonna tell you exactly what I've been telling you guys over there for the past six months. I closed the brokerage over a year and a half ago, and I haven't seen a paycheck since. If you read the notes, you'll see all of that. I was living on savings until it ran out. . . ."

"Hey, like I said, if you'll look at the notes, they'll answer all of that for you, Pal. . . . No. That ran out too. Yeah, yeah. Nope. Nothing's changed. Listen buddy, I know you're just doing your job and all. . . ."

"No, no. . . . I feel bad that you guys have to keep calling *me*. I never wanted to be in this spot. If you look at the ledger, you'll see I paid you guys like clockwork for what, eight or nine years before this whole mess? . . ."

"It's gotta sell soon. It's priced about as low as you guys would even settle for just to let me the heck out of this thing. You'll be straightened out then I'm sure. . . ."

"Hell, I'm the one that should be sorry. Call whenever you want. I'm not dodging you guys. . . . Yeah. Thanks, pal. I need all the luck I can get."

Well, that's the way most of my days have started for the past year or so. Still, I've gotta admit that I'm not really all that angry about it, even if I was for a little while there.

Today that first phone call seemed like it rolled in just a little too early, though. You see, I was up half the night with that goddamn storm. It was a real doozy. Lightning was bouncing off the Hancock Tower and the waves were splashing up onto the northbound lanes of Lake Shore Drive.

But the lake sure seems calm today. Just like glass. It looks like a perfect morning in the old Windy City.

I used to always hate it when that idiot Simon would say, *"It's always calmest before the storm."* I mean, he used to say it about almost anything, even when it didn't make an ounce of sense.

Like that time when my car got towed because I parked it in Cromwell's stall on accident. I was really pissed off too because Cromwell knew good and well that silver 911 was my car. He sure as heck knew that I had been parking in that same damn row next to him forever. Then one night he comes home all sauced up, sees my car in his space, and just has it towed? What a prick.

I was already fuming about having to spend the first two hours of my day getting my car out of hock, only to have that idiot Simon sitting with me on lower Wacker Drive sharing his theories about the nature of the universe and all. With all of his infinite wisdom, he explained to me how it's always calmest before the storm. Frickin idiot.

So, what even made me bring that up? Oh yeah. What a peaceful morning it is after that thunder and lightning show we had last night.

It's kinda funny that nobody ever says *It's always stormiest before the calm.* Dang that's good. Maybe I'll start saying it.

Maybe nobody says it because it isn't true. I mean, usually the things that people say have some truthfulness behind them, I figure. Maybe not. Maybe they just like how the words sound, like me. Hell, if I know.

That *It's-always-darkest-before-dawn* thing—I don't know how true that one is. *The squeaky wheel getting the grease?* Yeah, that's usually pretty damned tried and true. Cromwell ought to know that one for sure.

I guess that they really don't matter all that much anyway, all the silly things that people say about how the world goes 'round. At the end of the day, it was one heck of a ride, and I don't regret a thing about it.

I can't think of much that I would've done differently, other than maybe getting out of it a year or two earlier. But that's the deal with those kinda things.

I never was much good at spotting stuff like that anyways. If I were, I wouldn't be here in the first place.

The truth is that you never know when a streak is gonna end. And if you bail too soon, you might very well be kicking yourself in the ass. I happen to be quite an expert on getting kicked in the ass these days.

Funny thing about it is that you've got a lot of meat back there—on your ass, I mean. Everyone does. And I learned that it doesn't hurt all that much getting kicked in the ass by someone else.

It doesn't sting a bit when something that you've no control over or say-so about shoes you in the keister. It really doesn't. But when it's you kicking yourself in your own ass, well, that's when it really smarts.

I guess that I've come to learn that it's the *kicking yourself in the ass* that'll get ya in the end. Nobody else's ass whooping is going to do much to a guy who's already down on his luck. But if he lets *himself* get the better of him, he's all but done for.

So, I figure I'll share my story with you whether you give a shit about it or not. I would guess that you probably have your own problems and all going on right now. I mean, we all do with this damn economy and nobody in the oval office that has any idea of what to do to straighten the world out again.

But I'd bet you dollars to donuts that those bastards still manage to sleep darned good at night. Probably just like babies. I doubt that any of them have the phone waking 'em in the morning with some damn foreclosure department on the other end.

Still, I wouldn't trade shoes with any of those guys. Not one of 'em.

I figure that we've all got our problems, and for the most part, they're of our own making. And when all the cards are down, I think I'd just as soon stick with mine. At least I feel like I own 'em, as silly as that sounds.

Maybe it's just the way that I've learned to deal with this whole damn thing. I don't know. But they're mine. Start to finish. And if you can show me a fella who says that he hasn't got any problems, I'll bet you a hundred bucks that I can show you a liar.

As I was saying, I'll share my bullcrap story with you if you wanna listen. And if you don't, you can just turn it off any old time it gets too goddamn depressing for you. That'll suit me just fine. It's no skin off my nose.

That's the nice thing about listening to somebody else's story. If you don't like it, you can just turn it right off. Even if you're stuck at some dive bar, sitting next to that old drunken schmuck with his tales of heartbreak and what not. And you know he's gonna have problems, because they always do at those kinds of places.

You can be looking at him dead-pan, right in his old watery red eyes. His mouth moving a mile a minute spitting in every damn direction. And that poor bastard will have no clue that you turned him off long before he even got started jabber-jawing.

By now you've probably figured out that I've been through some stuff as of late. That sure as shit doesn't make you a rocket scientist. Sorry to break the news. But if you feel like sticking around, I could use a shoulder. And if not, that's just fine too. Like I said, it's not gonna ruffle my feathers none either way.

I'd be full of beans if I said that I'm glad about everything, that it made me stronger, or any of those other things that guys say when they've been through hell over something.

But the truth is that I never wanted to be all that strong anyway. I never really was the tough kind.

Clint Eastwood was a real tough guy back when I was a punk. My old man used to watch Brando and Pacino. He loved De Niro too. Those guys were tough, that's for sure.

I remember we had an old VHS tape of Rocky back when I was growing up. I thought that Stallone was the coolest, back when I was a little prick. It's funny too, because I used to dress like him.

I'd run around in a grey hooded sweatshirt with the sweatpants and Addidas. I remember how the kids on the playground used to bust my balls, calling me *Rocky Balboa* or the *Italian Stallion*.

They were probably laughing at me about it, but I sure wasn't. I wanted to be just like him. I really did. That was until I got into that fight with Mitch Moran in the fifth grade. That was really something. And I took him too. I mean it was completely over. I had him pinned with my knees on his shoulders and all. He couldn't get up. It was done. I won. He knew it. I knew it. What the heck did everybody expect me to do while he was down there squirming, with his legs kicking all over the place?

It was as though every single one of those kids in the circle wanted me to punch him right in the nose or something, when the fight was clearly over. Like I said, my knees were on his shoulders. All that son of a gun could do was jerk around this way and that, like a hyena in a bear trap. I mean, what kind of a person labels a fellow right smack dab in the kisser when he's already good and done for?

I let him up like the stand-up guy that I am, and while he was skulking away, every one of those damned punks on the playground started calling *me* a wuss. What the hell was I supposed to do?

I was the new kid at school, and I sure couldn't take all of them on. Moran knew what time it was, and he wasn't going to get back into it with me. I've gotta figure he knew that I really would've kicked his ass then.

But it sure made me wanna puke knowing that all those little bastards standing on the side-lines wanted to see somebody get good and hurt. They weren't gonna be happy unless one of us was lying in a pool of his own piss and blood or something. Kids can be so cruel sometimes. Even the grown-up ones.

That was the last fight that I think I got into. At least like that. I just never saw the sense in it.

I have a couple of buddies that say, *"Once in a while, you've just gotta cold cock someone in order to keep yourself from going insane."* But I never really bought into that. If that were the case, by doing the simple arithmetic you could figure out that we'd all be getting cold cocked once in a while.

And I know that I don't want to be picking my teeth up off of some bathroom floor, just because some jackass was looking to keep himself from going to the funny farm.

So, I figure *live and let live*. Other than this ass whooping that I've been getting for the past year or two, that philosophy has worked pretty damned well for me.

You see, I'd rather just talk. Talk my way into things, and talk my way out of 'em. It's what I do.

Sometimes I talk a little too much. Probably even now. Maybe I'm just being selfish in wanting to get this shit off my chest, thinking that anybody else really cares.

You might think *that's just like me*, if you didn't know me. And since you don't, you might guess that I'm looking for sympathy or something. But you'd be wrong.

I don't want anyone's pity. Never have. Over my dead body.

It's just that I have a feeling that some changes are coming at me, and I wanted to make some notes for posterity. That's a word that my mom used to use quite a lot when I was a punk, and I never thought that I would use it in my whole goddamn life.

But there you go. I'm sharing this crap for posterity. If you like it, then keep on reading. And if you don't, then don't. Like I said, I don't really give a shit one way or the other.

Either way, this is how the whole deal went down.

CHAPTER 2

I jumped in the shower that day just like every other godforsaken day before it. I brushed my teeth and did all the other stuff that thirty-five years will teach a guy. But I decided not to shave for the first time in ages. I figured, why should I bother?

I didn't have any fancy meetings or anybody to try and impress. I knew I wasn't going to be picking up any gals at the grocery store or the health club. I figured who the heck do I need to impress, Miles?

Oh yeah. Miles.

I guess that I ought to tell you about Miles. Miles is the greatest pal I ever had. Probably the best companion anybody ever did.

Now don't get me wrong. I'm not one of those fruity kinda guys that's all into his dog and carries pictures around to show everybody. I don't parade him down Michigan Avenue just to get people to stop us so that *they* can go on and on about how sweet their goddamn dog is or some crap like that.

I don't put any horseshit monogrammed sweatshirts on him or groom him like a frickin' sissy dog or nothing. I wouldn't do that to him. Over my dead body.

But I'd say that he is the only thing around these days that I care about other than Hope. Truth is, I don't know that I would even be here today if it wasn't for him.

He's getting older and all. The little guy has diabetes and sleeps the better part of the day. But we're family. And he's really the only thing keeping me going through all this crap. Well, him and Hope. But mainly him.

Miles is here for me all the time, and I only see Hope once in a while, even though I know she's always there if I need her. That means a hell of a lot to me too. It really does. But the truth is that I don't really need her all that much, even though I think she wishes I did.

Miles hasn't really been quite the same lately. I mean, I know he's just a dog and all. Still, he's got feelings, and he'll show 'em if he feels safe around you. I admire him for that. But things haven't really been the same around here for either of us since that thing went down with Jenny.

Jenny was Miles' mom in a way. That's the simplest way to put it. And he loved her. Heck, I loved her too. About as much as I can love anyone, anyhow. She was my best friend, and I couldn't even do that right.

We went through hell together, Jenny and me. And I'd be lying if I didn't tell you that I'd go right back through it again for her. She got me. And when I say that, I mean that she understood me. The good and bad.

Sometimes I hated that. In fact, most of the time I did. But I guess that's where you find your real family. They're the ones that get you and stick by your side anyway.

That was Jenny. And I got her too. And still, I let her do what she did.

Jenny used to be pretty damned sharp back in her day. She was on the evening news, always talking about this and that, telling everyone about what had happened each day out in the real world.

She was real pretty back then too. But I guess that you have to be, in order to get a job with one of those network stations.

Now, I don't really know all the particulars around it. All I know is that one day she was standing there in front of hundreds of thousands of people lying on their couches, telling them all that happened while they were at work. The next day, she was the one sprawled out on the sofa.

I do know that she lost something really important to her, and it knocked the wind out of her sails pretty good. I know that whatever it was that she lost that day, she never found again. I don't think that she ever really recovered from whatever happened to her, and that's probably what came back to haunt her a couple of months back.

I figured out long ago that the devil inside of your head will haunt you if you don't beat him. And if you don't beat him, you're more than likely gonna wind up joining him in the end.

Part of me still thinks that I could've helped her lick that devil, if I'd been in a good place myself. But I know that I did all that I could given the shit that I was going through.

At least that's what I tell myself about it. Still, I've come to figure out that you don't always get a second chance at being the friend you meant to be. And losing Jenny was worse then losing everything else that I've ever lost in my life combined. She was the kind of friend that was just there, no matter what.

Most of the time I hated the fact that she was always there. I must've caught her sneaking into my place a thousand times or more. And whenever something was missing, I pretty much knew that it was because she'd borrowed it.

It was funny too. Whatever she *borrowed* was never anything that you'd just notice when you walked in the door. It was only when you needed it that you suddenly figured out that it was gone.

There was one time that really rattled my cage. I'd been out of town at one of those retreats that I'd go to every now and again to get rewired.

I got home about eleven at night and was fit to be tied. I walked in the door fixin' to just get washed up and hit the hay. And when I sat down on the shitter to take a load off, I realize that there's no TP in the goddamn holder.

Now, I know that I didn't use it up before I left, but that's all right. It's when I opened the cabinet under the sink and realized that there wasn't any in there either that I just about flipped my lid.

I'm not one of those fastidious guys that takes inventory of all his bathroom stuff before he goes to the store once a week. I've been known to run out of toothpaste from time to time. Shaving cream, too. Heck, I've even run out of deodorant. But one thing that I don't think I've ever run out of is toilet paper. No way, no how. Maybe it's just etched deep in my subconscious or something, but I always know two weeks before when I'm getting low.

She'd deny it till the day she died, but I know she hocked it. Maybe I shouldn't have said that—but she took it. I just know it.

Anyways, I'd give all the toilet paper in the world to see her smile again. All the toothpaste too. I'd give my eye-teeth to have saved her from the devil, if I'd only known what the heck was going on with her. If I'd recognized that the world was swallowing her up whole, I would've done whatever the hell I had to do. And if we went down, at least we would've gone down together.

Maybe in some small way that's what's happening to me now. Shit, I don't know.

I guess we're all gonna be worm food or worse before too long, and there ain't no sense in going around all mopey about it. That's how she was right before she did it. All mopey. Morning noon and night, she was mopey. Half the people in this damn building are mopey all the time. I wonder if they think that I'm mopey all the time? I really don't think that they do.

You see, I'm more full of shit than most of them. Always have been.

I'm the jerk that always has one of those B.S. smiles on his face like everything is just peachy. Even when it isn't.

I know that I'm as much of a part of the problem as anything, but I can't help it. I guess that it's just the way that I am.

You know those pricky people who say, "What's up?" as they blow past you on the street? It's because of jackasses like me. When someone's all happy-go-lucky, people act like it's all right to ask the poor bastard a question even when they have no interest at all in the answer.

Occasionally, though, I'll mess with them, although they wouldn't know it. They're always far too busy paying attention to themselves and their busy little worlds.

Still, once in a blue moon, when there is a particularly pricky guy that I know from somewhere, who says "What's up?" out of the corner of his pricky little mouth, I'll stop dead in my tracks. I swear to Christ that I'll stop right smack dab in the middle of Michigan Avenue and speak loud enough so that everybody around me who gives a crap can hear.

"Oh, I'm so glad you asked. Quite a lot is up, actually. You see, I closed the brokerage and I have bill collectors calling me day and night, and my dog has diabetes, and

Jenny's gone, and my home is in foreclosure, and . . . Oh . . . Hey! Where'd ya go? I thought for a moment that maybe, just maybe, you actually gave a shit!"

I can be quite a prick myself, when I feel like it.

So, I decided that I was gonna spend the day doing all the things that I always used to like doing, back when I liked doing things. I was going to try to cram them all into one day as best as I could, so I could keep them safe in my head for a rainy day.

I thought I'd check and see if the world's worst baseball team was in town, and sure enough they were. It being a weekday in September, and the fact that they were more pitiful than usual, pretty much guaranteed me a seat in the sun. I figured that would be a great way to spend my last full day in the city, so I set my compass accordingly.

In preparation, I completed all my grooming rituals.

I put on my blue-faced Rolex Sub and folded the double clasp. It was the only good one that I had left, but it was also the only one that ever really mattered. I'd saved up damned near a year for it when I was just getting started, and it meant a hell of a lot to me because of it.

I fed Miles, filled the syringe to the eighth line, put the hammer down with his shot, and headed out the door. Surprisingly, it felt a lot like every other day. Even though I knew it wasn't. Not by a longshot.

"So, what's the good word, my friend?" I said to Sami in the building market where I always got my morning cup of Joe.

"Hollywood, Jack!" he chimed right back at me. "How's the world treating you on this sunny autumn day?" he asked sincerely.

"Getting by just fine buddy. No complaints." I smiled.

"Nobody would listen anyway," Sami said with a chuckle, just like he always did.

"That's right. . . . No one would listen."

It was the same old routine, and I doubt that he could've guessed that he wouldn't be seeing my sorry ass again. You see, that's the way I was playing this thing.

Still, I've gotta admit that I felt a little badly about it, all and all. Especially with the good guys.

I really liked Sami. He was a Palestinian who'd lived in the Gaza Strip till he was in his late 20s or so. I knew his story well, and I respected him.

He kinda got duped into taking over the market in this ritzy place, thinking that he could make some good dough. The truth was that this dump never made any money. I knew most the owners before Sami. There must've been three or four of 'em. None of them did any good with the place. Most probably went bankrupt trying to.

Sami was different than those other goofs, though. He was one of the good guys. You could just tell. With certain fellows, you get a feeling about them. And Sami was one of those people.

I met both of his children, and you could see that they were good kids. The boy was probably 18 or 19, and really good looking. But what I liked about the kid was the way that he listened to whatever his old man said.

His son would always work at the market during spring or summer breaks. And even though you could tell that he was confident—maybe even a little cocky when he was out with his pals—he always said "Yes, sir" or "No, sir" to Sami. And he wasn't doing it just to do it. It was obvious that this was the way that the family was.

I met Sami's daughter once too. She was only 15 or 16, but you could sure tell that he probably already had his hands full with her. She was a real doll, and pretty as all get-out.

I don't really wanna say much more about it, seeing as she was only a little girl and all. My mind can tend to wander sometimes. But the truth is that I'm not really that kind of guy. Let's just leave it at that. She was an angel, and Sami sure as hell knew it.

Anyhow, I got my usual coffee—the Columbia Supremo. I counted out seven quarters and handed them to Sami, just like always. He didn't count them as he threw them in the drawer.

"So, how's the screenplay doing?", Sami asked genuinely.

"You know I'm still waiting on the sequel."

Sami was one the few guys that had actually read my screenplay, or at least he told me that he did. That meant a lot to me. It really did.

"It's moving right along my friend," I said as though I was in a rush to get somewhere.

I really didn't want to get into it with him, and I think he could tell. I never was much good at goodbyes, and I didn't feel like making exceptions.

"Have a great one Sami," I said hurriedly as I put my sunglasses on.

"You too, Hollywood!" he hollered back as I skated out the street side doors and headed over to The Pier.

The Pier was basically in my back yard, so it really wasn't much of a hike to get there unless it was really windy. But this day was just perfect. It was crisp enough that the wind cut right through the humidity, and with the kids back at school, it felt kind of peaceful heading out there.

I took a small sip of my coffee, but it was still plenty hot. I blew into the little opening in the lid, knowing damn well that that wasn't going to do a thing to cool it down. Still, I did it anyways, out of habit.

Most mornings, The Pier has all sorts of people on it. For the most part, though, the bums are the only ones that'll give you the time of day unless you see someone you know. The tour-boat company always has their people lined up in red shirts and khaki pants, spraying down or sweeping the sidewalk and the decks on the ships.

It's funny. I don't know how much these lugs get paid for doing what they do, but they sure seem mesmerized by their jobs. They must be the easiest people in the whole gosh-darned world to keep interested in a nothing, dead-end gig. Either that, or they're just so damned bored that they're half asleep on their feet.

Then there are the power walkers. These zombies are in their own little world. They're usually in pairs, but I don't much see why. You'd think that they were together for the companionship, but you'd be dead wrong. They don't say a word to one another. They just shuffle around at about forty miles an hour, looking straight ahead at nothing at all. These clowns must go around the pier a hundred times or more in a morning.

About the time that I got to the entrance, I saw Moshe Lieberman. Moshe was a unique one out on The Pier, that's for sure.

He'd go out in his sweats like a power walker, but he'd just kinda drift around aimlessly. People in the building would make jokes about him because he was shaped kinda like one of the M&M characters in the commercials. I didn't laugh at him about it though. Truth is, I kinda felt bad for the old coot.

He was simply getting away from his pain-in-the-ass wife, who surely thought that he was out power walking. You'd think she could tell by the size of his waist line that power walking was one thing that poor old Moshe wasn't doing. He looked like Humpty Dumpty, and people used to say that behind his back too. I sure hope he never heard it himself, because that could really rattle a guy.

Now normally I would've doubled back before he saw me, but I sort of felt like chewing the fat with old Moshe. Truth is that I always kinda liked him. It probably didn't hurt that I knew that he always kinda liked me too, but I was sort of lucky that way.

Pretty much everybody in the building thought I was a decent guy, or at least it seemed like it. I didn't know of anybody that didn't like me except for Mrs. Belcher, and that was just fine. She didn't get along with much of anybody. Well, her and old Cromwell.

"So how are you on this fine morning, young man?" Moshe asked, just like he always did.

"Not too bad, good sir," I chided back at him.

I don't know how we got into this Old English crap, but we'd been going back and forth with it ever since I met him, way back when I first moved into the building.

"You going to the game today, old chap?" he asked.

"Actually, I do think I am gonna try to make it up there. I don't have my seats today, but I'm sure that I can get one in the sun from a scalper on Waveland or Clark."

I said it that way for a damned good reason. You see, Moshe is a state-of-the-art, top-of-the-line, professionally trained cheap ass.

Years ago, when I used to have dough, he would always throw a line out there, real casual-like. "If you've ever got an extra ticket...," he'd ask, figuring that I might toss him a bone.

Naturally, I presumed that old Moshe was just looking for a young guy to hang at the game with. I mean, if he's doing well enough to be living in this skyscraper with all the other high rollers, he's gotta throw a few bucks around now and again for a good time. And I'd like to think that I'm the kind of guy that you'd wanna hang out with at the Friendly Confines when you're pushing seventy.

So sure enough, I called him up a couple of times when I had a ticket lying around. And wouldn't you know, each and every time the sun was shining, he'd take me up on it.

But that son of a gun never offered up a penny in thanks. To make things worse, the cheap old bastard doesn't even buy you a beer.

That's right. There you are in good old section 242, baking in the sun with this bald old codger. You're just dying for a cold one, waiting like a first-class schmuck.

Finally, being the stand-up guy that you are, you ask him if he wants one, and of course he's gonna oblige. Then, wouldn't you know it? He milks it till the seventh inning when they stop serving.

Yeah, he's a real son of a bitch, Lieberman is. Still, I kinda like the old coot.

"So, what's going on with the sale?" he asked.

"There are a couple of people that have some real interest. It's just tough to get anyone to pull the trigger these days for a place in here. I guess when it's time, it'll be time."

"Well, were gonna hate to lose you my friend," Moshe said. "The building sure isn't going to be the same without you."

"I know, Moe. And I have a feeling that I won't be much the same without the building either," I said with a smile.

Moshe gestured over to the counter of the donut shop. I followed his lead, and we headed in that direction. "How about a bear claw my good man?" he asked pointedly.

"Sure," I answered with a shrug, not really knowing if he was actually going so far as to buy me a bite.

He ordered us a couple of bear claws. And what the hell do you know? That son of a gun paid—a whopping five dollars and thirty-seven cents. Still, that son of a bitch picked it up.

"Well, thank you, kind sir," I said sincerely.

Just then something weird happened that took me off guard.

Old Moshe grabbed my hand real strong with both of his and looked me dead in the eye. It was almost as though he knew that this was the last time he was gonna see my mug.

"You're welcome Jack," he said seriously. "We're sure gonna miss you around here."

I didn't answer. I didn't wanna lie to old Moshe and tell him that I wasn't going any time soon, because I sure as heck was. I didn't want the last thing that I ever told that old codger to be bullshit. I didn't want to tell him about how I was losing my place to the bank and all either. I just stood there and shook his strong, old, wrinkly hand like a regular two-bit schmuck—without saying a goddamn word. We sat down and chewed the fat about nothing at all for darned close to an hour. I heard about his sons and what they were doing to save the world and all. He rehashed a few stories about his poker nights on Tuesdays and his wife's Mahjongg games. He told me about all the two-for-one deals in town and all the senior specials.

To be honest, this was all that the two of us knew how to do together. And that suited me just fine. Just talking about the steals, deals, happy hours, two-for-ones, and buffets in town. If anybody was going to know them, it was going to be old Peanut M&M himself.

Finally, I told him that I had to run, even though I knew that I had plenty of time to make it to the game. I still needed to get home to take Miles out. I kinda needed to take a leak too, so I said goodbye to my old friend and watched him power walk down The Pier. At least that's what old Moshe would say he was doing.

I got upstairs and Miles was waiting at the door for me. He can hear the bell when the elevator stops on the floor and always knows when it's me. It's uncanny how he can tell, but he does.

It seemed he really had to go too, so I took a quick piss and then put his leash on for his turn.

We hopped on the passenger elevator. Some Chinese lady looked down her nose at me for not using the service elevator with a dog, but I didn't give a shit. I spent the last ten years following every damned rule in this place, and I figured they were welcome to write me up now for breaking a few on the way out.

Besides, this wasn't some oversized, drooling mutt in the elevator. So I just tried my best to ignore her and stare at the numbers going down.

I got Miles walked and all. When I got back upstairs, I grabbed my lucky jersey and was almost excited about having one more day in my city.

The clouds were rolling in on the lake like they often do in September, but they kept at a safe distance about a mile or two out because of the pressure from the Canadian fronts. At least that's what the weathermen say.

I've gotta tell you that the view sure is cool twenty floors up, watching how the clouds just kinda stop out there. It's almost like they're waiting in formation on some imaginary line in the sand or something. It may sound stupid, but sure as shit that's what they do. You've gotta see it to believe it.

I checked my wallet and saw that I had ninety dollars, which kinda pissed me off. I thought that I had a lot more. I'd forgotten that I dropped a few bucks the night before on someone who was way out of my league at The Pit Boss, my local schmokel watering hole. She got me for about three martinis before she had to leave to meet her boyfriend. That shit happens to me a lot these days.

Still, I figured that ninety bucks would get me a decent last day at Wrigley. And with that I filled the flask that Jenny had given me to the brim with Jim Beam, took the last swig from the bottle to finish her off, and headed down Grand to the L station.

I saw a lot of faces on the way to the Red Line. I made eye contact and nodded at most of them. I muttered a "hey" or a "hello" under my breath to some of them too. That's what I usually do. That's why a lot of people like me. Or at least I think that they do.

I passed by a few of the places that I used to go to for a beer or a burger before I jogged down the stairs to the station. I made good time and was careful to dodge any cracks on the way down the way I do. I know it's a stupid superstition, but I've been doing it since I was a kid.

About the time I was fumbling for my train pass, I ran into the last guy I wanted to see. It was that jerk off, Slick Ned. I knew that if I hadn't been so caught up in looking through my wallet and dodging cracks, I would've been able to dodge him. But I didn't.

"Yo, Pretty Boy!" he hollered from about forty feet away.

"Hey, Ned. What's up?" I shouted back as he continued walking towards me.

"You going to the game?"

"I'm not really sure," I told him, even though I knew that I was more than likely getting on the same goddamn train as him. "I have an appointment up that way and may swing by afterwards. Looks like a hell of a day for a game."

"Sure does," he cackled. "Especially if you're sitting first row box!"

Ned grinned from ear to ear as he waived two tickets in front of my face.

"Good for you, man." I said matter-of-factly. "How'd you score those?" I asked disingenuously.

"A client gave 'em to me. He can't make it, and I was gonna scalp one on the street. But it's yours for face-value and a couple of brewski's if you want, Jackie Boy!"

For a moment, I thought that I'd give him the forty-five dollars for the ticket. It would be a great way to blow out of the city, after all. Especially if it really was first row box.

You see, that's the thing with Ned. You never knew if he was telling the truth or not. He had a way of blowing smoke more often than the average guy.

But just then I got this feeling in my gut that made me wanna hurl that bear claw from an hour earlier. It was like a shiv to the belly. Right when I was fixin' to puke all over Ned's prissy black suede Ferragamo's and checkered shorts, I took a deep breath and held it in. Just the way I'd been learning to do for the past few months or so.

I didn't know if it was an ulcer or what, but it would come outta nowhere without warning. It was this thing that had been happening to me for quite a while. If I had any dough, I surely would've gotten it checked out. Whatever it was, it could make Mike Tyson curl up in a ball and cry like a baby. I'd kinda gotten used to dealing with it, and for the most part I could keep a straight face when it happened, even though it stung like bastard.

I figured by now that it was as much mental as it was physical, because it always hit me when I was having thoughts of something that really pissed me off. It never happened at night when I was sleeping or when I was watching a movie or just having a decent time. The pain only came when I was reminded of something I didn't wanna be reminded of. And that was exactly what was happening with Slick Ned right about then.

I remembered the ball games that I took that mooch to with my season tickets all those years. I remembered that he never bought me beers either. I thought of all the other times that we would be out on the town and how he was always gonna pick the tab up *next time.*

I recalled when we met some gals who were in town with their bosses from L.A. Ned made sure that we went drink for drink with all four of them, all the time knowing that the moment the check came, he would be out the door with the chunky Asian chick, leaving me behind with the blonde and the thousand-dollar tab.

Then I knew where that pain was coming from, and it just about made me wanna clock Slick Ned right in the kisser, for wanting to hit me up for a ticket that he'd glommed onto for free.

"No thanks, buddy," I told him. "I'm all set. I don't even know if I'm gonna make it or not."

I whisked my transit pass into the machine and pulled it out.

"If I get done with my meeting, I'll give you a shout." I just kept walking down the stairs towards the tracks as the 11:53 rolled up.

"Okay, Pretty Boy," Ned said as he darted to enter the first car of the oncoming train. I sauntered my way a good four or five cars back, where it was filled almost to capacity. I squeezed in and glided my way to the middle of the car, where I knew I could find a rail to grab.

I took a real deep breath as the train sped through the tunnel. I felt that tickle in my throat and swallowed to get rid of it. Although my thoughts were moving as fast as that train, I was at ease. Maybe even a little somber, I suppose. Watching all the buildings, cars and people go by, made me think about stuff.

Life really can make a guy depressed if he lets it. The key, I figured, was not to let it. Keep control of your thoughts and focus in on the good stuff. Stay away from all the darker places in your head.

I thought about how the train was a metaphor of sorts. It was merely a shell, carrying us from one place to another.

But that outside carriage doesn't remotely mirror what's being carried inside.

That's where we *really* are. Inside.

We were the feelings and the emotions. The brains and the guts. The soul.

That was us. Not the Goddamn fuselage.

If the train was dirty or old or run down or broken, the passengers weren't those things too. If the tracks were meandering this way and that, leading us to places that weren't on our itinerary, that didn't mean that that's where we were supposed to get off. Deep down inside, I knew precisely where I belonged, as well as where I was. And it was the same for all those other vacant faces, packed in like sardines on the Red Line with me, right then and there.

I thought about how the wheels on that train were a lot like life. We couldn't slow them down, and we couldn't back up and fix things if we needed to. We were just along for the ride.

I thought about how the tracks were some sort of path that we couldn't avoid even if we wanted to. As if it was already laid out for us long before got there. Sure, there were stops along the way. But deep down inside, we knew where we were getting off. And the conductor made sure to remind us of exactly where we were on our journey.

And as I was thinking these crazy things, I looked around at all the people on that train. All of them were going to the same place, just watching their lives go by too.

Strangely, right there and then. I didn't feel so crummy about all the shit that was happening to me. In fact, I didn't feel crummy at all.

It was probably all that goofy introspection that made me decide to get off a stop before the ballpark. I was early anyways and didn't really wanna run into Slick Ned again. I skipped down towards the escalator and heard a rapping on the window of the car behind me. Sure enough, it was Ned.

I smiled at him and gave him the thumbs up. I had a hunch that I'd never see him again, and that was okay. There were a lot of things that day that I wouldn't be seeing any time soon, and I was good with it. That feeling was about as close as I wanted to get, to actually saying goodbye.

I took a swig from my flask as I walked up Clark, peeking into all the stores that I always used to really dig. There always seemed to be the wildest shops on the way to Wrigley. Head shops. Secondhand book stores. There must've been four or five windows with all sorts of porn shit that I would sneak into when I was a punk.

I went into one that I thought I remembered, but when I got inside it was all different. As stupid as it sounds, I was kinda nervous, just like I was back when I was a schoolkid. I didn't really know why. It's not like I'm a prude or anything. Far from it. But I still felt really uneasy being in there. Especially peeking through the magazines.

The girls looked so young. But they were still sexy as all get-out. It dawned on me then that it had been awhile since I'd peeked through a skin mag.

I thumbed through the pages real slow and all, just as if I was twelve years old again and was peeking through my old man's Playboys. I glanced up at the cashier, hoping that he wasn't giving me an eyeful or anything, and was glad that he was watching the TV

Just then I felt my gut start to do that thing on me. Here I was, in my mid-thirties, thumbing through a porno mag like like I did twenty years earlier. Only this time the girls that I was drooling over probably weren't even born when I was their age. That made me feel rotten. Just goddamn awful. *Christ,* I suddenly realized. Any one of those gals could've been my daughter.

I didn't know what to do with those crazy feelings, and I really didn't want to think about them. Still, somehow those thoughts wouldn't let go of me. They just kept pounding at me like rain on a windshield.

So, I put the magazine down and scooted out the door. I've always been pretty good at controlling what I'm thinking about. I'd even gotten better at it since everything fell apart. But the thought of those girls rattled around in there for a bit.

It's a strange thing, what those skin magazines can do to a fellow. They made me feel naïve and innocent, but also like a dirty old man. I didn't like those emotions all mushed together like a peanut butter and jelly sandwich. I didn't like 'em one bit.

I figured I'd stop into the next little shit hole for a beer to get my mind on something else.

I ducked into a dive called COCKTAILS. I know what you're thinking. What a crazy name for a bar. But it kinda made sense. And with the blatent transparency of the name, it seemed like a good place to be dodging everybody's bullshit anyways.

I sidled up to the sticky counter and grabbed a napkin to wipe all the crap from the spot I chose. The fifty-something bartender just looked at me like I was crazy.

She didn't say nothing. She just stood there, sort of looking half in my direction and half at the tube. But I'd seen gals like this tending bar before noon before. I just assumed that this was the way that she did her job. I figured, who the hell am I to expect any different? So, I just decided to look only half way in her direction too. And with that, I rattled off, "Amstel Light."

"Shots are just a dollar, and mixed drinks a buck and quarter before the game," she shouted out in no particular direction. I told her that I would just take the beer.

Now I don't really know what I was thinking. I was on a tight budget, and yet I was ordering premium beer. I guess it was just force of habit. An Amstel was always my drink of choice, and I suppose it still was. But I sure as heck wasn't living in that big time world anymore. And nobody knew that better than me.

But now I was stuck with it and figured that was all right. If I was gonna be drinking a good beer at all this day, let it be my first one. After a few, it wouldn't much matter anyways.

She plopped the Amstel on the counter and didn't rattle off the price the way some bartenders do. "Four-fifty," some of these creeps will say as they're cracking the top off the goddamn bottle. As if you're really gonna stiff 'em over a beer. I hate that.

Then there are some that like to keep a tab because it's easier to slip an extra drink or two on there. I've gotta figure that it's pure profit when they can get away with it. But I reckoned that this girl knew I was only around for one or two before the game, so she wasn't up to nothing.

"I'll take a shot of Beam too," I told her while I was looking up at the TV. She chuckled.

I had a feeling that she'd seen a lot by the way she looked. She was haggard and rough, but she had a motherly side to her too. I could tell that she wasn't so bad.

"We don't carry that brand, sonny."

Sonny? Well that's not *so* horrible, I suppose.

"If you want a shot of bourbon, all I've got is Ten High." I should've known that was the only swill that they would have for a buck. My mind was somewhere else, that was for sure.

"That's fine," I told her. "Can you join me for one?" I asked hesitantly. I figured it was just the two of us in this hellhole, and the least that I could do was buy her something to get her mind off where she was.

"Guess so . . ." she said with a shrug.

She poured me one past the line, and it looked like she grabbed some blackberry brandy for herself. I plopped a twenty on the counter, and she held her dark glass up for a toast.

"To the fall of the empire!" I shouted with a laugh while holding my glass up to hers.

She looked at me like I was nuts, but she seemed to snarl something similar to a laugh out. I think that she thought that I was talking about the country's economic quagmire or maybe the Cubbies. We shot those down and she poured me another.

"This ones on me, sonny," she said sweetly. I didn't say thanks, and just nodded.

I think she knew that I was down on my luck, and for the first time in ages, I didn't care that somebody did. Stranger still was the fact that I didn't wanna try to fool her into thinking that I wasn't.

I knew that I'd never seen her before and that I sure as heck wasn't gonna see her again. In an odd way, that made who I was all right.

"So, what's your story, kid?" she asked.

Where do I start? I thought. I took a sip of my beer and felt a sort of rush. Two shots of shitty bourbon will do that to a fellow. So, I opened up. I figured what the hell.

I told her about the brokerage and how I kinda used to be a high roller. I didn't elaborate too much though, because I didn't want to get all misty-eyed and shit.

I told her about all the dough I'd lost in the past two years, although I don't know if she believed me. I told her about Miles and his damned diabetes too.

Finally, I got to the part that hurt the worst. I told her about Jenny. I put my sunglasses on when I did because I knew it was gonna sting, and I was right.

"I lost my best friend," I told her.

She didn't ask how or nothing, and I liked that about her. Although I think she might've figured it out. She just let me unravel, and she made me feel safe doing so.

I hadn't felt that way in ages. And I had a hunch that I wasn't gonna be feeling that way again for a while, so I took advantage of it. I don't think she minded. She handed me some paper towel from behind the counter. And even though I felt a little ashamed, she made it okay.

"Shoot," she muttered as she grabbed her purse. "I sure am sorry for all you're going through, kid."

She opened her purse and handed me some Kleenex that I could tell she had for safe keeping. I couldn't say nothing, or I sure would've thanked her. But I knew that she didn't need the words. We had an understanding the way strangers sometimes do.

I snorted really loud like you do when you're at the end of a cry and you're trying to act like you weren't blubbering like a baby. When you're pretending like it's just a cold or hayfever or something.

"I'm only human," I finally stammered. Knowing damn well that it sounded cliché.

"It's not all that easy being human," she responded. I just looked up at her through my dark glasses.

"We're outta here tomorrow though," I said. "Miles and I are heading west. We're done."

"Good for you guys," she said confidently, almost like she was giving me permission or something, offering the assurance that I was seeking.

"It sounds like you boys are already gone." She grabbed both of my shoulders, giving me half a hug.

I had fifteen bucks left on the bar, and in a different day I would've gladly left it all, especially because I knew I owed her far more than that. But she made it clear that five dollars was good.

I grabbed ten of it and nodded at her. I winked too, but I knew she couldn't see it with my sunglasses on.

"Safe travels, sonny," she responded.

"Same to you," I called back, not realizing how foolish that was to say. She just laughed, and I figured she knew that I was a little buzzed. And that was just fine with me.

CHAPTER 3

I made it to the game with about twenty minutes to spare. That was just fine, because you don't wanna buy a ticket till game time or else these bottom feeders will rape you.

I headed over to the corner where the scalpers all hang out, each one of them trying to take advantage of whomever came off the train or the bus lines. There are always a few little divey joints around that corner too where you can grab a cheap beer and a free shot or two if you know the right guy behind the bar. I knew most of 'em by face and a couple by name, so I figured I'd hit one up before grabbing a last-minute ticket after the anthem.

The Dugout was one of my favorite little dumps. It looked dead, so I headed in there like I had a thousand times before. Sometimes a bunch of us would go there after the game and run up a tab that must've been at least five or six hundred bucks. I oughta know because I paid it more than my share of times, that's for sure. But I didn't used to mind stuff like that. I really didn't.

I peeked around and felt a sort of chill. I recalled a lot of hot and humid days in there. But it was September and all the doors were closed, so it felt kinda damp and cold. I didn't see anybody that I knew.

I looked around for the bartender I used to flirt with, but she wasn't working. I wondered if she had gone back to school like she always said she was gonna do or if she'd gone home to Kansas City.

The only person working seemed to be this skinny kid with sideburns behind the bar, and he didn't seem too friendly. I knew the owners of this dive, and it sure as hell wasn't one of them. So instead of running right up to the bar, I decided to take one last walk around.

It stunk like cigarettes still. It always did, even though nobody had smoked in there since the ban. There were still the burn marks in the Golden Tee machine. I looked at the high scores but didn't recognize any of the old gang.

The pool table had a big rip in it at one end, which kinda broke my heart. We must've played a thousand games on that beat up, old six-footer. Half the time there was a ball or two gone or a cue stick missing its tip. There sure as shit was never any chalk around the place, but I remember that Billy or Jimmy would bring their own.

We always made do, somehow, but a big old rip in the felt was something that nobody could've played around. I guess it was just as well that none of the guys were there.

I decided to take a leak and get the heck outta there. I snuck in the old stall the way I always did. It was sort of a goofy tradition in my crazy mind. I walked in without breathing through my nose, and as usual, I was glad that I didn't.

I'd always wondered what kind of a megalomaniac doesn't flush after he does his business like that. I could go on and on about what must be in the head of a guy who decides take a dump and not flush. I used to have this discussion with the boys about it. I mean, it takes a special dude to leave that sort of a thing behind, and I really wondered about that fellow.

Truth is, it could've been almost anybody. It could've been Billy or Jimmy or Duke or Jeremy or maybe that old guy who was always sitting near the Mega-Touch machine.

I used to always wanna find out who the hell it was so that I could cold-cock 'em for being so damn inconsiderate. But today I didn't really wanna slug anybody. Today it just made this old dump seem like home in a strange sorta way.

As much as I'd always thought that there would be something that I could've said or done that would've left my mark behind for the next guy, I figured out right then and there that there was nothing. There wasn't a damn thing that one of these old bastards was gonna remember me by.

So, I took a leak and flushed. I almost puked when I did it, but I did it nevertheless. And then I walked the hell out of that old joint and over to the game.

There must've been a million empty seats because a ton of regular Joe's were outside by the Ernie Banks statue trying to unload 'em. I knew that wasn't where the scalpers hung out, and I figured that I was liable to find a cheap one.

The brokers always hawked their tickets by the L tracks since that was where they could buy and sell them at the same time, with people from out of town not knowing any better. I stayed away from them these days since dough was a lot tighter than it used to be.

Once in a while you can get a ticket for nothing from a nice guy who's afraid of getting busted for scalping. That's what I was hoping I could do. It seemed that I just might get lucky. There were so many extras that most guys were asking face or less for them.

I grabbed an Old Style from Murphy's and tossed it back really quick. I could be a pretty hardcore drinker when I wanted to be, and I had come to really like that buzz once in a while, especially when I'd knock it back with just a swig or two. Then it would hit like a freight train.

I got that rush and threw a fiver on the counter without asking what I owed. I figured that it couldn't be a five-dollar beer, and if they had the stones to charge that for a can of domestic, then the guy shouldn't get a tip on top anyways. If it was only three-fifty, then I didn't mind reaching out to the young kid.

The truth is that I figured it was a four-dollar beer that was worth five to me, and that was that.

I'd spent a lot of time in the past worrying about what somebody else said that I owed 'em, rather than putting my two cents into the equation. So, like I said, I threw a fin on the bar and headed over to the bleachers.

I've gotta tell ya that I was feeling that beer a bit, and that was just fine by me. I asked a couple of black kids if they had any extras, and of course they did. "Thirty," the taller one said.

I told him that I wasn't really looking to pay much of anything and didn't mind waiting until after the first pitch. He acted like he was giving away the farm by telling me that twenty-five dollars was the lowest he could go.

I just walked away. Damned if those two kids didn't keep following me right around the corner. Big surprise.

By the time I got back to the Ernie Banks statue, they were down to ten bucks for that damn terrace seat, and even though I had a hunch I could score a box for that or an upper grandstand for nothing, I kinda felt like sitting in section 242 for old time's sake.

"I thought twenty-five bucks was the lowest you could go, pal?" I said to him kinda snidely. I didn't wanna piss him off though. This punk was all muscle, so I smiled when I said it. He didn't bother answering me.

I handed him ten bucks down low and he slipped a ticket in my hand like it was a drug deal or something. I didn't think to look at it til I got to the gate, so it was a damn good thing that he didn't screw me the way some of these punks will do. It could've been a ticket from yesterday's game, but it wasn't. I thought to myself that the kid was more stand-up than pretty much everybody else that I had done business with in the past few years. That made me chuckle inside just a little.

I headed through the turnstile and handed the Andy Frain guy my ticket like I'd done a million times or more. I knew I'd seen him before, and on a different day I would've shot the shit with him. But I just wanted to get up to the sun.

"Hey, sugar. How you been?" I asked Cathy at the beer stand on the way up the ramp.

"Hey, Jackie Boy. What are you still doing here?" she said. "I thought you sold your place."

"I did. . . . I'm just catching a last game before I head outta Dodge."

"Well, be sure to stop by and see me before you bounce, okay? You promise?" she asked.

"Of course, babe. I wouldn't dream of leaving town without saying goodbye to my best girl." I winked.

We would always kibitz like that. She'd worked there forever, and even though she was a Sox fan, she fit in just like the rest of us. I heard that in her day she was quite a doll, but that day was many days before this one.

Life had beaten her up pretty good. She had a couple of kids or more, and I met one of them once. He was a punk, and I'd bet my bottom dollar that he drove her damn near insane . . . probably the way I used to do to my mom or Jenny. She always wore a ring, but she wasn't married. Cathy handed me a beer, and I threw a five on the counter. "See you in a bit, beautiful," I said.

"Okay, Hun. Have fun," she hollered back.

I headed up the stairs to my usual section without even looking at my ticket. It didn't much matter. Victor was there in full uniform checking everyone's stubs and he seemed happy to see me.

"Hey, hey Jackie! Better watch your backie!" he said like always. I peered over my shoulder cautiously and laughed with him. It was our standing joke.

"Heya, Victor. What's shakin', my man?" I shook his hand like a brother would and leaned in close for half of a hug. I breezed past him up to the old section, and it was damn near empty. I grabbed my usual seat, thinking it would be warm from the sun, but it wasn't. It wasn't warm at all. In fact, it was cold as hell. Well . . . colder than I'd ever remembered.

None of the guys were there either, and I reckoned that it was because the Cubbies were way out of it. Still, on a nice sunny day, I kinda hoped that one or two might just show up before the first pitch.

I reached in my pocket for my flask and carefully took a swig before I grabbed my phone and typed a quick text to Hope.

"Hey, you . . . I'm sitting in the old seats one last time. Wishing you were here." I hit the button, but as it was sending, I stopped it. I knew that she was probably hard at work in an executive brainstorming session or a science lab or something.

Besides, she was done with this city too. I didn't need her reminiscing along with me, and I didn't want to jerk her around anymore than I already had. So, I stopped that text before it could do any damage.

Just like those losers tossing the ball around the infield, I blow every good chance I get. Always have and probably always will.

I sat there in that bright Chicago sun and felt like Miles does when he's lying in his bed by the window, I'd guess. I sort of melted out there in the sunlight, and for a time I totally forgot everything that was going on. I was almost in a trance, alone in section 242. And it was great.

I drifted back to one of my happy thoughts, the kind my mom used to tell me to hold tightly to. I thought back to when Hope and I used to go to Lake Tahoe in September. How crisp it was, just like this day. How the sun would intoxicate us and how we'd drink cider at the bars with the locals and laugh till our sides hurt.

I remembered how we used to make love. And I'm not one of those pricky guys that normally calls it that, so don't get your panties all in a bunch or nothing.

God knows I've banged my share of women, but I sat there thinking about how Hope and I didn't do it like that.

I mean, we used to really make love, long before the love was gone. I recalled how we'd look at each other when we'd be doing it. Right into each other's eyes. I remembered how we'd breathe each other's breaths in and out, and how we'd really feel one another.

Somehow, it always seemed like nothing else mattered except that moment, right then and there. And that's exactly how I felt sitting in row three, seat two, section 242 in the sun. Just like nothing else meant a goddamn thing.

Everybody got up for the anthem, and the section filled in a bit. But still I didn't see any of the guys.

I waived at Marcy, the beer vendor two sections over, and she waived back and sorta shrugged her shoulders. I wasn't sure if it was her way of saying, "We blew it again this year," or "Where is everybody?" so I just shrugged back. I kinda hoped she'd come over and say hello since I was feeling sorta lame, but she didn't. I think she was still a little pissed off at me.

A few months earlier, we ran into her after a game at The Dugout, and I messed up and took her home. At the time, I knew it was a mistake. You see, she used to give us beers on the sly before that, and we all thought she was really a cool chick. I think she really dug us too. It was almost as though she was *one of the guys*, until I did what I did.

I know I should've called her the next day or at least the next week. I'm usually a pretty stand-up guy that way. But with Marcy it was weird. It was sort of like screwing your own sister (I would imagine) if you had a sister that was kinda hot like that. Either way, I should've called, and I didn't. Just like the prick that I am.

Finally, the game started. I'd be lying if I told you that I was paying a whole lot of attention. They were playing the Cardinals, which was usually a real rivalry. But not when the Cubbies are fourteen games out and the Cards are in first.

The Red Birds scored two in the top of the first, and the Cubs went down one, two, three. For the life of me, I couldn't recall a single time that season that one of the boys found that sweet spot on the old Louisville slugger.

You know that sweet spot. I mean, we all do.

That's where they pretty much lost me. I think I hung around for another inning or two before I figured that none of the guys were gonna show.

This must've been the first game in ten years that none of the boys were there to jeer at whomever we were playing against or scope out girls with me. Still, it was okay. In fact, it was just fine. I realized that I wasn't going to have to bullshit anybody out there on the right field line, and I felt kinda relieved about it.

I chugged the last quarter of my beer even though it was warm as hell. I'd gotten used to that out there, due to days that were much hotter than this one.

I finally decided to head up and see Lucy at the Stadium Club one last time. I didn't have my pass this year to get in, but the bouncers at the door always knew me anyway, so I didn't really think it would be an issue. As it turns out, I was wrong.

"Hey buddy . . . can I see your pass?" the bald bouncer, Chris, asked.

I was kinda miffed. I knew that he'd seen me before, and I was sure that he knew that I was a regular guy. Still, I could tell by the way this jerk off was staring me down that he meant it.

"I forgot it at home today, Chris," I said more respectfully than he deserved. "I wanted to sneak up and see Lucy before the season's over. Is that cool?"

He looked around as if he really wanted to make sure that nobody was watching. *What a load of crap,* I thought to myself. Nobody gave a shit what he did.

This bald son of a bitch had seen my mug for the last five or six years pretty much every Friday that the loveable losers are in town, and now he's gonna bust my chops about not having a pass?

So, I reached in my pocket and threw him a fiver.

I knew that I probably could've gotten by without duking him if I had been a persistent prick, but that's not my style. Over my dead body. Never has been, never will be. So, with the five spot in hand, he gestured up the stairs to the Stadium Club.

"Thanks a lot, Chris," I said with a sarcastic tone that he didn't catch. "You're a helluva a guy."

I got to the bar, and it was pretty damned full for the fourth inning. I saw a few of the faces that were always there, and I figured that most everybody was just at the club to drink. They'd already given up on a win, just like I had.

"Yo, buddy," I said to the guy behind the bar. "What's happening?"

I felt badly because he'd been back there with Lucy for as long as I'd been coming by, but for the life of me I couldn't ever remember his name. That happens a lot to me. That's how I got so good at breaching that empty space with either a "Hey, buddy," a "Hey, pal," or a "Hey, brother."

Sometimes just a bro-shake and a "Good to see you, man," can work too. It all depends on your confidence and the presentation.

"Another day in paradise," he said as he looked around the bar at his congregation.

"I see that!" I agreed a little more enthusiastically than was necessary. I think I startled the fellow sitting next to me, but he looked up and chuckled anyways.

"I thought you were outta here," the bartender said.

"Not yet, my friend, but I'm getting there," I told him. "Lucy around?"

"Naw . . . she doesn't work today. That's right, you're usually a Friday guy."

"I make it out to a few more than just the Friday games, but yeah . . . I guess I am a Friday guy," I said shrugging.

"The usual? Amstel?"

"Sure, pal. That'd be great," I responded.

I sat there and chewed the fat with Buddy for a few minutes while the Cubbies went down one, two, three again. Yeah. No shit. I'd forgotten. His name actually *was* Buddy, and I'd been calling him that all along. Sometimes things just fall into place for a guy. I didn't feel so bad anymore.

He gave me the lowdown on most of the regulars and told me that John Cusack had been in before the game started that day.

"No shit?" I said.

"Yep," Buddy told me. "He was right over there where Mickey and Pete are sitting." He pointed over in the general direction of a bunch of regulars that I'd never met before.

"I love John Cusack," Buddy said in sort of a fruity way, not that I have a problem with that or anything.

"Yeah . . ." I smirked. "He's all right."

I stayed up there for about a half hour, maybe forty-five minutes. My tab only had a couple of beers on it, but I was sure that I had at least three or four. Either way, it was time to go.

That goofy Groucho Marx song from a hundred years ago was going through my brain like it had been off and on for the past few weeks. Outta nowhere I would start singing it in my head, almost to the point that it was driving me crazy.

Hello, I must be going. I cannot stay, I came to say I must be going. It seems a shame, but just the same I must be going. I must be going. . . .

I swear that song had been driving me nuts. I thought that it was the dumbest thing I'd ever heard, but it was stuck in my cerebral cortex or something. I found myself singing it all the time lately, and it took all I had to not sing it then.

I must be going. . . . Groucho sang that final line in his monotone, nasal baritone. I could see him in my mind's eye with that caterpillar mustache under his nose, smoking a big old stogie, standing two feet lower than anybody else in the room.

With that, I got the hell out of the club like I'd done a thousand times before, but somehow it didn't feel like all the other times. Not one goddamn bit.

CHAPTER 4

So, the big day finally arrived. We'd been in the same damn condominium for the better part of the past ten years. And it really was something.

I wish that you could see it. It was far more than just your typical city flat, that's for darned sure.

When I bought it, the brokerage was kicking it pretty good. Originally it was two separate units that I put together right smack dab over Lake Michigan. It was roughly two thousand square feet, give or take and had everything that a guy could want.

There was a big Jacuzzi in the bedroom with a TV right on it. It had a pool table in the living room over Navy Pier with granite and marble damn near everywhere you could put it. There was one hell of a view of the beach too.

I'd be full or beans if I said that I wasn't going to miss it, because I sure as hell would, but I had a lot fewer regrets than most guys would have if they were standing in my shoes.

It's kinda crazy how you can accustom yourself to losing something if you know that it's inevitable. It's the same way that I was a few years back with my old man.

In lots of ways, I kinda built that place for him. Well, him and Miles.

Back when I was a little brat and my folks were splitting up, he used to laugh about it. He'd talk about us picking up girls together and shacking up as roommates. Still, when he'd go on about it, I knew that he was telling me straight, even though I was just a kid at the time. He really meant it.

As he got older, I could tell that it was kinda keeping him going through all his stuff. Like it was giving him something to look forward to.

So, when I knocked the walls down, I hooked him up with a real sweet set up. I got my old man the walk-in shower and all the other stuff that he needed for his day to day—the handicap seat on the shitter, the bars to hold onto. Hell, I even got that fancy coffee maker that he wanted built right into the wall. But in the end, it didn't much matter.

The truth is, if he'd licked that thing, I probably would've done whatever I had to in order to save the place. But he didn't. And that's that.

"Hey, Milo" I said gently. "You ready?" I could tell that he was a little on edge.

"It's gonna be all right. We'll be together. But we're done here fella. . . . Come on, let's get this over with," I said, patting my thighs to get his attention.

He came swaggering out of our bedroom, and I put his leash on him. I felt my throat clench. I mean, I'm not a frickin' pussy, but I'm not a tough guy either. I built this place for us, and I never thought we'd be leaving, especially like this.

So what if I shed a tear? Does that really make me a pansy or something? I'm sure that you would too, so don't be so goddamn quick to bust my balls.

We headed down to the car by way of the mailboxes next to the dry cleaners. "Hey, Rochelle," I said.

"Hello, Mr. Woof." She never could get my name right, but that was okay.

"You look good with that stubble on your face. Makes you look kinda rugged," she smiled, with a strong Mexican accent.

"Thanks, dear," I said as I discretely dropped the keys in the mailbox.

I smiled back at Rochelle. I really liked her. She always had something nice to say to you even if there wasn't anything nice worth saying.

I admired her a little bit too. I knew that she had two kids that must be teenagers now. I was always amazed that she was at that dry cleaner window every hour that they were open, and she wasn't even the owner. The owner was some Chinese guy who was there every once in blue moon.

The days that Rochelle really blew me away were the ones when I used to take my old man to the doctor's office. I had to leave before six a.m. in order to get out to the hospital before his seven a.m. appointment. Rochelle was there every morning for the drop offs and every evening, even after seven p.m., for the pickups too.

I also knew of a few people in the building that would call on their way home to ask her to stick around another half hour or more just so that those selfish bastards could get their dry cleaning for the next day. I mean the fricken' inconsideration.

This lady is on public transportation with two kids. She's already been there for thirteen goddamn hours, and you can't rearrange your schedule to make certain that you can get there before they close to get your Armani suit?

But she always stayed, and she did it with a smile. I always respected her for that. I really did.

So, we dropped the keys in the box without flinching. To be honest, I was a little proud of myself. Not because of all the ways that I screwed this deal up, but because of the way that I handled it.

We headed out to the car. I spied a few of the usual nameless acquaintances that you accumulate over years of living in the same building and nodded hello. I felt good because none of them had any clue what I was going through. Nobody would've figured in a million years that I'd fallen down. And that suited me just fine.

Most of them recognized me. They knew that I had the brokerage in the building. Quite a few of them knew me as the guy who would have the wild parties around New Year's Eve or the Fourth of July, and I didn't mind them seeing me that way at all.

I'm sure that a lot of them knew me as the guy that was usually with some young girl—often a different one than the last time they'd seen me. Some of my neighbors surely recognized me as the guy with the silver 911, and a bunch knew me as the guy with the funny looking terrier.

But to the best of my knowledge, none of the people I saw that day recognized me as the guy who was losing his home, was flat broke, and was never going to be seen in that godforsaken building again. In some odd way, that made me feel pretty damned good as I got to my parking stall and started up the engine. Miles sat shotgun, panting a bit, ready for whatever journey we were on together.

Yeah, we were in this together, all right. And I was happy to just be with my little guy this crisp morning in September. I scratched behind his ears the way that he likes. It was kind of odd that this took the tickle out of my throat and ceased the battle to hold back a tear or two. It seemed to put Miles' insecurities at bay too. Together we drove out of that garage and away from that goddamn place for good.

I double parked on McClurg and put the hazards on. I patted Miles on the head and hopped out of the car. It really wasn't a car. It was more like a rocket with four wheels. And even though I didn't drive it like that much, it was good to know that it had the balls when I needed them.

I walked into the bank and felt that damn tickle coming back again. But I just swallowed and that seemed to make it go away.

"Hullo," the security guy said in his usual friendly way. I think he was from Bulgaria or Romania or Bosnia or Macedonia or some place that ended with a couple of vowels or more. I had gotten to know him over the past few years. Never said more than "hullo" on the way in and "have a nice day" on the way out.

Nonetheless, I liked him. He wasn't full of shit like so many of the other bullcrap security officers in the city. Every goddamn police academy dropout or overweight cop wanna-be—they all have these egos like they are some frickin' gang-banger with a license to bully you around. They spend all day trying to impress the girls that are half their age and stick their flabby chests out at all the guys that walk by 'em. They make me sick.

Who the hell does the hiring for these two-bit security companies anyway? An absolute moron could sit there all day and act tough. These guys couldn't chase an old lady down if they needed to, but they'd sure give her an evil look just for peering in their direction.

But I always kinda liked this guy, and I thought that he liked me too. Not that I should really care one way or another.

"Hey, Jackie. How are the ladies treating you?" my usual bank guy said when I got inside.

"Hey, hey. Not too bad Bill. Thanks for asking," I responded.

Bill had been the commercial teller ever since I started banking there, but he'd always take care of me even after I closed the shop. We always talked about the ladies, and I had the impression that he kinda admired me for some of the hotties I'd brought in with me over the years.

"So, what can I do *you* for?" Bill asked like always. *What a dumb expression,* I thought to myself. He'd used it damn near every time I've walked up to his window over the past ten years. Still, who's the idiot? I was the one chuckling with him like always.

"I hate to break your heart, my dear friend, but I'm closing it out today."

"No shit," Bill muttered under his breath leaning into me over the counter. He couldn't let the other tellers hear him talk to me like a regular guy, but it was all right. Bill and I were always good that way.

"You must've finally sold the place," he said. "It's about time. What was it, a year or more?"

"Yeah," I told him without wanting to get into it.

"Here's the slip, Jack. Just need for you to sign it," he said pointing to the line. "I tell ya . . . we're sure gonna miss you around here. It's been a long time."

"Yeah," I said with what seemed like a deep introspective breath. But it really wasn't a deep breath at all.

I had gotten good at keeping things a secret. It wasn't something that I had always been good at. But I'd gotten it down pat over the past few months.

You see, I was really taking a deep swallow to get rid of that damn itchy throat thing that I had going on.

But Bill didn't much notice. That poor old dolt thought I was taking in a breath, like I was contemplating the complexity of all that is The Goddamn First National Bank of Whatever the Hell it was. But I really was just swallowing to get the damn pineapple out of my throat so that I could say goodbye to everybody without looking like a goddamn fool.

Bill counted out $1248 to me as if it was my last handout from some family inheritance or something. He did it real slow too. For a second I almost felt like he was getting the itchy throat thing too, but I doubt that he really cared.

Since he was being all slow handed in giving me my dough, I pretended for just a moment that he was the cashier at some fancy casino cage giving me my winnings from some hot night of blackjack or craps. It kinda took the tension out of room. And it worked too. I felt like a big shot again for a second or two. I really did.

"Well that'll do it, Jackie," he concluded. "Like I said, we're sure gonna miss you around here." He looked at me real serious like. "You're off to Vegas then, huh? Good for you man. You're living the dream!" He smiled.

"Yep. Got Miles in the car. Just two bucks heading out on the road," I said confidently. "I think we're taking Route 66 most of the way there. That seems like the way to do it."

"Milo!" he exclaimed. "Good for you guys!"

"Give him one of these for me," he said. "I'm gonna miss that little bugger."

Bill handed me a couple of Milk Bone's that they had lying around for when someone brought in one of their foo-foo dogs.

"And you take care of yourself my friend. I'll look you up next time I'm out there," he said a little solemnly.

I stuck my hand out and he grabbed it firmly.

"We will meet again, my faithful financier," I said with a slight English brogue, like I would've done with old Peanut Butter M&M. Neither of us laughed though.

At the moment, I wasn't sure why. But neither of us even smiled. I just turned and headed out of that bank as if I was making a getaway. "Have a nice day, sir," the guard said to me through his thick accent. I just looked at my feet and got the hell out of there just the way that Billy the Kid would've done.

And with that, I hopped into the silver bullet.

"Dammit, Miles!" I shouted. He'd taken a dump in the corner of the passenger side.

"Goddammit!" I hollered again. He cowered in the area right under the passenger seat as if he was trying to get under it, but he was far too big.

He could tell that I was pissed. And I was. I was really upset for about a tenth of a second.

But today wasn't an ordinary day, and I wondered how I could be so damned selfish. I had some paper towel, so I picked it up and pulled up next to a garbage can to throw it in.

"Hey there, buddy . . . it's all right," I assured him.

"It was my fault, Milo. I'm sorry," I told him. He licked my hand cautiously.

I've never once hit him. Never. Over my dead body.

He knew I would never hurt him. Not in a million years. I scratched behind his ears the way he liked and merged onto Lake Shore Drive right before a big semi blared his horn at me, startling the crap out of us both.

It was right about then that the tears hit me, the way that I figured they would. And they started coming down pretty goddamn good.

I put my sunglasses on and let 'em roll. They kept pouring down my mug, but I really didn't give a shit. Just like the pussy that I am.

It was probably about the time that I got to the Skyway that I realized what hurt so bad.

You see, the entire world had been shitting on me for the past year or two, and I took it. I could handle it from all of them. All the goddamn bastards who reveled in my ruin and kicked me when I was down. I could take it from them, and it didn't sting all that bad.

All the guys that used to look at me with contempt and disdain until they finally got what they wanted—I could take all that in stride because their day was coming too. And if it wasn't, more power to them. I'm not a vengeful kinda guy.

But Miles was the one thing other than Hope that hadn't shat on me. And it made me feel crummy as hell that, because of my selfishness, the poor little bugger had to take a crap in the only home that he had left.

I knew in that moment that I didn't blame him for what he did any more than I blamed the economy or the President or the real estate bubble for what happened to me. I didn't blame that shitty disease for what happened to my old man or the world for what Jenny did.

I recognized in that instant that I blamed myself for all of it. The whole lot. That's what really hurt. And that realization stung like a bastard.

CHAPTER 5

We got to St. Louis about five in the afternoon. Even though I had the sleeping bag, I figured we'd just crash at some dump in town.

I pulled into a Red Roof Inn that said they had rooms for twenty-nine dollars a night and hopped out of the car. Miles darted out of the driver's side door between my legs and found a light pole to christen. He really had to go. I didn't realize that we had been on the road almost six hours, and my legs could really feel it.

I tried to talk the front desk manager down a little, but twenty-nine dollars was about as low as he was gonna go. So, I paid him in cash for the room. He wanted a credit card for incidentals. For the life if me I couldn't imagine what I could charge to the room. Maybe a nice dinner at the swanky lounge off the lobby? I guessed not.

I reckoned that a lot of truckers came in and bought porn off the TV. That was probably the one way a guy could run up a tab in this place besides damaging the room.

I knew I had a Visa that I didn't wanna use just yet. I also had an Amex that wasn't expired on the front, but they'd cancelled it a few months back.

"I don't run it unless I need to," he said reassuringly. Trying to put my mind at ease, I think.

It did make me feel better about handing over Amex. Obviously, I didn't care since there wasn't anything he could do with it. I just didn't want him having his hands on that Visa since there wasn't a lot left on there. I needed it for the rest of the trip, and I didn't wanna have a problem crashing here if the card didn't work.

I handed the Amex over to the guy, and he seemed fine with it. He ran an imprint and gave me the key. I thought to joke with him about wanting a room with a view, but I didn't think he was the joking kind, so I didn't bother.

Miles and I navigated the steps to the second floor like we'd never used stairs before. And that wasn't too far from the truth. The little guy certainly had elevators down pat, but stairs were unchartered waters for him, so we took our time.

"Man . . . there are sure a lot of little things that you haven't experienced before," I muttered under my breath to him. He was too busy figuring out what to do to pay me any mind.

He'd hop onto one stair and then look around before he'd size the next one up. It was kinda funny to watch, but I tried not to laugh at him too much.

He did it three or four times before I figured I'd help the little bugger out. When I finally picked him up, he licked my face as I scratched behind his ears, and we made it up to 211.

I started to slip the card into the slot, but it didn't matter. The door wasn't latched all the way, so I just pushed it open. I'll level with ya. That did kinda freak me out for a moment before I could find the light switch.

But once the lights were on, I could see that the bed was made, and it didn't seem that any bums were crashing there. I figured that the maid must've accidently not closed the door all the way when she was done cleaning up, and that explanation suited me just fine. Still, just to make sure, I checked the bathroom right away.

Miles followed, stopping to sniff everything within those sleazy walls. I realized that he really hadn't seen anything like a twenty-nine-dollar hotel room before, and I could only imagine that his canine senses were going off the charts.

And if there was any doubt that this was a twenty-nine-dollar hotel room, the bathroom certainly confirmed it.

The toilet seat had six or seven randomly spaced cigarette burns accenting the piss stains around the rim. I yanked the shower curtain aside like James Bond would have done and was glad our only nemesis that night was a dead bug near the drain.

"Okay, Milo . . . whatcha feel like for dinner tonight?" I knelt down, petting his head.

It's kinda funny. I always sort of figured that once we made the break, we'd be a couple of cowboys on the trail, ropin' and ridin', picking up gals, and drinking whiskey till dawn. Rabble rousing and what not.

Yet here we were. It was our first night on the road, and all I wanted to do was order a pizza and pass out.

I thumbed through a few of the tattered pamphlets on the dresser and found a local place that wasn't a chain. I ordered a medium pie and an Italian sausage sandwich. With the local news on the tube, and Miles at the foot of the bed, I guess I drifted off.

CHAPTER 6

The jazz was a little looser than most people usually enjoy, but that was just the way that I liked it. I always had. I'm sort of an aficionado of that kinda crap. Or at least I think that I am.

I could tell that damn near everybody else around us thought that he was playing a trumpet . . . even Jenny did. But I knew it was a godforsaken flugelhorn.

"The tone is just a little richer," I explained, as if I could tell.

The truth is that I couldn't really hear the difference. But I was being a hotshot and couldn't let anyone know I was anything otherwise.

I probably should've just kept my mouth shut, but that's the kind of jerk I can be.

As it was, Jenny and I were quite the spectacle out there. Man, were we stoned. I had scored some mushrooms before we left, and she'd never done anything like that before. Hell . . . she was so darned square that she hadn't even smoked pot.

I handed her a blackish blue cap after we'd gotten good and settled in. She looked at me the way that she used to— with such unconditional trust.

"Are these legal?" she asked innocently.

"They're organic . . ." I responded with a smirk.

We'd eaten them an hour or so before, or at least that's what I figured. And man, we were baked.

The sun was so bright there in Sedona, and the jazz was coming from every direction. The cliffs were like rust in their vibrant shade of dirty red. It was really something. And I was so gosh darned glad that I could share it with her.

We had been there since the show started at eleven in the morning, and for the life of me I had never seen anything like it. We couldn't stop laughing at this one big guy that was about two blankets away from us. Jesus, that son of a bitch could eat. It must've been damned near three hours that we had been there, and this 300-pound guy just ate and ate and ate everything that those poor bastards had dragged up the hill. Jenny was the one that noticed it first, right before we started laughing our asses off.

"Look at that bowl full of salsa that that guy has. Man, he's piling it on," she whispered. "It's like he hasn't eaten in days."

And it sure as hell seemed that way from where we were sitting. All he did was shovel one plate after another into his sweaty old mug.

Little did we know, that was only the beginning. Then came the chicken wings and the ribs and the potato salad and the coleslaw. Some sort of an Italian sub followed by a cold pizza. Then a salad.

"A salad!" We laughed our asses off. "Like he's really watching his weight!"

Still he piled it all down his pie-hole like it was his last supper or something.

A little while later he had a big old hunk of some sort of chocolate dessert in the plastic bowl where his salad had been, and by then we were laughing it up pretty good. If one of us so much as pointed in his direction, we would both burst into tears at the expense of the poor schmuck.

It was really terrible, and I don't usually laugh at other people. But with this guy, we just couldn't help it. He was sweating like a goddamn wild boar or something, and still he just kept stuffing his sweaty, fat face.

"You do know who that guy is, don't you?" I finally asked Jenny, far more sincerely than she'd ever expected out there on that red hill with a belly full of mushrooms.

It was all I could do to keep from cracking up. And for a moment she really thought I was being genuine, that it was somebody there for the jazz festival that she should've known about.

Being high tends to mess with your mind a bit anyways, and in the right shadows, he did look a bit like a fat Forrest Whittaker or that guy from *The Green Mile*. So, I kept it going without much of a struggle to do so.

"No . . . who is he?" she asked, having somehow found that same serious tone inside of all the laughter.

"Seriously? You don't recognize him?" I asked, fighting off the urge to break into gibbering laughter.

"Should I? Is it somebody famous?" She stared glassy-eyed but intently at me. I just smiled and waited.

"Who is it? Who is it?!?! Tell me!" she prodded while pulling at my shirt collar.

I grabbed her shoulders, using all the composure that I had left in me to not burst apart at the seams. I stared squarely into her eyes like some evangelical minister giving some bullshit sermon to a hundred thousand brainwashed believers.

"Well . . ." I said slowly. "Since you obviously don't recognize him, I'll tell you. But you have to promise that you won't embarrass us by asking for his autograph or fawning all over him. Can you pinky swear it?" I asked, sticking my right pinky finger up for her to grab.

"I swear! I swear!" she insisted while wrapping her finger tightly around mine.

"Alrighty then," I conceded. "I'll tell you," I said peering intently in her eyes, not wanting to come undone.

"That's the ugliest man in the world."

Well, I've gotta tell you straight away that we are lucky as hell that we didn't both get our asses handed to us out there on that hill in Sedona that day. I swear that the whole goddamn crowd must've heard us break out into a roar. I think that even the guys up on stage thought to stop their playing, just to find out what in the heck was so goddamn funny.

We must've laughed for the better part of fifteen minutes. For the life of us, we just couldn't stop. It was terrible.

The poor sap a few blankets over had no idea that he was the brunt of our joke. But that didn't stop him or everyone else around us from glaring our way like we were some frickin' lepers or something.

I can't say I blame them though. I'm sure that we were disrupting the concert darned good. It wasn't that we wanted to, but they didn't know that. We were just stoned as all get-out and couldn't help it.

Finally, we fell back on the grass in exhaustion and just laid there. I took my shirt off in that warm Arizona sun, and Jenny put it over her face like a little child would. I think she thought that if she couldn't see all the people around her, they couldn't see her either. It was kinda cute.

We just laid on our backs there for the next hour or so, listening to the sounds of sweet jazz bouncing off the mountainside.

Then, all at once, I snapped to attention. I'd been way out of it. Although I wasn't asleep, I also knew that I wasn't fully awake either. I was definitely in another world. The sun was so bright. And even though I was high as a kite, I could tell that Jenny was getting burnt and didn't know it. I realized that we needed to stay hydrated up there, but we didn't have any water. And in that moment, I sorta panicked.

I knew that she didn't know any of this stuff. She wasn't accustomed to being out at these kinds of things and certainly wasn't used to being this stoned.

I glanced around and saw that we were sort of swallowed up by everyone else. There must've been a few thousand people around us, and I figured that they all knew exactly who *we* were after our outbursts earlier.

I also recognized the distinct possibility that I might have just been freaking out because of the mushrooms. Either way, I had to get her some sunscreen and water, or she was gonna be in dire straits.

Jenny was lying there with my shirt halfway over her face, hiding from whatever she thought that she needed to hide from, and I grabbed her hand. "You all right?" I asked her. She half nodded.

"I think I've gotta get us some water," I said as coolly as I could.

"Yeah . . . water would good," she answered sort of groggy and all. "Water would be *really* good."

I could tell that she meant it too. I saw that she was parched by the way she answered, and I didn't wanna get her riled up. In truth, I was a little worried myself.

I reckoned that I could figure out how to get outta the spot that we were in, but I wasn't certain that I could get back so easy. We'd been there for a few hours or more, and the hill had filled up with a ton of people. But I knew that I had to do it. I needed to take care of her that day. I had to make sure that she was all right. I was responsible for her, and I couldn't let anything happen to us. "Over my dead body," I said calmly to myself.

I recognized right then and there that I had to get going and find her some water and some sunscreen. I got up slowly, put my sunglasses on, and headed out into that vast sea of people and jazz.

I tried to put my mind at ease and put aside the fears that were battling me. As I started walking, I sized up where I was in relation to the stage. I spied that I was three-quarters of the way to stage right and maybe a hundred and fifty feet back. If all else failed, I had to remember this.

But still . . . I was high. Higher than a frickin' kite. And I had to straighten out. If only for a half hour, I had to come down. I couldn't let the loonies take over.

I made it to the back of the crowd without anybody knowing that I was shrooming. At least I don't think that they did. Shit. I don't know. I was shrooming after all.

Finally, I found the concession area and thanked God nobody was in line. "Can I get two of the big ones?" I asked, pointing to the large bottles of water.

"And . . . uh . . . do you have any sunscreen?" I muttered while trying to speak as clearly as I could.

"How strong do you want?" the guy asked me.

I'd never bought sunscreen before, as crazy as that may sound. When I was a kid, my mom would have some around the house, and she'd sure as hell make certain to always put way too much on me. I guess that the rest of my life I sorta rebelled against using sunscreen because of that.

I vividly recalled looking like such a dork as a young punk, all covered from head to toe in it.

"I dunno," I answered like a genius would. "Whichever is the strongest, I guess."

I guessed the guy could tell that I was baked by the slow way he was talking, but then again, it could have been me. I really don't know.

"Well . . . this is for babies, so it's as strong as they make," he explained while holding up a bright pink plastic bottle.

I chewed on that line for a second, and something dawned on me.

That's what we were out there on that rusty old hill— just two infants a million miles from our mothers and fathers. Just like orphans, we were far from everything that made us feel safe.

Jenny was helpless somewhere in that ocean of people, just like a baby plucked from the womb. So goddamn innocent.

She'd never been high before, and she'd never really been in love before me, I don't think. She trusted me so goddamn much to take care of her.

I thought of her dehydrating out there on that rock with people all around her, too wasted to even ask for help, just keeping faith that I'd be back before she'd all but shrivel up and die. I recognized what an asshole I was to leave her all alone.

"I mean . . . adults can use it too . . . it's just really protective if that's what you're looking for," the guy explained. I just stood there.

"You still with me buddy?" he asked, snapping his fingers in front of my face like a doctor might do with a patient that was drifting off.

"Yeah. Of course. I'll take it," I told him knowing that it must've seemed like I was on another planet.

"Just give me fifteen dollars," he said. "That's fine."

I panicked.

I could feel the perspiration shoot from the pores underneath my armpits, and I started to get dizzy. My skin went cold even though I was burning up in the heat.

"Hey . . . you all right man?" the guy asked. "Here. Sit down."

He got up from his lawn chair and gestured for me to come over to it. I made it behind the folding table where the T-shirts were laid out and carefully sized up the folding chair.

It didn't look stable at all, and I knew that if I just plopped down in it, I would more than likely break the damned thing. I turned around, and while peering over my left shoulder, I grabbed one of the aluminum arms.

Then I looked over the other shoulder and grabbed the other one. My forehead was clammy, and my heart was racing a mile a minute.

"Are you on something, kid?" the guy asked as he put his forearms under my shoulders and gently helped ease me down.

"Yeah," I said kinda sheepishly.

"My girlfriend and I took some mushroom caps a few hours ago, and she's down there somewhere near the stage," I told him. "I've gotta get her some water, or she's gonna die," I said with all the urgency I could. Maybe it was even a little too dramatic.

To say she was gonna die is pretty damn serious. But at the time I was really scared shitless.

"Okay. It'll be all right man," he assured me. "Just relax and take a sip of this." He opened one of the bottles of water and handed it to me.

He had a way of making me feel safe, almost like my old man. No judgment. I didn't expect that out there, and it sort of took me by surprise.

"No . . . Here's the problem, man," I said as I peered at him intently. "My wallet is out there with her. I don't have any cash for you."

I pointed in the general direction of the hill where the music was coming from.

"Relax," he said calmly. "Just straighten up with me before you guys leave today. Cool?"

What could I do? I felt like a bowl of Jell-O sitting there in this guy's rickety old lawn chair. The colors were coming at me pretty fierce, and the music all sounded like Bitches Brew or Agartha. It was all warpy.

I didn't know if I should hug the guy or shake his hand. He didn't give me much of a choice. He just put the sunscreen in the pocket of my cargo shorts.

"Go ahead and take care of your girl, man. She needs you," he said as he picked me up from under my shoulders and got me out of the chair.

He handed me the two bottles and scooted me out of the tent.

"Thanks, man," I said, sort of baffled but grateful. "Thanks so much. I'll be back in a bit," I tried to assure him as best I could, considering everything.

I stumbled out into that abyss of colors and sound without looking back at the guy. Just keeping my focus in front of me as much as possible, meticulously placing one foot in front of the other.

I don't recall a whole heck of a lot about how I got back to Jenny that afternoon. I remember looking around and feeling lost for what seemed like an hour or more, even though I know that it wasn't nearly that long.

The crowd had taken on a whole different vibe it seemed. There weren't people anymore, at least not to me. There were just patches of bright reds and oranges, with some blue and purple spots that would come out of nowhere.

I breezed by the blankets of color as if I was on air. I stopped using my head to navigate and instead just relied on some weird compass that was suddenly inside of me. I couldn't follow the music anymore because it seemed as though the music was following me. It was everywhere. It was all around me and coming from inside of me too. Just like the colors were.

I held those two bottles as tightly as I could while traversing the hill that day. I didn't see a single person in that tapestry of color and sound until, all of a sudden and without warning, my legs found something big and heavy, and I met that red dirt head on.

"Oh! 'Scuse me!" I said as a knee-jerk reaction, not knowing if I'd tripped over a person or a dog or a grill or whatever. I was mortified while doing my best to find my feet again and gain some composure.

"Are you okay?" a deep voice asked in a startled fashion. I scrambled to get back up, still clenching tightly to the bottles of water.

"I'm fine," I tried to sound confident and un-fazed.

"Just need to pay a little more attention to where I'm going," I said half-laughingly as my defense mechanisms kicked in.

"Okay . . . just as long as you're all right," the deep voice resonated in a warm gentle fashion.

"Your girl has been passed out over there, and I bet she'll be glad you're back," he said.

Sure enough, there I was—face to face with the ugliest man in the world, brushing off the red rock dust from my shorts and shirt. And you know what I realized right there and then? He really wasn't so ugly after all.

I just smiled and nodded. I needed to get over to Jenny and make sure she was okay.

"Hey, Jen . . . you all right?" I asked, slowly brushing her blonde hair from her forehead. "I'm back."

"I knew you'd be back," she muttered. "I was worried I was going to die up here on this mountain, but then I remembered you were coming for me," she said slowly.

I opened a bottle, leaned the back of her head into my palm and poured the water down her parched throat.

In that moment I felt something that I couldn't put my finger on. I've thought about that moment a whole hell of a lot since then too.

What it was, I think, was connection. Real connection.

There was a connection between Jenny and me then, and it didn't ever really go away after that. At the time, I guess I just didn't know what it was the way I do now. I still feel it. Wherever the heck she is, I still feel her in the palm of my hand, the way I did that day. I can feel how she knew that everything was going to be okay. That we were safe. That it was all right.

The day was pretty darned easy after that. We made idiots out of ourselves by putting way too much sunscreen on our mugs, but it was okay.

We started coming down slowly, and the sun set more magically than either of us had ever seen before. We cherished those bottles of water as if they were Dom Perignon, and we wound up sharing some white-chocolate-covered strawberries with the big guy whose cooler I tripped over on my way back from the concession stand. This time that fat son of a gun was laughing with us, and damned if those didn't turn out to be the best laughs of the day.

After the final act, we got up and bid our new friends goodbye. I grabbed Jenny's hand so that we could make it back down the hill to the concessioner, but he was already gone.

I looked all over, but the only tent still up was the first-aid area. We walked back and forth and forth and back, but he just wasn't there. Jesus . . . I sure felt bad about that. I don't like owing people. Never have, never will. Over my dead body.

CHAPTER 7

"What the hell!?!" I shouted. I awoke startled and confused. Miles jumped about two feet into the air.

"It's just a little hotel room!" I yelled towards the door. "You don't need to kick the frickin' door in!"

"I called three times, and nobody answered. I didn't know what the deal was," a whiny little voice said from the other side of the door.

Sure enough. I looked at my phone and the son of a bitch had called a few times. I had the ringer on vibrate like I usually do, and it was lying on the floor.

"Oh . . . okay. Well I guess that's a good enough reason to scare the shit out of me and my dog," I rifled back sarcastically. "I mean, it's not like you could just knock normally first or anything before you punch a hole in the door."

The delivery guy and I both looked at the door, and sure as shit, there was a big dent in it. It looked like knuckles—it really did—even though it could've been most anything.

"What do I owe ya?" I asked a little snittier than I should have.

"Sixteen eighty with delivery," he chimed back.

I grabbed the twenty I had on the table and folded it in thirds the way I always do, like I was duking some casino host at the old Stardust.

"Here's twenty," I said snidely. "Just keep it partner," I told him.

"Okay," he mumbled back while looking awkwardly at the way that I handed him the bill.

I could tell that he wasn't accustomed to somebody paying that way, and for a moment I sort of wondered why I did. He opened it up and analyzed it closely. Obviously, it was a twenty. I certainly wasn't gonna slip him a five or something and pretend it was twenty dollars, especially not here.

Still, I can't say I blame him for looking at it really good to make sure. What kind of a jerky guy folds a bill in thirds to pay for a pizza? But like I said before, that's just the kind of prick that I can be sometimes.

Before I opened the grub, I got Miles' insulin out of the thermos and was happy that it still seemed chilled. I did what I always did and rolled the bottle in my palms to mix it up a bit and get it close to room temperature. I filled the syringe up to eight units, put the orange cap back on the needle, and set it on the dresser. By the time I turned around Miles, had come out from under the bed where he'd been hiding after that goofy delivery guy showed up.

"Okay, buddy . . . I know . . . I know. I bet you're starving," I said, rubbing his head as he stood on his hind legs. I got in and around the ears, right in the sweet spot where it feels the best.

I opened the Italian sausage and broke it into little bite-sized pieces. With the smell of meat hitting the air, Miles pawed at my leg, but not in a pushy way like some other dogs. Miles wasn't like other dogs. He never had been.

Other mutts would be begging and all. But with Miles, it was more like he was saying thanks, even before you did anything for him. He'd always been that way, ever since he was a pup. I guess that's why I decided to keep him way back when.

I think I always knew that he was special, and in some strange way it sorta made me feel like I was special too, even if it was only him that saw me that way.

I put the bite-sized pieces back in the Styrofoam container that the sandwich came in and tore off a bit of the bun too. I knew that the bread wasn't good for him with the diabetes and all, but I worried that the sausage wasn't going to be enough for the little bugger.

"There you go, buddy. That's the good stuff," I smiled.

I grabbed the syringe, took the orange cap off, and gently put it in without him caring. Like usual, he was far too busy gobbling down his chow. I pushed the hammer down, pulled the needle back out, and then rubbed the scruff of his neck like I always did.

"You're such a good boy, Miles," I said as if he gave a hoot. "Such a good boy."

He didn't much pay me any mind. He was far too busy enjoying his Italian sausage. But rubbing the scruff of his neck always made me feel good, probably good enough for the both of us, I reckoned.

I opened the pizza box and realized that I wasn't really that hungry. My mind was elsewhere.

I figured that I ought to give Hope a shout just to let her know that I was all right, but I didn't really want to lie to her. She was probably asleep anyways. I decided I'd reach out in the morning when I was on the road. Even if I got her voice mail, at least I'd leave a message.

But the truth is that Jenny was really on my mind. It stung really bad, knowing that I couldn't just call her. She was always up for a phone call no matter what time it was. She'd always be there to talk to, even if it was about nothing at all. We could talk more about nothing than anybody could.

The pizza didn't really taste all that bad considering. I was a little bummed when I opened it up and the cheese was all orange, the way it can be when you're not getting pizza in Chicago or New York. These small towns will do that to you. They put cheddar or some other kind of weird cheese on their pizza, and you won't even think to ask about it until you open the goddamn box in your sleazy hotel room long after the young punk delivery guy has left.

Just about then, you realize: *Shit! They put that orange crap on my pizz*a. But by then it's too late.

I picked off most of the orange spots and ate two and a half slices.

I headed down the hall with the garbage can from beside the bed and grabbed some ice from the machine with all the mosquitoes, flys, and other bugs around it. I made it back to the room, filled the sink with cold water, and dumped a bunch of cubes in there for the insulin.

I knew I couldn't let it freeze, but I had to keep it cold. I put the vial in the sink right about the time that I realized that I hadn't brushed my teeth yet. So, I sat on the side of the tub and brushed 'em as good as I could.

Then I grabbed one of the washcloths from the back of the door. I tore off the plastic wrap of the cheap crap that they call *facial soap*, lathered it on my face and neck, and rinsed off under the large faucet on the grubby old tub with the bug in it.

By the time I was done, Miles was already conked out at the foot of the bed, and I reckoned I ought to do the same.

"Goodnight, buddy" I mumbled into the night. "Sleep tight." I don't think he really gave two shits. He was out like a light.

CHAPTER 8

I don't think I had any more crazy dreams that night. I was zonked the second my head hit the pillow. I can't remember the last time I slept so soundly. It felt like it was the first night that I'd ever really slept. Or at least the first night in almost forever that I had.

I figured that it must've been the last couple of days that finally caught up with me. Maybe even the last couple of years. Either way, I slept right through, and before I knew it the sun was shining bright as can be through the slits on those cheap hotel blinds. Miles looked like he hadn't moved an inch, and I could hear him snoring by my feet.

I knew that we had to get the day started, but I wanted to just take a minute first to appreciate the moment. As corny as it may sound, I didn't know how many more we'd have like this, so I decided to take it all in.

Without moving my legs too much, I propped my head back on the pillow and just watched Miles sleep. There was something so perfect about the way that little bugger was when he was really under.

I don't think I'd ever even caught him snoozing until he was at least five or six years old. Back then, he was always running and jumping and playing the way that terriers do. But you could catch him sleeping a whole lot more often these last few years. It always made me feel at peace. I don't really know why. It just did.

I watched his whiskers move and his upper lip go in and out. I wondered if he had dreams too and what they might be about. I knew that I'd seen him flinching and flailing from time to time. He'd even let go of a little bark every now and again while he was under. I imagined his dreams were so much simpler than mine.

Throughout all we had been through over the past nine years or so, I figured that his dreams were always pretty much the same. Maybe it's selfish, but I guessed that his dreams were always about just being with me.

I thought of all the different dreams that I'd had myself over those years. How they'd changed so goddamn much.

It always seemed that there were so many important dreams careening through my mind over the past decade. Money, cars, girls. Whatever.

But this day, as we lay there in a twenty-nine-dollar hotel room in St. Louis, the only dream that really mattered was the one that I figured he was having all along. And I realized in that very moment that his dream was the very best one of all.

"Okay, buddy. Time to get going," I said as I maneuvered my legs out of the still tightly made bed. He awoke and immediately scampered up to my face to give me some sugar.

"Okay, okay . . . that's enough," I said sternly. I always acted like I hated it when he would do that sort of crap.

He'd lick me right on the kisser, and that was just a little too much for me. Always had been. I know that some of those foo-foo dog owners enjoy that sort of shit, but I always thought it was damned disgusting. No matter how much you might care about your goddamn dog, his tongue sure as heck doesn't belong anywhere near yours. Over my dead body.

We were out of there in sixty seconds, I would say. Maybe ninety at the most. I grabbed the insulin from the sink and filled a syringe up to eight. After gently putting the vial in the thermos, I brushed my teeth with some of the facial soap even though it tasted like shit.

I scraped off the cheese from some of the leftover pizza and put a whole slice in my mouth. Truth is, it wasn't half bad.

I took the little pieces of sausage and pepperoni that were on the four remaining slices and threw them in the Styrofoam container from the night before and tossed it in my bag. Then we were gone.

We had a long day ahead of us, and I was filled with a buzz that I hadn't felt in far too long. I think Miles had it too. He had a real skip in his step just like he used to. When I saw our reflection in the windows of the rooms as we walked by, I realized that I did too.

Once we got to the parking lot, he ran over to a fern at the edge of the drive. I threw the bag in the pocket seat of the Porsche, set the Styrofoam container on the passenger's side floor, and started up the engine. Once Milo did his business, I picked it up in a leftover napkin and threw it in the dumpster.

With that, I opened the door and he hopped right in. I pulled out the syringe, grabbed the scruff of his neck and put the hammer down.

Then we were off. With Townes Van Zandt on the stereo and us ropin' and ridin', we were gone.

I plugged Albuquerque into the GPS as I rolled out of the driveway. While Miles fidgeted with the leftovers in the makeshift Styrofoam bowl, I managed to grab a handful of kibble and threw it into the container.

I knew that I had to keep his sugar level in check, and that wasn't going to be as easy on the road. But I was sure we'd manage. Just like we always did.

Then I thought about the road before us. Seventeen hours seemed like a helluva day. Even if we could drive it, why the heck should we?

We didn't have anywhere that we needed to be. We were just two bucks on the road with no agenda. It felt kinda free. Like Pancho and Lefty, the two of us were. Like I said, ropin' and ridin'.

I yanked out an old road map that I had in the glove compartment from when Jenny and I drove around the lake the year before. Although it was a map of the Great Lakes, the back-side did have the whole U.S. and Canada. That gave me some sort of an idea of where I was, and where I wanted to be.

I spied a few different ways that we could get to Vegas by way of New Mexico. Oklahoma seemed like the most logical one, and sitting right about halfway between us and the Land of Enchantment was a town called Okemah. So, I plugged it in with one hand while keeping the other on the wheel.

It took a minute or two for Matilda to get the route calculated. By the time she did, I was already heading the wrong way down the frontage road, but that didn't much matter. I did a U-turn and whipped around with Miles sitting shotgun. Townes' raspy voice was louder than it oughta be, and a billion thoughts were cycling through my head.

Now the truth is that I picked Okemah for a reason, even though I pretty much figured it was going to be a shithole. There were certainly more metropolitan places that a guy could hit somewhere between St. Louis and Las Vegas, but Okemah was a place that I always wanted to check out.

You see, Woody Guthrie was from Okemah, and my gut was telling me that walking the same streets that he walked a hundred years before or whatever might just have a bit of him rub off on me. At least I knew it couldn't hurt.

Woody and all his hard travelin'. You know, that's where all of his stories came from. The whole Dust Bowl thing started somewhere down there right around the time of the Great Depression.

I never was much of a history buff, but I sure knew Woody, and that was plenty of history for a fellow, I supposed.

I'd always sorta resonated with the stuff he sang about and the life he lived. Seeing Okemah pop out on the map felt for a moment like it was just meant to be. Even though it probably wasn't.

Either way, we were headed there by our own volition. Nobody else's call. Just ours. And that felt free. Damned free.

We were on autopilot the whole way it seemed. It must've been darn near the flattest place on earth. I don't think I saw a single hill or lake the whole way, and the four or five times that I realized that we were pushing 105 made me thankful as hell that there didn't seem to be any cops out there either.

It sure was a desolate stretch, that four hundred miles or so. Sometimes it seemed like an hour or more that I didn't even hear a peep outta Matilda on the GPS. If I hadn't been so damned mesmerized by the road, I can see how a guy could feel kind of alone. But I sure didn't.

I tried to call Hope a handful of times, but there wasn't a lick of service out there in the middle of nowhere. I reckoned it was just as well. She'd probably be busy in some important meeting at work anyhow.

I figured out that there are a whole lot of places that a fellow's mind can wander when he's in the middle of nowhere. I thought about Woody, and how he probably traveled these same stretches with Lead Belly, Seeger, or Cisco back in his day. The only difference was that he was in a boxcar on some rickety old freight train, and I was behind the wheel of a German sports car. He'd probably hate that.

Yeah, we were free. Just about as much as we weren't.

He had his choices, I reckoned. Hell, he could've jumped off one line and hopped on another going in the opposite direction at any old time if he wanted to. But while he was on that train, he really didn't have a whole helluva lot of say about where to ride. And here I was, sitting on autopilot following Matilda's instructions to the T.

Both of us were on a road to find something that we didn't even know was out there. We were in the middle of nowhere, longing to be somewhere. Searching for an answer or even a clue. Lost—trying to get found.

My mind was really wandering, and I realized that I couldn't remember the last time that I wasn't at least just a little scared deep down inside. I wondered if Woody was frightened too when he was writing all those powerful songs.

I was doing a hundred or more when Matilda told me that the exit for Okemah was in four hundred feet, so rather than dying in a fireball along the interstate, I blew past that exit and decided to turn off at the next one instead.

There sure weren't a lot of signs lining the highway near Okemah. And the next exit was a good five miles up at some rural route. We got off, and I decided to fill up the tank at a Valero so we'd be ready to do it all again the next day.

Miles woke up as soon as I stopped at the pump and made it clear that he had to go. He hopped out of the driver's door as soon as I opened it, and I grabbed him in mid-air.

"Hey, hey, buddy . . . be careful!" I scolded.

I knew that he couldn't just be leaping out into nowhere without knowing where he was going. Still, I recognized that he wasn't accustomed to not recognizing his surroundings. He'd probably never really worried about all that much before. He didn't have to. He never knew the real world, and he was going to have to get adjusted to the way that things were going to be from now on.

I sort of held him up so that he could analyze everything around him. So he wouldn't become roadkill.

When I set him down, he ran right over to one of the yellow guard poles for the pumps and started peeing on it. I didn't think anybody would really mind. There wasn't much of anyone there anyways.

I yanked out my credit card to put in the pump before I realized that there wasn't any place to slide it. The pump must've been fifty years old or more. It still had the reels like a slot machine and a lever to reset it on the side. I stood there kinda bewildered like an idiot or something.

"Go ahead and pump your gas!" a voice yelled from the doorway of the aluminum shed nearby. "You can pay when you're done!" she hollered.

I gestured to the grey-haired woman and reset the pump the way I used to back when I was a kid. It was almost like riding a bike. You never forget.

The reels spun around and around, and I stood there entranced by the ticking. It reminded me of when I used to fill up my old VW as a teenager.

Before I knew it, the pump shut itself off. Instinctively I pumped a few more dimes in to get it to the top, just like I used to do.

Miles was off sniffing around the tall grass near the frontage road, and I called him back. I figured that he'd taken a dump. Although I probably should've looked closer, I didn't really think it much mattered. The way that the grass and weeds had over-grown I doubted that anybody'd been over there in years, so I called off any reconnaissance mission.

With that, I opened the door and he hopped right in like he was a puppy or something. I started her up and went inside to get the gal paid.

"Whaddaya owe me?" a smoky voice said.

At first, I was kinda taken aback. I was wondering what the heck she was even talking about. But I could tell right away that she was a sweetheart. She was saying it in a warm way. Still, with that country accent, I really wasn't sure at first.

"Oh . . . I don't know exactly . . ." I stuttered.

"That's all right sweetie. I'll go check," she responded. I think she could tell that I wasn't used to the process. She headed outside to get the numbers from the pump.

I was looking in the cooler for a pop when I realized that there was a baby in a crib behind the counter. It must've been her grandkid because she was way too old to be the mom of a new born, I figured. I grabbed a Frostie Root Beer out of the fridge. I hadn't seen Frostie since Boy Scouts a million years ago.

"Sixty-eight seventy," she said. "That yours too?" She pointed to the chilled can of root beer.

"Yep . . ." I smiled. "I haven't had a Frostie in years."

"What you oughta do is head down to the Tasty Queen and get yerself a scoop of soft serve in a big old cup. There ain't nothing better than mixing that up." She sounded like my old man back in the day.

I handed her my card and she pointed to some chicken scratched sign on the register. *Cash Only*, it read. "It says so on the pump too, sonny," she smiled gently. I should've known she'd call me sonny.

I didn't have a whole lot of cash left, and I really hated to be using it. If all else failed, I knew that I had to hold onto the real thing.

"Okay . . . I'll be right back then," I told her assuredly.

I popped the hood and dug into the side pocket of my duffle. As I did, I thought of something. And the more I pondered it, the more I realized that the idea didn't seem so bad.

The gal was more than likely paying attention to that little red-headed bundle of joy in there. I reckoned that she didn't own the station, and I knew that I could be a mile down the road past the cornfield before she'd even know it.

I figured that if they didn't have digital pumps, registers, or even a credit card machine that they sure as shit didn't have surveillance cameras out there. It seemed like a no brainer. Just like Pretty Boy Floyd, we'd be gone.

I peeked back over my shoulder and didn't see her head in the window at all. Truth is, with the goddamn price of gas these days, this would easily be a night's stay at some shithole in Okemah.

My heart started to race like it used to, and I could even feel the perspiration in my pits from adrenaline. I felt just like a kid about to run off with a pack of gum or a *Playboy*. The 911 was already running and ready with about 450 horses, and I was jazzed up at how easy this was gonna be.

Just then I stopped.

What the hell am I thinking? I asked myself. "I'm not that kinda guy," I said under my breath to nobody at all.

Over my dead body am I gonna screw somebody outta something. Never have, never will. And none of any of this bullshit is gonna change that.

I walked in with a hundred dollar bill folded three ways like I was duking the maître de at The Pump Room and handed it to her. "We'll just call it seventy," she smiled sweetly as she got up from the crib where that little piece of shit was lying in its own feces, I guessed.

She handed me back a twenty and a ten. I didn't say nothing as I headed out to the car, leaving the root beer behind. Wondering what had come over me for that moment.

"Sir, sir" she hollered in my direction. "You forgot your Frostie!"

"You enjoy it." I told her. "It's on me."

I can't say that I was proud about those feelings that I was having. I began thinking about just how thin that line is between doing the right thing and doing the wrong.

I realized that it wasn't about whether or not I could've gotten away with it, because I know in my gut that I could have, at least the way that most of us would define getting away with it, that is.

But to get away with it in the conventional sense of the word maybe didn't mean getting away with it with yourself, you know? That's the person you've gotta answer to when you're lying in bed alone at night or staring at in the morning while you're brushing your teeth. Shit. What the hell did I know anyway?

All I can tell you is that I could've gotten away with a lot of stuff over the last couple of years if I'd set out to do so. I could've stolen and cheated a whole bunch of people if I had it in my blood. But the truth is that I don't. And I wouldn't change that one bit even if I could.

I drove up and down the three or four blocks that is Okemah, Oklahoma. It was more abandoned buildings than much of anything else. Between the vacancies, was a jewelry store that advertised that they bought gold and sold Wittnauer watches. That really cracked me up. I wondered who the hell would be proud of that.

I saw an old five and dime that seemed like it might still see some traffic and a movie theater called The Crystal. That was pretty much it.

The weirdest thing though was that there wasn't a soul out there in that old Dust Bowl town. I must've seen at least ten pickup trucks parked along that drag, but not one person walking or shopping or even pan handling. Nobody was out there walking a dog. It was deader than a doornail. Whatever that means.

By the time I got to what seemed like the end of the strip, I finally saw a little hustle and bustle. There was a Dollar Depot right next to a liquor store, and a block away I spotted some sort of a locally owned grocery called Homeland Foods.

I figured I'd head into the liquor store and grab a beer, but I gave it a second thought when I saw the two drunks sitting out in front of it. At least I figured they were drunks. They sure looked like it. I didn't want any trouble, so I made the hard right and headed down to the Homeland place and parked the 911 in front.

"No, buddy . . . I'm just running in for a second," I told Miles as I gave him a stroke along the backbone. He was good that way. He always knew what I was trying to say.

I walked through the double doors, and it stunk like old gizzards or something. It's funny how you never forget what one of these old bumblefrick grocery stores smells like. I swear to Christ that I would never buy anything that wasn't packaged, canned, or bottled outta one of these dumps. Over my dead body.

Even if I lived in one of these towns, which I doubt I ever would, I'd eat fast food for the rest of my life before I bought anything from a deli or a butcher at one of these places.

You forget all about the stench when you're living in the city, but the second you walk into one of these hick places, you remember really quick. It doesn't take much. I'm sure that the ninety-four-degree day with ninety percent humidity wasn't helping it much either.

I headed back to the cooler and grabbed a forty-ouncer of some goofy looking malt liquor with a dragon on the can and was surprised to find a bottle of Fiji. I snatched it up too and headed to the front of the store.

The gal at the register sized me up really quick. I could tell from the sneer she gave with her pierced upper lip that she didn't much like my kind. On a different day I would have given a shit. But today I didn't.

"That's four fifty," she said without even punching anything in the register. Like I said, on a different day I would have given her a hard time, but today I didn't much care.

"Do you take plastic?" I asked more genuinely than she deserved, showing her my credit card.

Now of course you've gotta know that this snoot rolled her eyes at me. I mean I reckoned that they must take EBT for the people in town on food stamps, so they must accept some sort of card. I knew that there must be a system in place. But I wasn't a local, and I know that makes a whole hell of a lot of difference in these types of places.

I handed over my card, and you would've thought it was killing her. She punched a few numbers in the register and swiped it. It came up to four-dollars and eighty nine cents, which was fine I figured. She was close enough the first time, so I bit my lip. She couldn't have been more than sixteen years old, and probably not much snittier than I was at that age.

"You need to sign it, mister," she said down her nose at me. I grabbed the pen and scribbled on the slip.

I smiled at her, and she actually smiled back. I have a hunch that she didn't expect a grin outta me, and I caught her eye as I slid the slip back to her too.

"Where's the nearest motel that'll take dogs?" I asked her reluctantly. I could tell that she must've thought I was nuts for wanting to spend any more time in her godforsaken town than I needed to.

"Well," she exhaled deeply. "There's really only one motel in town. You've gotta take a left out of the lot onto Guthrie, and it'll be on your right about two miles down past the water tower."

"That's it?" I was kinda shocked that a town could only have one place for a fellow to flop at.

"Yep. That's it, mister. Nobody much comes to Okemah unless they've got to," she said as if she was proud of it in a strange way.

"Well . . . either that, or if they've got nowhere else to be," I smiled.

"Tell me about it," she chuckled, almost as if she'd warmed up to me.

"I guess that sometimes you've gotta go to the middle of nowhere to find what you're looking for," I chimed like it was the line from a song that I'd memorized for a school play or something. But the truth is I just pulled it outta my ass. Still, it was good.

The more I thought on it, the more I realized that it was damn good. Once in a while I can do that when I'm in the zone. When things flow, I can say some pretty goddamn profound shit.

"That's good, mister. I gotta remember that," she said kinda respectfully in a weird sorta way.

I mean not too respectfully. Don't get me wrong. She really was a quirky little punk. But still, she seemed like a different kid than she was when I walked in. Maybe not, what the hell do I know? But I could tell that she was digging my shit right then and there, and for some odd reason that was important to me.

I hopped in the Porsche and started her up. I scratched Miles behind the ears the way he liked while he sat there in the co-pilot's seat. I cracked open that beer without even bothering to look around to see who was there, and I took about the biggest darned gulp I'd ever taken.

And sure enough, there it was: Woody Guthrie Street, staring us in the face right smack dab in the middle of downtown Okemah, Oklahoma. I took a left as the tires kicked up dust on the gravely blacktop, and we headed on down the road.

I chugged another big swig down to about half of that forty-ouncer. I still had that buzz from the kid at the food mart, and I started singing to myself a little. At first it was just in my head, just like that old Groucho Marx song from *Animal Crackers*—the one that had been driving me half nuts as of late. But then I started mouthing it, and then I guess I started singing it out loud since it was just the two of us with nobody else around.

"This land is your land. This land is my land. From California to the New York island. From the Redwood Forest to the Gulf Stream waters. This land was made for you and me."

I rubbed Miles head the way that he likes, right in and behind the ears and all. Right in the sweet spot.

Miles just sat there, loving his loving. And I sat there loving mine right back.

It was strange, but it was one of the few things left that made me feel at home. No matter where we were, being with him made me feel connected. Don't ask me why, because I sure as shit couldn't tell you. But it made me feel safe.

As we drove down Guthrie, I realized that it felt like forever that I'd had people bugging the shit outta me. Bill collectors and the IRS. Phony-ass friends trying to rip off whatever meat was still left on my bones before it was all gone to the rest of the vultures. Hope wanting more than I could give. Shit . . . even my own goddamn mother wanting to know what the hell I was gonna do with my sorry-ass life now.

But in that very moment I recognized that I finally got what I'd been wishing for. Miles and I were all alone without anybody bothering us for anything. It was just the two of us.

And as much as I'd wanted that, it still stung like hell. Right in my gut. And the only thing that made it any better was rubbing that little guy right behind the ears.

"As I went walking that ribbon of highway, I saw above me that endless skyway. I saw below me that golden valley. This land was made for you and me," I mumbled as I took another swig.

I put my sunglasses on because I knew that I was going to start pissing in my pants again. Miles looked up at me because he knew it too. The way he always does.

I just rubbed inside of his little ears with my thumb and middle finger real hard but gentle, and I could feel him taking it all in.

I felt those pansy-ass tears start a-coming down. But I was okay with it. I guess that, right then and there, I didn't mind being a wuss.

There was a shitload of stuff going on inside of me, and I figured that it needed to come out somehow, some way. So I cried and I sang. Just like the pussy that I am.

"I roamed and rambled, and I followed my footsteps, to the sparkling sands of her diamond deserts. And all around me, a voice was sounding. This land was made for you and me."

Miles looked up at me and I realized I wasn't really singing as much as I'd started hollering. Still, you could tell that there wasn't anywhere else that he wanted to be.

He didn't miss nothing. He didn't miss the old place with its fancy granite and marble. He didn't care much about Egyptian cotton or gold-plated fixtures. Home wasn't any of those things to him. To him, home was wherever I was, even if it was Okemah, Oklahoma, windows down and sun roof wide open, the wind whipping through our hair, drowning out our horrific crooning.

"There was a big high wall there that tried to stop me. A sign was painted, said 'Private Property.' But on the backside, it didn't say nothing. That side was made for you and me. That side was made for you and me."

We kept looking at each other as I unraveled. But he didn't feel awkward in that moment. My most faithful companion. My Robin. My Tonto. Or was I his? Hell, if I know.

In the end, it didn't really matter all that much who was Robin or Tonto. All that mattered was that we were there together. And we were.

CHAPTER 9

I saw the water tower off to the left and kept my eyes out. Sure enough, there was a Days Inn that looked like it should have been torn down about a hundred years ago.

At first, I thought to just drive on to the next big town, but something had gotten us there in the first place. I wasn't gonna start rethinking it now, especially considering all the shit I'd been feeling driving down Guthrie then and there.

I pulled into the lot and saw that the office was a free-standing building in front of the motel. I spied somebody's head inside but didn't wanna go in just yet.

I pulled around back and grabbed a few squares of the paper towels that I had lying in back seat and peeked at myself in the rear view. I was a mess, just like I figured. I rubbed my eyes really good, took a super deep breath, and thought for a brief moment about Hope. That always got me outta these things when they came on. She really was an angel.

Cleaned up as best as I could be with that paper towel, I pulled up in front of the office. The door was wide open and the guy inside seemed startled for a moment. I don't think he really expected to see anyone, but he smiled warmly, and I could tell that I liked him.

I walked in and it was hot as hell. Either he didn't have any air conditioning, or he was too cheap to be using it, which really is the same thing. He was probably the last person you'd want to be getting a motel room from, because you could tell right off the bat that he was a cheap ass. But then again, if you're looking for an inexpensive place to crash, he might be exactly who you'd be looking for.

He had a couple of fans blowing the dust around, and the guy's forearms sort of straddled his desk. It was almost as if he was using his arms to hold down papers on either side of him as he was reconciling the books or something. Just then, he grabbed them all and shuffled them in some sort of half-assed way before putting them in the top desk drawer.

"Welcome," he said warmly. "How may I help you?"

"I have a reservation for the Presidential Suite," I smiled with a cocky sort of laugh.

He looked out at my car and then back at me. "They are all Presidential Suites at my motel, sir," he mused back at me.

I could tell that he was East-Indian or Pakistani.

"Of course, they are," I said cheerfully. "How much for one of them?" I asked.

"It's forty-nine dollars a night plus tax, sir," he said rather seriously.

I told him that was fine and handed him my card.

I heard a little bustle coming from one of the rooms inside the office, which I figured to be his family. The door opened when he called, and a middle-aged woman with a red dot on her forehead came out to instruct him in their native tongue which room was best for me. He handed me an old metal key for the deadbolt and pointed upstairs to my room.

"Let me know if it meets your expectations, sir. If you should need anything at all, my name is Sanjay, but my friends call me Jay," he said as I shook his hand.

"And I suppose that if I shouldn't need anything at all, that your name is still Sanjay, and your friends still call you Jay," I said joking, but in an affectionate sorta way.

He got the humor, and I was glad he did. He probably understood more than most the goofiness of the English language.

"I'm sure it will be just fine," I told him knowing full well that it wasn't going to be the Ritz. But I really didn't care. With that, I hopped in the Porsche, and we pulled into the space in front of room 201.

We hobbled up the stairs with our bag, and I looked back at my new friend. I realized then that I didn't tell him that I had a dog. But somehow, I didn't think that it mattered. As he watched us unload and go inside, he just waved and smiled. I waved back, and I knew he was all right. I have a sense about those kinda things. I always have.

I fumbled with the deadbolt for just a second. It had been a while since I had used one, and they all seem like they're temperamental in their own ways, especially when you throw a humid, late summer day into the mix.

But we made it in okay, and I went straight for the thermostat to turn it down as low as it would go. The unit kicked right in with air that took about sixty seconds to get cool, but I was relieved when it did. We were fine. We had a roof and a bed, at least for today.

As if it were a routine that I had practiced for years, I unpacked the necessary stuff. I yanked out Miles' bowl and filled it with water from the tap, which I quickly poured into the bathtub and replaced with Fiji once I saw the best that Okemah had to offer. I dumped some of his kibble on a paper plate that Jay had evidently stocked the room with, and he started gobbling it down like he hadn't eaten for days.

I pulled out the thermal bottle, and it was still cool. All the ice had melted, but the insulin was still chilled. I closed it up quickly and set it next to the door so that I wouldn't forget. I pulled out my bag of bathroom stuff and brushed my teeth with some of the remaining Fiji.

I didn't trust the stuff out of the tap, but I did let it run anyways thinking that it might clear up a little. It kinda did, which made me feel a little better about the idea of taking a shower, but I still just rubbed some deodorant under my pits and splashed some cool water on my face instead. When I finished, I chugged almost all of the remaining forty-ouncer, which was getting warm quicker than I would've liked.

Miles seemed to find a spot by the TV that suited him just fine. He had dozed off, so I figured I'd let him be. When we were back in the condo, he'd sleep damn near half the day. I figured that being on the road and all must really be throwing him for a loop.

I could hear his little snoot snoring ever so quietly, and that made me feel good. I reckoned that I could really use a little time to myself anyways, and this town didn't seem like they would take too well to some city slicker with his little foo-foo dog. It's not like he was a pit bull, Rottweiler, pinscher, or shepherd. Either way, I thought that I'd head out for a spell and grab a bite to eat.

I almost tripped on the thermos on my way out the door. "Shit!" I yelped to no one.

"Well . . . I guess that's why I put it there," I said to myself.

I grabbed the ice bucket and slipped off my Diesels. I slid one between the door and the frame and darted off down the hall barefoot like I was a ten-year-old on a family vacation

I could hear the walkway rattle as I ran, so I slowed down. I knew that I must be about a hundred pounds heavier than I was the last time that I ran down a second-story motel hallway. I didn't wanna make too big of a ruckus, even though I presumed I was the only one in the whole goddamn place besides Jay and his family.

I got to the machine and filled the bucket all the way, even though I didn't really need that much. I jogged back to the room and made my concoction of water and ice in the sink, and popped the insulin in.

Miles was still snoozing, so I took a few treats from the side pocket of our suitcase and set 'em in front of his little snoot. He didn't stir a peep, so I felt good about leaving the little guy alone for a bit. Still, I knew that he needed his medicine before I left, so I got it ready and shot him up.

He barely flinched. But he did manage to open his eyes and gobble up the Milk Bones in about a second. I put the plate of kibble in front of him in case he needed a little to offset the insulin a bit. He just closed his eyes and went back off to dreamland.

I rummaged through my stuff and found my favorite shoes: a pair of Mark Nasen's that I'd had for the better part of the last ten years. They'd gotten a little worn, but they fit like a glove and looked cool as heck.

I slipped 'em on and headed out to see what the night had in store. The whole time my heart was racing like I was off to the prom or something. I didn't know why. I just felt something inside that was picking me up, so I figured I'd go with it. I didn't have much else going for me at the moment, so I knew I'd best take whatever I could.

I'll tell ya right now that a Friday night in Okemah is probably quite a lot like a Monday night or a Tuesday night.

I'd bet it's the same as Saturday night in Okemah, too. There wasn't a whole hell of a lot to do, but I figured that was all right. I didn't really come there for the nightlife anyhow. I headed to the only place there was to head to, I reckoned. I took Guthrie to Main and hung a left. I knew that was about as much of a downtown as I was gonna find. Cruising down the main drag, I noticed there was a bit more activity than earlier, especially around The Crystal.

When I got there, rather than driving up and down like some school kid cruising the boulevard, I decided to just park. There were plenty of spaces, so I nabbed one right out in the open in front of a vacant store.

Even though I was taking everything in and appreciating it, I sure as shit felt out of place. I hadn't noticed earlier, but every single car or truck in this town was American made, and damned near all the pickups had shotguns straddling the headrests.

Among the people milling about, it seemed that there wasn't a single guy that didn't have a cowboy hat on. They were really nice ones too, not like the ones you'd find in a truck stop or something. And everyone—I mean everyone— was dressed in blue jeans and boots.

Now, I don't normally mind being different. The truth is that I'd always been a little different than the average Joe. I wore my hair a little longer, and I'd try to dress a little more stylish than the other guys. I was always sharp, and I prided myself on that.

Even back in grade school I listened to The Beatles and Dylan when everybody else was all caught up in whatever the latest boy band was.

When all the guys went off on their parent's dime to some four-year university in Pricksville or wherever, I went to Oakhurst, the local two-year place. And I worked at the burger joint in town to make ends meet.

When all my buddies ran off and got married, I ran off and stayed single. They bought starter homes in the suburbs. I bought a condo in the heart of it all, where all the action was.

I never thought twice about being a lone wolf, but I'd be lying if I said that I was crazy about being so goddamn different here in Okemah. This seemed like a town that you wouldn't wanna stand out in all that much. I did my best to not make eye contact, but I could feel everyone staring at me.

I thought for a second about looking up with one of those crazy-eyed glares that I'd perfected a long time ago in the city, but I didn't. I was glad I didn't too, because I could feel that I came up to about the knees on a most of these dudes.

The truth is that I half expected them to say something to me. But nobody said a word. Not a gosh darned thing.

They might not have even noticed me walking by them for all I know. I could've been just imagining it. I can do that sometimes. Jenny used to say it was because I was insecure. Insecure my ass. I've got nothing to be insecure about. I knew I could run circles around most guys. But she always used to say that I was, even though I know I wasn't.

Just past The Crystal there was a place that didn't look half bad for a beer or two. The name on the old brick building caught my eye, and I figured that for a guy who didn't really fit in, this could be a place.

It was called the Fink Building, and I reckoned that seemed about right for me. I stepped into the old dingy basement where they had a bar, although I guess you might call it a tavern.

In the corner, I saw a guy and a gal setting up some sort of a microphone and amplifier. They had an old banner up over the stage that read "Bonnie and Clyde," but it surely had seen some much better days.

I could tell the walls were filled with stories. I just needed somebody to tell 'em to me, I figured, so I copped a squat. This place must've been a hundred years old if it were a day. You could feel it in the damp air.

I spied a couple of cute girls at the end of the bar, but figured they were with the young punks next to them. They were dolls though, especially for this town. I instinctively did what I always do. I made eye contact with them.

The one smiled back a time or two, but I knew to back off before I wound up in a mess. I wondered what the hell they were doing with those young goofs before I finally figured out that they were probably the same age as the guys. That's when I really backed off.

It's funny how the chicks that I tended to go after hadn't changed all that much in twenty years. I just kept forgetting that *I* had changed.

If there was a lineup, I'd still go for the eighteen-year-old blonde with blue eyes or the brunette with long legs. The guys looked like kids to me more and more these days, but the gals always looked just right. It's nucking futz.

I couldn't recall the last time I'd hit on a girl my own age. It must have been ten or twelve years ago, I'd guess. Half the time I'd start talking to 'em and find out that they'd never even heard of Led Zeppelin or Pink Floyd or whatever. About the time that they'd say, "I think I've seen a picture of him before," I'd wonder if I was banging their mom about a nine months before they were born.

At least that's what's going through my mind half the time. Shit. One of these days I'm gonna get my ass kicked by some gal's father. But what am I gonna do? They still look like my next girlfriend no matter how old I get. Always have, always will.

"Hey, pal. Can I grab a shot of Beam and a light beer from ya?" I asked real coolly as I looked in the direction of teenage kid behind the bar.

The punk looked up at me from under the brim of his white cowboy hat like he wanted to slug me or something. Truth is, he probably did. Or maybe I was just imagining it because of my insecurities.

He didn't say a word. Not a goddamn thing.

It was funny too because I was sort of shaky about it. I looked right into the brim of his hat for a second that felt like an hour. Then I turned around real quick and started peering back down the end of that bar again before I realized that probably wasn't a good idea either.

So, I swung around three quarters and pretended that I was looking to see how Bonnie and Clyde were doing setting up their equipment. It was sort of an awkward few moments there, but I didn't let on to anyone that it was.

I watched those two go back and forth with each other and figured that they must've been married. They probably had been for the last hundred years, the way that they were bickering.

He was busting her chops really good about leaving something at the house that they needed. By the time they finished rattling each other's cages, I realized that I had entirely forgotten about the situation with this young, cowboy-hatted, brass-rodeo-buckle-wearing, crooked-green-teeth-smiling twit behind the bar.

I figured that I would just get the hell out of there anyways since I certainly didn't wanna make a scene or nothing. I could tell that I wasn't welcome, and that was just fine with me. It really was.

There were enough places in my life that I fit in just fine, and I realized that if I had to come all the way out to the middle of nowhere to find a place that I didn't belong, I was luckier than most of the sorry pricks out there.

I imagined how all the guys lined up outside The Crystal to see last month's top-grossing movie would probably feel more outta place at my regular joints than I did in this little dump. So, I figured that I didn't have it so bad.

But enough time had passed, and since I was sure as shit I wasn't gonna get any service in this joint, I knew it was time to go. I turned around to take one last peek at that jackass before I scooted out of that tavern. It was then that I realized that I had a half-filled high-ball glass of bourbon, and a bottle of Bud in front of me after all. They'd been sitting there gathering dust.

I peered down the bar and saw that young kid yacking it up with the gals at the end. I tried to give him a nod, but he was too busy setting things up for himself. I was glad that he was too, although I did kinda wish it was me. But for the moment I was just happy to have a shot and a beer staring me in the face.

I peered around the dimly lit room and took a real deep breath. I had learned how to calm myself down when I was really going through hell with the brokerage and all. Back then I couldn't sleep. I couldn't eat. I couldn't even shit. Hell, I couldn't even get outta bed half the time. And like I said, when I was in bed I couldn't sleep. So, I really was in quite a spot.

I finally went on a few appointments that Jenny had scheduled up for me with a goddamn shrink that she knew. Only she said he wasn't a shrink.

I kinda doubt that he was because he didn't have any fancy diplomas on the wall. You know that those types are sure as heck gonna have all their highfalutin pedigrees staring you right in the kisser while you're sitting on the couch. But he didn't, so I don't really know what he was.

I remember that I didn't really wanna go, but she made me. I was quite content lying there in my own little puddle between the sheets. But she dragged me up outta there one day before I even had a chance to say no.

I'd be lying if I told ya that I was pissed off about it, though. I mean maybe I was for about a minute in the cab on the way over to the place, but at the end of the day, it probably saved me.

He didn't say much. I don't suppose that any of those guys do. I kinda figured that it wasn't his job to be telling me how I felt.

At the time, I thought that it *was* his job to let me tell him how I felt about everything. But now I know different. Now I know that all he was doing was letting me tell *myself* how I was feeling. And somehow by doing that, it did something.

Now I'm not the sharpest guy out there, but it might have saved me a few bucks if he would've just had a sign out in the lobby that read "All I'm gonna do is show you how to talk to yourself." But then again, I guess that he would've been outta business a long time before I walked in his fancy waiting room if he did.

The truth is that I'm glad as hell that I'm a tad brighter than your average Joe, or I could've pissed away a lot of dough on that guy. I'm sure that a lot of people do. Regular guys will get addicted to going somewhere that makes 'em feel good. Probably a lot like the cowboys that come into the old Fink Building every Friday night. It feels good to have a few pops and catch some gal's eye when the lights are low enough that people don't feel intimidated to glance over.

That was the thing about this guy, though. He let me talk without feeling intimidated. That felt good, to not be on edge. Kinda like the way that shooting back a snort of Beam or Maker's Mark will do.

But still, I've gotta think that they are all encumbrances of one kind or another. Like a crutch, preventing you from feeling like a wuss and what not, when you're facing the person that you really should be looking in the eye. The one that you really need to be talking to.

But I learned how to talk to myself pretty good once I figured out that was what it was really all about. And damned if I didn't find out that I kinda liked myself too. I mean, not every single little thing. But for the most part, I learned that I wasn't such a bad guy at the end of the day. The funny thing was, once I figured that out, everything else was okay.

I let that breath out real slow and picked up that shot of whatever the heck kinda bourbon or whiskey was sitting in front of me. It smelled like poison, but the truth is that most hard liquor does to me anyway. Even the good stuff. It doesn't much matter. So, I stopped breathing through my nose, and I shot that half of a rocks glass down like Keith Moon would've done.

I thought it was gonna burn, but it really didn't, so it wasn't so hard to keep a straight face for all the locals.

I took a big swig of the beer in front of me and turned around on the barstool real cool in order to take another peek at the girls. Then I set my sights keenly ahead on Bonnie and Clyde over in the corner finishing up. *It really isn't so bad in this dump*, I thought to myself. It had a sort of energy, for lack of a better term. It felt real.

God knows I'd spent plenty of time in clubs that do their best to make you feel like you're somewhere else. They have their fancy murals, waterfalls, lights, and music. There were places in Chicago that made you feel like you were in Vegas and places in Vegas that made you feel like you were in New York or Paris. There were clubs in the city that made you feel like you were on the beach and places on the beach that made you feel like you were in heaven on a cloud or something. I even went to a place once that made you feel like you were in the middle of Antarctica in a goddamn igloo.

There's big money in making people feel like they're somewhere that they aren't. But not here in Okemah. I sure as shit felt just like I was in a tavern smack dab in the middle of nowhere. And since that's exactly where I was, I kinda liked that honesty.

A bunch of kids walked in and started hanging around where I was sitting. They didn't pay me any mind, and it sort of made me feel like I was part of something, even though I wasn't. I didn't wanna stare at them too much, so I kept to myself while taking a few quick peeks just to see what they were all about.

They were young as hell. They couldn't have been twenty-one, but I didn't think that really mattered. The bartender came over like he knew them and just threw a bunch of bottles of beer on the counter. By the time I'd sized them up, I realized that he'd filled my glass three quarters of the way with that mash. And I reckoned that the least I could do was oblige.

I took it down in two gulps and almost instantly felt the kick. It was good. It was really good. I just sat there for a while, enjoying the buzz and taking it all in.

Then, *boom!* I was down on the floor trying my damndest to get back up.

I didn't know what the hell had happened. I could tell I hadn't been slugged or anything, but there was all kinds of noise coming from all around me.

"Come on, you son of a bitch! Come on! I'll take you right here, right now!" I heard somebody yell, but I knew that it couldn't have been at me.

I couldn't seem to find my feet to get back up, so I tried pushing myself with my arms to get the heck out of there. My trusty Mark Nason's were trying to find some traction on that old concrete floor to get back up, but instead they just sort of pushed me further away from the altercation.

Even then I couldn't really get out of the way like I wanted. That's when I decided to just stay down low and out of sight. I started crawling, figuring that nobody could cold cock me if I just kept moving.

I was glad to see that all the scrapping was going on where I'd *been* sitting, rather than where I found myself. And I was happy to be on the sidelines for whatever kinda show the local talent was putting on that night in the old Fink Building.

There stood two of the kids that I had been sizing up not long before. But they didn't look much like kids anymore. The one fellow must've been six foot five and fit as can be. He was skinny, but not like bones. He was built pretty damned good, and I knew that I sure wouldn't have been mixing it up with him no matter what the scuffle was all about.

The other one had high cheek bones and a scar on the side of his face. He wasn't nearly as tall as the first guy, but he sure made up for it. His chest must have been the size of whiskey barrel, and he was showing it off like a peacock would. His flannel shirt was unbuttoned about half the way down, although it may have just been torn that way from whatever was going on.

"I told you to stay the hell away from her, man! She doesn't want nothing to do with you!" the stockier fellow bellowed.

"Oh yeah!" the taller guy questioned him in a mocking sort of way. "What the hell do you know?" he hollered back.

"We've been together for six months. You'd know that if you were coming around to pay your goddamn child support!" he yelled back. "But you're too busy toking up on that shit to worry about getting a job and paying your bills. You're just like your old man. You're a deadbeat. Nothing but a two-bit dead beat!"

Just then the beefy dude grabbed one of the beer bottles by the neck and cracked it on the counter-top. Glass shattered everywhere, and it left him with a pretty hefty gash around his right wrist. But he didn't seem to notice.

He waved that bottleneck around like he was in some sort of a trance. It was kinda spooky the way that his eyes were all glassy with rage or whatever the hell had taken over.

I looked over and saw that the bartender was slowly heading back to the other end of the bar, almost as if he'd seen this all before a few too many times and didn't need to stick around for the ending.

"Oh yeah? So, you think that me and my old man are deadbeats?" he said as he flailed that broken bottle around in a figure eight, all the while keeping his crazed eyes on the taller guy. "Then I guess that I'll need to show you what it's like to screw with a deadbeat!" he yelled as he thrust forward at the tall one.

The kid got out of the way, and there they stood, now on the opposite corners of a fight ring that had formed. They looked ready for round two.

I finally found my feet and pushed myself up. "Damn!" I cursed under my breath. The pinky finger on my left hand was all bent outta shape and looked like a branch on maple tree. I tried to touch it, but it hurt like hell. I figured I'd fiddle with it a little later, since there were more pressing issues at hand.

It seemed like this wasn't the first time that either of these punks had been in a scuffle by the way that they were handling it. I couldn't remember the last time that I'd seen a bar brawl, and I had forgotten how scary it could be. I'd forgotten the way that the adrenaline kicks in and the testosterone comes out.

I had long ago dismissed that animal that comes out in the heat of a jungle fight, the one that's deep inside and just waiting to pounce.

Mitch Moran was the last to see that beast in my eyes, and that was twenty some odd years earlier. I had worked hard to keep that side of me under lock and key ever since. It's just been pacing the cage all these years.

The stocky guy charged. The tall guy parried. The stocky guy swung. The taller guy ducked. Finally, the bruiser just came at the other with all his might and tackled him head on.

They rolled around on that floor, swinging at each other wherever they could, just trying to land one. The taller guy was quicker and nimbler, and fortunately the broken bottle had found its way rolling over to the opposite corner of the tavern. One of the gals picked it up and put it on the end of the bar, far away from those two.

The sound of scuffing boots drowned out most everything else in that moment. Although you could still hear a good thud every few seconds as one of the two would land a punch or collide with the concrete floor. They started to roll over in my direction, and I moved back towards the bar, this time farther down near the kids that were there when I arrived.

As I looked around, I couldn't help but notice all the different ways that people were reacting. By now, a group of about twenty locals had gathered around in a circle of sorts. It didn't seem that anybody was trying to do anything to stop one of these guys from winding up in a body bag.

Some of the kids even egged the two guys on. One girl was screaming, "Kick the shit out of him, Cory!" or whatever the heck his name was. A couple of the guys were chanting something like they were frickin' animals or something.

"Oomp, Oomp, Oomp, Oomp!"

I pulled the phone outta my pocket almost out of instinct. I was getting ready to call 911, when I did a little bit of a double take. Before I dialed, I kinda cased the whole bar from one end to the other. I looked at the couple that had been setting up their equipment. The man sat stiffly behind his keyboard, watching the brawl intently.

Bonnie was behind him, rubbing his shoulders to keep him calm it seemed.

The kids that I had been eyeing when I walked in were on either side of me staring at the two cheering. The bartender just stood behind the counter, only half paying any attention to the fight going on at his bar.

Everybody else was simply enamored by the possibility of someone winding up with a toe tag by the end of the night.

As I started to dial on my phone, a thought hit me. *Who the hell am I to walk into their bar and call the shots?*

As much as I wanted to do something to help, I knew all I should do is take one of those deep breaths and hope silently that nobody would get hurt. I put my phone back in my pocket where it belonged.

Now, I know that the whole thing couldn't have gone on for more than a few minutes, but it felt like an hour to me. They rolled around on that floor the way that I felt like I had been doing for the past year or two. Back and forth, forth and back, each of them hoping for some kind of break or at least a window to jump on and get back on top.

The beefier guy's flannel shirt was all torn and covered in dirt from that grubby concrete floor. There was even some blood from the cuts they both had. I felt bad for both of 'em.

It seemed that they weren't really fighting for anything worth fighting for. It kinda seemed like they were duking it out because that's what they thought they ought to be doing, like it was all they knew. To me, that was sad.

Like I said, nobody was doing much of anything to stop them either. It seemed like everyone was enjoying the show, almost like seeing somebody laying in their own blood and piss was entertainment or something. Truth is, that made me wanna hurl.

Sure, I remembered how me and my old man used to go to those boxing matches back when I first started making real money. We'd throw some dough on each of the fights to make it interesting. Sitting ringside was really something for a young punk. The possibility of seeing a guy get knocked out that close up could really get your blood pumping.

Once, me and my old man were sitting in the second row, and some Russian guy who was just off the boat knocked the bejesus outta this local kid. That was probably what changed it all for me. We were standing up on the backs of our chairs with everyone else, hooting and hollering for some action like we'd always do. The crowd was really on their feet too because it was the third or fourth fight of the night, and nothing had really happened yet.

We were all yelling for the home town kid, telling him to go for the gut or for the jaw.

"Bob and weave!"

"Stick 'em. Stick 'em!"

You know, all that crap that a crowd of people who don't know what the heck they're talking about will tell a fighter.

So anyways, he's bobbing and weaving like we were telling him. He's swinging high or low depending on what us jerks are yelling. But you could tell that he was getting winded pretty good. Still, it seemed like it was scored evenly going into the last round.

That was when all hell broke loose, at least for the local kid.

I think he was weaving or maybe he was bobbing. I really didn't much know the difference. All I know is that it looked like he kinda stumbled just a half of a step or something. But when you're in the ring, that's sometimes all that it takes.

That was when the red-headed Russian threw a punch like I'd never seen before. It was almost as if we could all feel it, and it felt like a goddamn freight train. Even in the second row.

I still remember it like it was yesterday. That kid went down like a sack of potatoes. His eyes were like slits while he was falling, and you could see his big old purple lips just kinda quivering in slow motion. Hell, you could even see the spit splattering while he was going down.

By the time he hit the canvas, he was lying flat on his back, shaking like a frickin' leaf.

At first everyone was hooting and hollering for him to get back up, until we all realized that this poor son of a gun was really good and hurt. Then we all got real quiet. I mean the whole lot of us. We just went silent.

When they finally got that poor kid outta that ring, they had him on a stretcher with some sort of a goddamn wooden spoon in his mouth so he wouldn't swallow his own damn tongue. He'd stopped shaking, finally, but none of us knew if it was because he was dead or not.

Sometimes I still think about that poor kid and wonder if he made it or not. But the truth is part of me doesn't really wanna know anyway.

Just then, I did something really stupid. I mean, I've done a lot of dumb shit in my life, but this has to take the cake.

I know at the time I felt like I didn't have a whole lot to lose, even though I did. Maybe not realizing what I had is what gave me the stones to do it. Whatever it was, I did it. I jumped right in the middle of those two kids. I'd seen an opening and I made my move.

I figured that they never expected somebody to get in the middle of them since nobody else in that town was as stupid as me. So, dumb as I am, I jumped in the damn center of it all. Once I did, there was no turning back, even if I knew then what an idiot I was.

At that point, I didn't have much choice but to do what I was able to do. I got in between those two slabs of beef and pushed as hard as I could. I just kept pushing out and away, out and away. It was like trying to separate two locomotives from one another, I'd have to guess.

These guys were all muscle, but I'd caught them by surprise. And even though it seemed for a second like I wasn't doing any good, I could tell that the space in there was getting just a little bit bigger and that the swinging had slowed down.

"Come on guys! Come on! Break it up!" I hollered like a buffoon. "If you really wanna kill somebody, kill me!"

I knew full well that this might make them stop, even if just to laugh at my stupid ass. But it didn't.

I just kept plowing my way in between the two behemoths, pushing and ramming my shoulders in really good.

I caught an elbow in the ribs and a punch on the cheek as blows kept bouncing off them. I felt one of their palms push against my forehead trying to wrestle me away, but I found some leverage on the floor and thrust forward to wedge myself even deeper between the two of them.

I think that the crowd of people must've been floored by what I was doing, because the noise in the room seemed to pick up quite a bit. I heard a couple of gals saying shit about how I was crazy or that I was gonna get killed, and it's not like they were wrong. I heard a whole lot of stuff that would have made me pretty scared if I wasn't already up to my neck in that mess.

I started swinging low. Left, right, left, right . . . just hoping to wedge the two guys apart. By now the pain in my left hand should have been crippling me, but it wasn't. Nothing was fazing me at all. Not my finger or my gut. Not a damn thing was hurting.

For the first time in ages, I felt like I had some skin in the game, and being in the game felt damned good right then and there, as nuts as that might sound.

I couldn't tell which guy was which anymore, but one of them grabbed my hair and yanked a pretty good chunk out. Still I kept fighting like it was my life on the line. I was duking it out like I was drowning in the ocean or something. Like it was all or nothing. Just like I had everything and nothing to lose, all at the same time. Nothing could make a guy feel more alive than that.

By the time that I got on top of the taller guy's shoulders, I'd dug my elbow really good and deep into the huskier guys belly. I felt it hit something hard, and I know it must've stung, no matter how big he was.

Now I'd love to tell you that he backed off because he didn't want any more of me, but that's probably not exactly the truth. Still, whatever it was that got him to get out of the ring was just fine with me. And I figured that if I had the other one on the floor alone, just maybe I could stop this thing cold. Even if the odds were stacked against me, I still stood a chance at fixing the world in some small way.

I straddled him, but I didn't wanna swing. I knew that if he really thought I was out to get him he'd sure as shit kick my ass. I put my forearm right on his Adam's apple and shoved up into his jaw. He was squirming a bit, but I think he knew that I wasn't really gonna do nothing.

"Come on, man . . . it's over," I said. "It's over."

I looked at the hefty guy, who was hunched over trying to catch his breath. "It's over, pal," I said, peering over at him.

"I'm good with that," he stammered back at me through his huffing and puffing.

Then another voice called out from over my right shoulder. "That's right. You boys get the hell outta here. I don't wanna see the two of you in here at the same time together again!"

I recognized the loud cock of metal against metal and looked up. There was the bartender kid pointing some sort of a shotgun at the two of us on the floor. "Go on! Get outta here before they have to shovel you out!" he hollered.

I let the guy up and he didn't even look at me. He just turned and headed out the door like a tomcat that had just lost the girl.

I turned to the other guy and nodded. He nodded back and then just looked down at the floor and headed out slowly. He gave the other guy some space so they wouldn't wind up going at it again in the alley outside.

I started walking behind him while the bartender cracked the shotgun over his knee and took the shells out of the barrel. "You can stay if you want, stranger. You didn't do nothing," he said.

I peered up at him with half a grin. He handed me a couple of napkins and gestured back to the washroom.

I washed up as best I could and looked at my hand. Sure enough, it was swollen pretty good, but I knew it wasn't broken. The more I fiddled with it, the more I realized that it was probably close to nothing. I never was much of a tough guy, so I really didn't know. And with that, I headed back out, feeling kinda high.

I moved down a few seats closer to the center of the bar. I was feeling like I could pull it off now. It didn't seem like I was so much of an outsider anymore, especially when my new pal behind the bar had a shot and a beer waiting for me when I sidled up.

"This round's on me, stranger," he said.

I looked up, and he sort of smiled. Maybe it was a sneer, but it sure felt like a smile to me. Before I could say anything, he was gone, down by the punks at the end again.

I sat there for a spell. I had quite a kick from the booze, but I wasn't quite drunk. I could certainly drink a whole lot more than three shots and a few beers before I started feeling loopy. But I was definitely buzzed and pretty damned rattled over what had happened.

I figured I oughta be. I wasn't used to anything like that, and it was really hitting home. It was a lot to process, what I did and all.

I started thinking about my old man and how proud he would've been of me for getting in the middle of that. My mom would have kicked my ass. Hope would've been screaming like a goddamn school girl until everybody's eardrums were popped or something. But Jenny would've jumped right in there and scrapped it out with me.

I really did wonder what the heck had come over me. It just didn't make sense. But maybe it did. There was a small part of me thinking that it made all the sense in the goddamn world.

Just then my phone started vibrating. I could feel it buried deep in the pocket of my jeans, and prying it out hurt like a mother with my left hand all screwed up. It was Hope. Of course it was.

I held the phone there in my hand, just staring at it like I didn't know what to do. I knew that I was gonna feel like crap if I didn't answer, but the truth is, I didn't know what the heck I'd say if I picked up.

It had been awhile since I'd talked to her. Too long probably. I figured she was probably worried about me, and I owed it to her to let her know I was all right. With all those thoughts running through my brain, I watched my phone vibrate for a good thirty seconds or more.

I watched and watched until it stopped its buzzing, knowing full well that once it did, I was gonna wish that I'd picked up. It had to be bedtime back in Boston where she was. She'd probably washed her face and brushed her teeth just perfect and all. She'd more than likely just crawled into that impeccably made bed and peeled back the covers without disturbing the rest of the spread.

I'd bet she'd propped two pillows up at forty-five degrees to watch the evening news, and after seeing first-hand that all was still perfect in the world, she decided to check in on me.

And the jerk that I am was too damned self-absorbed to take her call.

Instead I tilted back that beer and chugged about three quarters of it while motioning to my new pal in the white cowboy hat for another. I had a hunch he was quite accustomed to guys who drink too much in this dump, so I reckoned I was all right getting good and drunk if that was what I felt like doing. And the truth is, I did.

I'd be lying to you if I said that ignoring Hope's call didn't eat me up a little, though. She'd probably been waiting to hear from me for longer than she should've been.

But I just didn't know what the hell to say. And she sure didn't deserve to hear any more bullshit outta me. That was for certain. She'd always been so damn generous with me, and I'd always been so frickin' selfish with her.

I knew that all that she ever wanted was for me to let her love me. But I was always on to other things. I mean, I always figured that there would be a day that we'd wind up in some little cottage in the middle of nowhere together. Her changing my diapers and wiping the cream of wheat from my kisser. Still, I'd always felt a little guilty about the way things had been.

Shit. She probably had some regular thing out in Boston anyways, I reckoned, as beautiful and smart as she is. I knew damned well that there's no way a gal like that just sits around her apartment waiting for some schmuck like me to call. A girl doesn't just hang around the house baking cookies and reading romance novels.

Thinking about that made me feel even more awful about not taking that call, especially when I realized that she didn't leave a message. I was debating whether or not I should sneak outside and ring her back or wait till the drive to Albuquerque the next day. Then the cocky, young bartender swaggered down with my beer.

"This one's on Jessie," he said as he looked back at his friends.

A girl sort of giggled and waved. So, I waved back. I lifted the bottle, tilted it in her direction and mouthed, "Thanks."

She smiled and sorta hid behind the group that she was with. I smiled, took a swig, and looked around the room.

And for a moment, just the blink of an eye really, I felt like I was home.

I mean, not *home* like the place that you keep all the crap that you've collected over the years, or *home* like the place that your mail comes. But *home*—where everybody that you give a shit about sits around a table and eats Thanksgiving dinner or watches the Super Bowl or whatever. The place where you can be you, not the you that you think that people wanna see. The you that's underneath all of that.

The couple on the stage had pretty much finished their tuning up and finally started going into something that a regular guy could recognize. It was a song that I remembered well, and recalled Freddy Fender's eight-track being in current rotation on my mother's car stereo.

I'd heard it a thousand times at least, maybe more. The old lady singing was just warming up, but you could tell that she had some damn good pipes.

She peered around the dimly lit room as though she was performing at Carnegie Hall or something. And to her, you know, it probably was.

She must've been wearing a wig, I figured. It was sort of strawberry blonde or maybe even red, and it was propped on top of her head like a hornet's nest. She had makeup caked on too, and you could see the crease where one shade of eye shadow would end and another would start.

But what that really floored me were her eyelashes. They must've been an inch and a half long. They were all pasty black, and I kinda thought they were gonna start running any old minute out there under those hot lights.

I'll be honest. I thought it looked terrible. But you could tell that she sure didn't. She thought she was the cats ass. You could see by the way that she carried herself.

She had big boobs. I mean knockers. And in her day, I've gotta believe that she could stop a bus. But that day was long ago. Still, I was impressed that she didn't seem to let on that her time had passed. She strutted up to that microphone just like she was the belle of the ball, and I really respected her for that.

Through that dimly lit room, with my buzz going strong, I saw what I'd bet she sees when she looks in the dressing room mirror. Damned if I didn't spy a twenty-four-year-old bombshell. Even if it was for just a second. But sure as shit, I saw it. I really did.

She strutted up to that old, Elvis-style square microphone with her lashes and her makeup and two-foot-high hair, and she took a solid scan of everyone in the room. She had that place in the palm of her hand.

It was the last thing I expected in this little dump, yet it seemed just right. Nobody took a sip of their drink and nobody peeked at their phone. Nobody got up to take a leak, and not one person looked anywhere else in that tavern except into the eyes of old buxom Bonnie.

"If he brings you happiness, then I wish you all the best. It's your happiness that matters most of all," she crooned. "But if he ever breaks your heart, if the teardrops ever start . . ."

I looked around even though I knew I shouldn't. Even her husband was sitting there in the dark of the stage, his bald head barely reflecting the spotlight that his wife had entranced.

". . . I'll be there, before the next teardrop falls."

I felt a hand on my shoulder. It was the gal that had sent the beer down my way.

I grabbed her hand and started to mouth her name, but she put her finger up to my lips to silence me. She placed her right hand on my ass, pulled herself real close, and guided me over to a little corner that seemed like some sort of makeshift dancefloor to the right of the stage.

We swayed back and forth to that old country ballad. Strangely, it felt like we'd done it a thousand times before.

This girl smelled fresher than anything I'd taken a whiff of in a long time. And she seemed to fit just right next to me. Just like the missing piece of some jigsaw puzzle that got lost between the seat cushions years ago.

She sang along softly in my ear, almost as though it was a lullaby that sent her off to sleep each night.

I just let her. Even on the last verse where I knew the words as if they were scripture, I let her have 'em. I could tell that she needed them all to herself. And so, I let 'em be.

I have a hunch that old Bonnie and Clyde saw us over in the corner stage and decided to make it real special by playing the first verse again before the last chorus. It didn't seem that anybody in the old Fink Building minded. I know that I sure as heck didn't.

Finally, the eight-minute version of that old song ended with everybody in the place singing the chorus. People started applauding, and even though I figured that it was for the band, part of me imagined it was for Jessie and me.

It wasn't until she leaned in and kissed me that I figured out that those claps really were for us. Because when she did, everybody started hooting and hollering like a circus crowd or something. I'd be lying if I told you it didn't feel just fine by me. Because it did. It felt just right.

I grabbed her by the hand and pulled her back towards the bar. By the time we started making our way, Clyde had jumped right into that old George Jones song "The Race is On," and everybody got all jazzed up in the moment.

Somehow it seemed that old dank basement had come alive with energy, and I sure as heck wasn't the exception. I wanted to dance, but I also wanted to get to know this girl. I wanted to get drunk or high, but I also wanted to stay focused in each and every moment that came to me. To stay present. To be caught up in the whirlwind.

She gestured to the bartender, and he brought both of us something in a highball glass. It was a light orange and yellow concoction that sorta reminded me of piss. But I didn't really care.

"You doing one too, Billy?" Jessie asked.

"Ehhh. What the hell," he hooted.

He grabbed a big plastic jug, poured himself one, and held the glass up. Jessie looked at me, and I looked right back as we raised our glasses to his.

"To the fall of the—" I started to say instinctually, almost as if it was my duty to make the toast. But before I could come up with any of my horseshit dedications, Jessie looked at me.

She stared right through me right then and there almost as if she'd known me her whole life.

"No toasts, Rockstar," she said earnestly. I bit my lower lip.

At first, I thought to be offended. But she smiled so sweetly that I knew it wasn't meant to upset me. I smiled back and looked at Billy. We clinked our glasses and downed that poison in one fell swoop.

For every bit that the earlier shot didn't burn, this one sure as hell made up for it.

"Dang!" Jessie said, wincing. "That's a hell of batch you got there, Billy. That'll put hair on *my* chest!"

Billy smiled. "That's the one I've been telling you about," he smirked. "I told ya," he said proudly.

Billy turned around to some of the regulars on the other side of the bar, and Jessie leaned in again real close. She put her little hand up to the side of my face and started caressing my hair.

"What was that?" I asked sort of slyly. I wasn't really sure if I should've loved it or hated it.

"Oh . . . Billy and his brothers bootleg sour mash," she said. "Although, it's probably more like moonshine than anything else. His family's been doing it for years, and they're kinda known for it around these parts."

"Oh. It's good," I said with all the bullshit I had left.

"Well, I don't know if it's good, but it'll get ya there," she winked.

Right when she said that I did what I do best. Or at least I'd like to think that I'm the best at it. And some days that's really all that matters.

I looked real deeply into her eyes the way that other guys don't, especially in a town like this, I figured. I peered deep into her pupils and right into her soul. I felt her looking back. Trying to read me, while still doing her best to hold onto the control.

I pulled her in real tight, not letting go of the power. Neither of us taking our eyes away. Neither of us letting go. Jessie and me in an all-out stalemate to see who would blink or look away first.

Damn. I thought to myself. This little doll couldn't have been more than twenty one, and even though she seemed a little tough at first, she was anything but. Sure, she was rebellious. I was at that age too. But I knew that where there's a rebel, there's gotta be a cause.

It wasn't difficult to get her in my spell. I mean, she wanted to be there and all. But still, it seemed like so much more. She was staring right back, and I'd be damned if this kid wasn't trying to put a spell all her own on me.

It had been a long time since I felt this sort of thing, but not long enough for me to have forgotten what it's like. I mean, don't get me wrong. I've gotten laid more than the average thirty-five-year-old fellow. There weren't all that many nights that I went home alone if I didn't want to.

But it's those nights when you're just minding your own business and the magic finds you. They're the ones you remember. I could tell already that this was gonna be one of those times.

The music was a little loud and I was flying a bit off that swill that Billy had poured me, so conversation seemed like a little more than I was up for. Jessie didn't seem to mind. She seemed to be happy just staring into my eyes and whatever the heck she thought they were hiding.

We must've gazed into one another for five minutes or more. I thought to lean in and bury my tongue down her throat about a million times, but I held back. I guess that I didn't wanna ruin the moment. Plus, I sort of liked the anticipation, too.

There had been a day that I would have just gone in for the kill. But I was wiser than that now, I thought. At least smart enough to know that the foreplay starts the moment that you set eyes on a gal. And I wanted that to last.

It had been awhile since I had something to really look forward to, and I'd be damned if I was gonna rush a good thing when I found it. So, I stared at this beautiful girl and cherished every goddamn second of it.

Jessie had the deepest brown eyes I'd ever seen on a gal with skin so light. Not that she was pale, because she sure wasn't. Her skin was perfect. And it made me wonder what the hell she was seeing staring back at me.

She stroked my hair. I could tell that she liked it a little longer. That was probably why she called me Rockstar, I figured. Shit, I don't know.

Her hands were exactly how I like them. Soft and small. Her nails sure weren't long, but they weren't too short either. I think that they had some clear polish on them, but I was never too good at telling that kind of stuff. All I know is that they were sexy as hell without trying too hard. And that's exactly what I like.

Just when I thought that I was going to cave, she beat me to it. And I've gotta tell ya that I was glad that she did. She cupped the back of my head with her right hand, but she didn't pull me in the way a young kid would do. Instead, she pulled herself to my mouth, never taking her eyes off me.

When our lips touched, she didn't do anything. Not a goddamn thing. And although my first thought was to go in full force, I stopped myself.

Instead we stood there with our lips resting beside one another. Not really kissing, yet every bit as passionate. Maybe even more so.

I felt her breath as she exhaled over my lips and into my mouth, rolling over my tongue like satin or velvet, her gaze never leaving mine.

It was right about then that I realized how aroused I had gotten. *Christ, that came outta nowhere*, I thought to myself. I was turned on. So damned turned on.

I rubbed up next to her, not wanting to make it too obvious, but I figured that she ought to know what she was doing to me.

Hell, who was I fooling? I'm sure she knew damn well what she was doing without my needing to poke her in the belly.

As I pulled her body in closer, I felt her lips part ever so gently next to mine. With such goddamn anticipation, I longed to taste her. But instead she clenched my lower lip with her teeth and gently pulled me even further in towards her.

At first, I thought to fight it, but I decided to succumb and let her pull me in. Like a lion to his lioness, I knew that I would love this foreplay, this survival of the fittest. I would take it all in for each magnificent moment that it brought without question, judgment, or even interpretation. *Over my dead body*, I thought. She deserved so much more.

"Get a room!" some jackass hollered from the other side of the bar.

I glanced over and saw some goofball leering at us while laughing with his buddies. Shit, I probably would've said the same thing back at one my shitholes in Chicago if some out-of-towner was making it with one of the regulars.

I could tell that she knew who he was just by the way that he was giggling. But she didn't react. Her gaze never left my eyes.

Shit, she was good. She was sure playing me like a fiddle. And I was loving it.

At the end of the day we probably wanted the same thing anyways. One of those nights. That's all that I wanted, and maybe all I needed to. Just one of those nights. You know those nights. At least I hope that you do.

"So. Whaddaya think?" she finally broke the silence.

I was sort of taken aback, because her voice was a little raspier than I thought that an angel's would be. I could tell that she didn't smoke, but it almost sounded like she used to or something. Still, just like the rest of her, it was sexy as all get out.

"What do I think?" I said inquisitively. "I think that you are the most beautiful thing I've ever seen."

"That's not what I meant, silly," she giggled. "Should we get a room?"

I'd had enough, but I still wasn't ready. I didn't want to blow my opportunity because I knew that despite her giggling, she meant it. She sure as shit meant it. She would've left with me that instant and banged me in the car if we couldn't make it back to the old Days Inn. But like I said, I wasn't ready yet. I just wasn't.

You see, I'm what they call a *pleasure seeker*. I saw it in a movie once. I wasn't always that way, but I guess I'm different now. I like to carry the anticipation out as long as I possibly can without exploding. It can be tough sometimes, but it's worth it. At least for me it is.

Back in the day, I was the guy that would grab a gal from the club, take her out to the parking lot or the alley or whatever. I'd like to think that I've come a long way since then. All I know is that I get more of a kick outta dragging it out and making it last.

So, I didn't say nothing. I just smiled. Because that's what I do when I don't know what to say.

She smiled back, but I could tell that she was getting a little antsy. It seemed that she was a little confused too, since I hadn't given her any kind of an answer to her question.

I reckoned that all the guys in this town that she'd ever come onto jumped in her pants as soon as they had the chance. Just like I would've probably done if I lived in Okemah. And I sure as shit didn't want her thinking for a second that she didn't have me, because she did.

So, I caved a little. Just a little. But it's because I needed her to know that I was into her.

I leaned in real gently, parted her lips with mine and pushed my tongue softly inside of her mouth, licking her upper lip as I did it. With that she grabbed the back of my head and shoved her tongue in with all her force.

She opened her mouth real wide and turned it sideways, almost upside down. I felt her suck my tongue in. Then she pulled her body next to mine and started to straddle me, inching up to where she could feel me next to her.

I went along for a few seconds, maybe even longer. I remembered what it was like. It really hadn't been all that long ago that I would try to impress a girl with my kissing prowess.

Grinding harder and feeling how turned on I was, she groaned, opened her eyes real wide and smiled. Even though I figured it was sort of an act, I pulled her back and forth and rubbed myself against her. She closed her eyes and rolled her head back as if she was on the brink, even though she certainly wasn't.

I knew I had to slow down. For a bunch of reasons, I knew that I had to. So, I pulled my hands up to the sides of her head and took control.

I brushed her hair away, sort of pulling it back into a makeshift pony-tail. That seemed to bring some temporary distraction to our foreplay.

I pulled her back and began to breathe really slowly and deeply into her. I moved my right hand down along her neck and shoulders until I worked my way to the small of her back. She moaned and kissed me slowly, working her tongue down my chin to my neck.

"I'll be right back, Rockstar," she said with a smirk. "Don't you go anywhere."

She pulled herself away, winked at me and headed off towards the hallway where the bathrooms were located.

I glanced around, and you'd have thought that I'd killed somebody by the way that they were all staring me down. There were at least seven or eight guys around the bar getting their rocks off pretty good watching the action. I could tell that they all must've thought that I was the devil incarnate, scoring with this doll. I'd be lying if I said I didn't kinda understand.

I mean, I'd bet that they came to this dump at least two or three times a week thinking that each one of those nights might be *the one.* They'd probably been doing it for the past twenty years or whatever and went home empty-handed every time.

Then, out of nowhere some long-haired kid from some big city rolls into town and winds up scoring with the young chickie that they'd been creaming over for God knows how long. They *knew* exactly what was gonna happen.

So, I get it. I really do. But there just wasn't really a whole hell of a lot that I could do about it even if I wanted to.

Nevertheless, I smiled at them the way that not many other guys would do. They all kinda looked down or away, but not one of them smiled back. Maybe they felt like they had been busted or something. I don't know.

Finally, I spout out, "I'm sorry, guys," real sincerely. Nobody even thought to look in my direction.

"There really isn't a need for such a public display like that," I went on, loud enough for them all to hear beyond the bustle of the bar. "You fella's didn't need to see that."

Still, none of them looked up. I figured that they didn't wanna let on that they knew I was talking to them. I saw Billy sort of looking over too, wondering what in the world I was doing even talking to these locals.

"It's just that we couldn't control ourselves," I continued, really trying to drive it home. "You see, I haven't seen my niece in over a year, and we really missed the heck out of each other," I said as straight-faced as I could. It took everything I had to maintain my composure.

At once they all peered up at me as if I had done the undoable. As if I had really found a place too extreme for these guys. And you know what? I had. In that brief moment, sure as shit, I had.

Billy chuckled quietly covering his mouth, but none of the guys noticed. I recognized that these goofs thought I was serious. And I was loving it.

"Your niece!?!?" one of them exclaimed.

The others stared intently now, almost as if they were ready to take me out back and kick the snot outta me or something.

"Jessie's your niece?" another one said as if he didn't hear his buddy ask the same goddamn thing.

I sat back smirking. I knew that I had these dumbbells right where I wanted them and figured that I'd be just fine as long as they had some sort of a sense of humor.

"I'm just messing with you guys!" I finally exclaimed, laughing confidently. "Of course, she's not my niece!"

"You son of a bitch!" the one guy cackled. "You got us!"

I saw his buddy turn and look at one of the others and say, "What did he say? Jessie's not really his niece, is she?"

They started laughing their asses off the way that I hoped they would.

"Dammit, sonny, you got us real good. Shit! I believed him too!" he said as he slapped his friend on the back.

I sat back on the barstool and laughed with them. I'd stuck the landing.

"I didn't know whether to shoot ya or pat ya on the back!" one of them said jokingly.

"All I was thinking was that if you were my brother, you'd be waking up in a pine box in the morning!" the one guy exclaimed from behind his beer.

"How'd you come up with that?" the bearded guy asked.

The truth was that I didn't know how I'd come up with that one. I mean, I always knew how to work a crowd, but I'd never used that line before. And even if I had, you could never get the timing down perfectly the way that it came out right then and there.

Somehow, I was always the guy with the one-liners. I must've had a million of them over the years. But the truth is that I don't remember any of 'em.

I was sure that this one would be no exception. These guys would probably recite it for the rest of their goddamn lives. I'd always be the stranger who came into town, made out with Jessie in the old Fink Building and told them that I was her uncle. But for me, even if I remembered, I doubt I'd ever recall the delivery.

And like most things in life, I've found that the delivery is damn near everything. Well, that and the exit.

"Shit, kid, what are you drinking?" one of them asked.

"A beer would be great," I said to my new friends.

"And her?"

"The same I think," I said, even though I really had no idea.

"Hey, Billy. Get those two a drink when you've got a second," the bald guy directed. Billy just nodded.

"Thanks, friend," I said real politely. He was a big guy, and I didn't mind being the joker for a minute or two. But I sure as shit didn't want these guys thinking that I was a wise ass, because there is a world of difference between the two.

Jessie came back looking perfect. She'd put some gloss on her lips, and I wondered how long I could go without ruining it. She placed her hand on my waist and kissed my cheek, almost the way that old lovers do. I felt the warmth of her breath next to my ear. And I knew I was right where I wanted to be.

"I want to make love to you all night, Rockstar," she whispered.

I grabbed her thigh and squeezed it tightly in my hand a few times.

The local guys turned back to what they were doing before we started rocking the tavern, although I figured that they were mostly hoping we'd get back into it.

Billy brought me a beer and had a glass of something for Jessie, and just smiled at her. I had a hunch he'd seen this before, but I didn't give a shit. She was great, I thought.

Now, I know that I'm not the brightest guy to come out of the Academy, but I also know that I am sharper than the average thirty-five-year-old fellow. So I recognizd that I was at a real fork in the road. This thing could go one of a couple of ways, and I knew that I didn't wanna blow it.

I reckoned that I could actually introduce myself, learn all about her messed up childhood, and tell her about mine. I could probably find out that she used to be on drugs or gave a kid up for adoption last year. I could hear all about the guys that she's banged and "the only one that ever really mattered," too.

Or I could just imagine her to be everything that I needed her to be. And I could let her do the same with me. So, I decided to just keep my big old mouth shut.

I chugged that beer and grabbed that little girl's ass. Together we walked out of that old place and into the dark, probably the way Bonnie and Clyde did a hundred years before. Just like two thieves escaping into that damp, cold night. Intent on robbing one another of what each of us needed in that moment.

CHAPTER 10

When we headed outside it wasn't really raining—more like the sky was spitting on us. Once we got to the street, Jessie took my hand and started leading the way.

"My car is back there," I said, but she didn't seem to care. It seemed like she knew where she was going, and that was all right with me.

When we got down past The Crystal, she pulled me into a doorway that was part of a storefront, I'd guess. She started kissing me again the way that she'd been doing before she'd gone to the restroom a few minutes earlier.

"I want you so bad," she moaned before pulling me back outside into the misty night. Grabbing my hand again, dragging me down Broadway.

"Wait a minute," I said as we passed a little makeshift courtyard. "What is that?" I asked her in the moment.

"It's some sorta statue of one of the guys that built the town," she said sharply, pulling firmly on my arm. "It's nothing . . . come on."

"No . . . wait," I said. This is what I came to see," I told her.

"What? That stupid rusty old thing? Stop kidding around. Now come on. I need to feel you," she whined like some poor, deprived school kid.

"I'm serious," I said. "Do you know who this is?" I asked her.

"Well I can read, silly," she mused while looking at the engraving on the bottom. "It's Woodrow Wilson Guthrie, whoever the heck he was." She sounded really serious and all, despite the funny face she was making while she said it.

"The street over that way is named after him too," she said while rolling her eyes. "He sure is funny looking. . . at least that's what I've always thought. Now let's go!"

Ignoring her tugging, I walked over slowly and looked closely at the figure. She was kinda right. He was sort of funny looking in that statue. But he was Woody for Christ's sake. You sure don't call him funny looking, no matter what he looked like in some goddamn artist's rendering.

I held my hand up to the bust. It was just regular old American steel, although I'd thought I might feel something more powerful when I touched it. But I didn't.

Jessie didn't say anymore. She came over and started running her hands through my hair and kissing my neck. Out of the corner of my eye, I could see her perfect complexion looking up at me in the moonlight like I was somebody special. And I liked that. I liked it a lot.

I reached up and touched Woody's guitar. The metal was wet from the mist and felt cool to my touch.

Jessie started working her way down my body. She opened my shirt and began kissing my chest. I felt the cold moisture cling to the goosebumps that I already had.

"Oooh. I guess I'm not the only one who's turned on," Jessie giggled as she gently nibbled on my nipple.

I peered down intently and leaned in to kiss her as passionately as I had ever known. Shit. Probably as passionately as anybody's ever known.

I started to undo my fly when she grabbed my hand and put it between her legs. Then she grabbed my zipper and had my pants to my knees in what seemed like less than a second. She crouched down and yanked them the rest of the way to my ankles, pulled my underwear down to my knees and started.

I stood there for a good five minutes it seemed, just staring at old Woody Guthrie and his guitar, while I had the most gorgeous girl in the world taking care of me.

I thought about a lot of things right then and there too. I'd be lying if I told you that I didn't feel a little guilty pondering stuff while this girl was doing what she was. But the truth is, I kinda justified the way my mind was wandering in that moment. I guess that I reckoned that I was doing her a favor in a way.

You see, I knew that if I hadn't had my thoughts careening all over about all sorts of other things, that I probably would've been done long before I should've been. And this girl deserved a whole hell of a lot more than that. But part of me still knew that I should've kept my mind where it belonged.

Over in the corner, a picture of Woody holding a guitar caught my eye. Woody didn't look funny at all in that picture. To me he looked real. To me he looked damned real.

Written on the guitar above soundhole was "This Machine Kills Fascists." For the life of me, I didn't know what the heck a Fascist was. Nor did I want to own a machine that killed anybody or anything. Still, I thought that statement on his guitar was pretty damned cool. I liked the idea of a guitar being a machine that could fix things. An instrument for change, both literally and figuratively.

I thought about Miles too. And I thought about my old man.

I reckoned that he would've really enjoyed this story. Who knows, maybe he was enjoying it. Peering down from a fancy leather bar-stool somewhere with a big old high ball in his hand, all ready to reach down and high-five me.

I pulled Jessie up and unbuttoned her jeans. I pulled her shirt up over her head and started to suck her perfect breasts, as she gave in to the sensation of my tongue darting around. I went back and forth, sucking and then kissing, licking and then sucking again. She moaned like an alley cat in heat.

I turned her around and brought her pants down to her knees. Then I rubbed her wet panties and slipped in my middle finger past her G-string. "Ah-ahhh . . ." she groaned as I rubbed.

Finally, she clutched my hand and pulled away momentarily. She picked up her left leg and pulled her blue jeans over her black boot, leaving the other leg of her pants around her right ankle. She put both hands on that wall, right where old Woody's mug was, and peered over her left shoulder at me.

"Fuck me," she said.

I pushed aside the string on her tight little panties and felt how warm she was. How perfectly we fit together.

It seemed like the whole goddamn world stopped right there on its axis for a moment or two. I was on the precipice of something that was bigger myself. It was almost spiritual in a weird way.

I felt like I was fucking for every goddamn thing that ever meant anything to me. Like I was fucking for peace and fucking for freedom. Fucking for truth. Like we were fucking for every goddamn injustice that we'd ever experienced. Every way that the world had shit on us.

We were fucking for salvation. As silly as that sounds, I felt like I was fucking to be saved from the big mess that I knew I was smack dab in the middle of. In that moment it seemed as though fucking this girl was the only way out.

When I came, it was as though every burden I had was washed away. I felt my soul break loose from my body. My imprisoned spirit became liberated. My most hidden and enslaved fears, emancipated.

I grabbed Jessie and pulled her down on that wet pavement. I clutched her tightly on the cold, cold ground. And I held her.

Sobbing.

Yeah, that's right. Sobbing.

Maybe I am a wuss. I don't know. The truth is that I have no frickin' idea what the heck came over me, and I know that she sure didn't either.

"What the shit, dude?" she asked, almost offended, as I lay there trying to pull it together.

I tried to look up at the half moon, and I felt the mist get colder on my cheeks and bare chest. My eyes were filled with water or tears. I rubbed them real hard to try and clear them as Jessie pulled away.

"What the heck is your deal?" she asked pointedly.

I mumbled something but couldn't really get anything out. I pulled myself up to my knees, my jeans and underwear at my ankles, my face in my hands. I just balled like a goddamn sissy.

"Dude. What's up with you?" she asked, momentarily sounding concerned.

I just looked up at her and shook my head. The words wouldn't come, and I knew better than to keep trying.

"Are you okay?"

I just sat there in the rain staring blankly, completely dumb.

"Hey man . . . this is too much for me," Jessie said, finally breaking the silence. "I'm sorry man. I've gotta roll."

Of course, I thought to stop her. But there didn't seem to be a damn thing that I could do. I was like a bowl of jelly out there.

Even now I can't figure out what came over me. The only thing I could do was lie there in my own little puddle like some helpless pansy.

I fell to my side and curled up in a big old ball, wailing like some goddamn baby.

I couldn't blame Jessie for getting the hell outta there in a hurry. I probably would've too. I'm pretty sure that she said a few things to me before she ran off, but I really don't recall. All I remember is lying there staring at that lonesome moon over Woody's steel shoulder and feeling so helpless and alone. It felt as though I was stranded up there on that crescent, and mission control had left me there to die.

It seemed like hours that I laid there and had my big sissy-ass cry. Just me and that old crescent moon out in the middle of nowhere. With nobody and nothing giving a shit.

I peered up at Woodrow Wilson Guthrie with his Fascist-killing guitar. I could see the purpose in his eyes. I could sense that he believed in something bigger than himself, the way I used to.

I finally hopped to my feet, yanked my pants up, cinched my belt one hole tighter than I usually go, and buttoned my shirt. It was soaking wet and felt cold as ice. I started to run to the Porsche with everything that I had left in me. I could hear the bottoms on my blue jeans snap each time that I took a stride, being so wet and heavy, but I just kept on running.

My boots slipped a bit on some of the loose gravel as I ran down Broadway, but that didn't slow me down any. Instead, I sprinted even faster, just concentrating on going straight rather than trying to dodge any cracks or rocks or anything. I knew I'd wind up on my ass if I did otherwise.

I got to the car and grabbed the keys out from under the driver's seat where I'd left them. I started her up, did a U-turn right in front of the old Crystal, and headed back to Guthrie. I took a right past the convenience store and gave a little honk and a wave for the heck of it, all while tears rolled down my sorry mug.

Two minutes later I pulled into the Ritz and parked. I couldn't get to the room fast enough.

By the time I managed to open the door, Miles was already waiting for me, panting like he used to do when he was a puppy. Loving me all unconditional and what not.

"Hey, buddy. How you doing?" I patted him on the head and scratched behind his ears the way that he likes. He just sat there, taking it all in the way he always did.

CHAPTER 11

E ven though I felt like my head had just hit the pillow, I knew that we had to get a move on. The sun was pretty high in the sky, and I was glad that Miles took care of his business without any pacing or prodding.

I figured that it probably had something to do with me not taking him out when I'd gotten home the night before. He really was good at holding it. He always had been. I picked it up in a baggie and threw it in the nearby dumpster.

The shower wasn't nearly as bad as I'd thought it was gonna be. I left my Sub on my wrist while I washed up, and it came out clean and shiny just like the day I got her, the blue bezel sparkling and the crystal clear as day.

My head wasn't pounding the way you would have guessed, and we made it up and out of there as if we'd done it a thousand times before.

I wasn't too hungry, but I knew that I couldn't be too careful with Miles. There was about a quarter of a bag of kibble left when I packed things up, and I didn't wanna take any chances with his sugar and all. I remembered seeing a Sonic about a mile back into town, so I headed that a way.

"Welcome to Sonic," a deep voice resonated through the speaker. "This is Mary. How can I help *you* Sonic today?" I chuckled at the stupid question, and her southern accent sort of threw me for a loop. Miles appeared startled too. I don't think he'd ever been through a drive-thru before.

"I'll take two breakfast sandwiches and an order of the chicken strips," I answered loudly towards the speaker.

"Ooop, Mister," she said kinda gruffly. "Let me make sure we can still do that."

"Do what?" I asked, Miles looking at me like I was frickin nuts or something. Nobody answered, and I sat there feeling like a fool.

I rifled through our music on the iPod, not really knowing what would be good for the road that day. I knew we had a lot of driving ahead of us, and that could be a good thing.

As I shuffled through my library, I was figuring I'd just throw any old thing on. The turn of the dial stopped on an album that was important to me a million years before. So, I hit it.

I'd come to learn that sometimes the thing that you need finds you, rather than the other way around. And I'd been meaning to revisit Blind Faith for quite some time. They were a one album, one tour, supergroup that my old man had turned me onto a long time ago. I always liked the idea of putting it all out there on the line, and then calling it a day. Not giving a shit about a follow up or a sequel. Just giving it everything you've got, without worrying about the next chapter.

Plus, the name seemed like something that I was in need of right then and there. Blind Faith, that is. I had a hunch that it was going to put us in a zone, but that was all right.

I was ready to just drive off when Mary came back. She explained through a little feedback on the micro-phone that they would still be able to do breakfast after all. I looked at the dash, and sure enough it was a little after 10:30. Then I really knew we had to get the heck outta there.

"Can I get a large coffee and a cup of water too, Mary?"

I didn't get an answer.

"That'll be nine-eight-two," she finally replied. "Please pull up to the window," she directed hurriedly.

I pulled around to the drive-thru window and laughed. "So, is this what it's like to be in your shoes, buddy?" I asked Miles, scratching behind his ears.

I looked up at the window. It must've been three or four feet above us. I reckon it's because everybody else in town has a pickup or a four-by-four. Yet here we were in Okemah, Oklahoma, in our little German sports car. We probably looked like dwarfs in it.

And there she was: Mary. Her tits sticking out a foot in front of her while sporting sideburns and a peach fuzz mustache. She had her headset strapped right on to the side of her head just like she was born with it.

I could tell that she was taking somebody else's order when I pulled up but figured she was used to multitasking. That didn't stop her from looking down at me with more than a little surprise.

"Oooh!" she squealed while mid-sentence with the car on the other end of that headset.

"Nice car, mister," she eyed us up and down. "What you be drivin'?"

"It's a Porsche," I said sorta modestly. I'd guess that they really didn't see too many Porsches in Okemah.

"Looks like a race car to me," she said seriously, more seriously than seemed warranted.

"Well you ain't gonna be able to reach up here in that," she chuckled.

I stared up at her and nodded.

"I'll pull up and get out," I told her.

"No, no, no, mister. I'll bring it out to ya," she said warmly.

She must've been 300 pounds, with most of it being in her belly and her boobs. She jiggled her way out the door, and I pulled up and away from that window a bit. I needed to. She never could've squeezed between me and that building.

I reached in my pocket and gave her a ten.

"Just keep it, my dear," I said with a big old smile.

"Oooh. You gots a dog!" she shouted. "So cute!" she cackled in a real shrill voice.

"That a boy or a girl?" she asked while leaning into the window.

"He's a boy," I told her. "His name is Miles."

"Hey there, little man. What a sweetie. Here's your breakfast." She handed the food over and waved at Miles through the window.

I kept up my big old smile and got a giant grin in return. "Have a great one, Mary!" I said loudly.

"You too, mister. And Mister Miles too!"

I pulled back around the building to avoid parking in plain view of the drive-thru window. I reached into to the thermos, grabbed a syringe, and filled it to the eighth line.

With that, I unwrapped the two breakfast sandwiches and threw the buns out the window for the birds. I didn't think anyone would mind.

I set them both down on the floor where Miles started to inhale 'em. He was clearly famished, and it made me feel good seeing him enjoy something so much.

"Slow down, buddy," I told him. "Save some for the road," I chuckled.

He didn't pay me any mind. He was plenty preoccupied, I guess. So, I grabbed the scruff of his little neck, slid the needle in, put the hammer down, and pulled it out. Just like we'd been doing for over a year.

Like I said, it made me feel good seeing him enjoy his breakfast like that. I watched him for a minute or more while I tried to sip my hot coffee. Then I put the car in gear and stepped on the gas, with Clapton, Winwood and Baker already doing their thing.

"Come down off your throne and leave your body alone. Somebody must change. You are the reason I've been waiting so long. Somebody holds the key. But I'm near the end, and I just ain't got the time. And I'm wasted and I can't find my way home."

All I could do was smile. Well, smile and take a deep breath. That stabbing in my gut was coming on again.

I figured that it must've been the crappy, bitter coffee. What can you expect from a place like Sonic at 10:45 in the morning? So, I set it in the holder and listened to Matilda get me back to the road heading west.

Since we had a full tank, I just put everything on autopilot for the most part. It was a fairly straight shot once I was on the open road, so I didn't need to put a whole lot of thought into the drive. Miles was crashed out on the passenger seat for the better part of the trek, and I was able to just be alone with my thoughts for awhile before we made it to New Mexico.

By the time the fuel indicator turned on, we'd put over three-hundred and twenty miles between us and old Woody Guthrie Boulevard. Jessie too, I reckoned. I hopped out and slid my card into the pump. I was glad to see that it worked.

I knew that I didn't have a whole lotta room left on it and needed to hold onto as much cash as I could. I figured that as long as I had a few bills in my pocket, I could make things work out. And whatever was still on credit was gravy at that point.

I put just over fifty-five bucks in the tank before I noticed that Miles was panting and leaning on the window as though he wanted to get out. The station was a little too busy for me to feel good about him running this way and that. Somebody had spilled some gasoline at the stall next to us, and I didn't want him getting into that mess.

I carried him over and set him down in an area that seemed particularly green. Not that he really cared, I just always thought that the greener the grass, the better. But what the heck do I know about where a dog wants to do his business?

When he was done, a loud voice yelled in my direction.

"Hey, jag-off!"

I turned around and saw a big burly guy in overalls with a light blue attendant shirt walking in our direction. It seemed like he was staring a hole through me as if he was ready for a throw down or something.

"You talking to me?" I asked, feeling a little cocky. I sure as shit didn't want any problems, but I wasn't gonna bend over for this guy either.

"You think your little mutt can just shit anywhere he feels like?" he barked, pointing over to the grassy area.

I looked him square in the eye, at least much as I could from a hundred feet away.

"Listen, pal, I'm cleaning it up." I told him without hesitation.

He stopped heading in our direction and just stood there, arms folded.

"Okay, big shot," he said firmly. "I'm watching you."

I could tell that this guy was an asshole, but there was nothing that I could do to change that. Besides, he could've kicked my ass with his eyes shut, I figured. Most of these big guys in these small towns can. They don't really have much else going on, so they're all pretty good at getting into a scrap with a fellow, especially a guy from out of town.

I walked over to where the paper towels should be and saw that there weren't any. There wasn't any fluid for the squeegee either, and I knew right then and there that this big jerk was a lazy bastard too.

I headed over to the other bay where there was some older lady pumping her gas who'd obviously seen my little discussion with the attendant. She did everything she could to avoid eye contact with me, just like I was some sort of a two-bit hoodlum or something. Sure enough. No paper towels there either.

As I walked back to the car, I could see Bubba or Cletus or whatever the hell that asshole's name was monitoring my every move. I could feel the smirk he was smirking, the grin he was grinning. I really could. I knew that he was getting a hard-on from how he'd straightened shit out with me, and I'd be lying if I told you that I wasn't burning up inside over it.

I was about to head into the station and ask him for some paper towel until I thought better of it. I wasn't gonna give this prick the satisfaction. Over my dead body. So, I walked back to the car.

Sure, as shit. Out of the corner of my eye, I could see his shoulders perk up as he walked to the station door and open it half way. Staring at me, he seemed ready for an altercation if I even thought to start my engine. But I just popped the trunk instead.

I knew that I didn't have any paper towel in the trunk, so I went through my duffle, not certain what I was looking for. I could feel his cold glare coming from over my shoulder, and I knew I had to come up with something.

I rifled through my stuff and grabbed an old ratty Cubs jersey that I'd purchased way back when. It wasn't folded correctly, and when I pulled it out it was pretty wrinkled. So, I decided I'd just use it. I opened it up and held it out by the shoulders, feeling deflated.

"They're the shittiest team in the National League anyways," I muttered under my breath.

I folded it back up in squares and headed to the spot where Miles had taken care of his business. I could hear the station door close from a couple hundred feet away, and my throat started to clench. My pride was defeated. The slump in my step had taken over. And it was then that I remembered when I'd gotten that old ratty jersey.

It was that 104-degree day about eight or nine years earlier when Jenny and I went to a Friday game. We were burning up in the sweltering heat and humidity, but Jenny still needed to get a goddamn jersey.

You see she'd never had a Cubs shirt before. She'd grown up a Cardinals fan. But she'd made it clear from the start that if she was gonna go to a Cubs game, come hell or high-water, she was going home with a jersey.

So, she bought one and made me buy one that matched. We got hats too. Mine was blue and hers pink, but they both had the same retro sort of Cubbies emblem on them.

We all but died out there in section 242 with those damn jerseys on over the shirts we'd shown up in, laughing and drinking and cheering the loveable losers on to yet another one-sided blowout of a loss.

I found the spot that Miles had done his business, and it really was a doozy. I crouched down on one knee and picked it up, before I headed to the garbage can near the bay where the pumps were located.

"Dontcha be throwing your dog's shit in my garbage can, big shot," I heard that jerk-off say from out of the doorway of the station. He was really itching for a fight, I could tell.

"I don't need to be emptying shit-filled garbage cans on account of your little mutt."

I felt that pain in my gut and that tickle in my throat. I just looked up at him and swallowed.

He'd won. He knew he'd won. I wasn't gonna fight him. He was twice my size, and he knew it.

"You just go take your shit-filled shirt and your fancy car and hit the road," he sneered in my direction. "See the sign?" he chuckled and pointed. "No loitering!"

He laughed, thinking that he was so goddamn clever, and closed the door behind him. I looked around, and when I did, the few people who had been watching all turned away. So, I headed to the driver's door and got in the car with my shit-filled shirt. Humiliated as hell, burning up inside, I took a deep breath the way that I'd learned to from that shrink that Jenny had sent me to. It helped. It usually does.

With that, I started the engine up, looked straight ahead, and pulled out of the driveway with that shit in my lap. It was still warm, and if Miles weren't already asleep on the passenger's seat he would've been looking at me like I was nuts.

I took a right down the frontage road, feeling the gloating stare of that asshole on the back of my neck. I pulled back into the trucker's entrance about 500 feet down, out of sight from that stupid little mini-mart window.

There I waited about sixty seconds, gathering my thoughts, searching for my composure.

By the time I caught his eye, my arm was cocked and ready. I'd pulled up in front of the window and caught him with that good old element of surprise—that thing the world had thrown at me so much as of late.

I hurled that pile of shit against that station window as hard as I could and watched it splatter as it hit that wall of plate glass head on.

Like a giant bug on a windshield, that crap exploded. And before it could start its slow decent down that double pane window, we were outta there. Before that son of bitch knew what hit him, we were heading west, just two bucks on the road. The Lone Ranger and Tonto, ropin' and ridin'. Before that bastard could do a goddamn thing about it, we were already gone.

CHAPTER 12

I was only half listening to Matilda's voice on the GPS as she directed us to Albuquerque. We were heading down Highway 40 just out of Santa Rosa, when I saw the sign for Cimarron. I'd forgotten all about this place, and I figured, what the heck? So, I took the exit north.

I shut down the GPS and set my internal compass to auto-pilot. I knew the signs would get me there—they always had before—so I just went along for the ride.

I took a left where I saw the marker off 64. It couldn't have been more than five minutes later that I saw the Tooth of Time peering out at me. And it seemed like Miles could feel it too.

He was standing there on all fours. Panting at the great big world out there as if he knew precisely what I'd long since forgotten.

I opened the sunroof and let that big world in. Miles looked up at the sky coming through, and his little tail wagged just like a puppy getting a rawhide for the first time.

I slowed down to thirty-five and reveled in the sights, the smells and the sounds just like I was a kid again, coming here for the first time, not knowing all that life had in store for me.

I passed the old lodge on the left where the Phillips' used to vacation. Waite Phillips, the petroleum guy, was dead long before I'd ever come here, but you could still feel the energy of a man with wealth beyond anything I'd ever known.

He'd donated this whole place to the Scouts, and in doing so had become quite a legend. He was a real inspiration to young punks like me back in the day.

And suddenly there it was, looking just like it had over twenty years before: Tent City.

I pulled the 911 into the dirt lot and parked in front of a concrete marker, seemingly a parking space. Before I could open the door, what seemed like a giant dust cloud engulfed us. Even with the doors shut, dust blew in through the sunroof. I covered Miles' face so that none of it got in his eyes and closed the roof. By the time the roof sealed, the dust had settled, and with a deep breath, I opened the door.

I hadn't seen Miles so wound up in years. He jumped out of the drivers side door before I could even plant my leg on the ground and darted towards the mountain. He probably couldn't tell that we were a couple of miles from it. I mean, how could he? He'd never seen anything like that before.

He just ran and ran, so far that I couldn't see him anymore. But I wasn't worried about him. Nothing could happen to us here. I don't know why I felt that way. I just did.

I saw the vastness around me, and I felt kinda free too. Freer than I had in as long as I could remember. And that felt pretty damned good.

The sky seemed bigger than I'd ever seen it. The clouds were whiter too. Almost as if they'd been bleached out there in the high desert of New Mexico.

The sky was a cobalt sort of blue, and the trees were an emerald kinda green. I hadn't recalled everything being so damned vibrant the last time that I'd been there. But a whole hell of a lot had changed since then, that's for sure.

I looked around and saw that there were a couple of cars over by what I remembered to be the quartermaster's building. I wondered who would still be there in the middle of September. By now all the guys would've gone back to school or whatever. So, I slowly started walking over, all the while keeping half an eye out for Miles.

It took me a good ten minutes to make my way. The truth was that I didn't really have a fire under my ass to get me over there or anything. It still hadn't hit me that I was even there. An hour earlier I'd forgotten all about this place. And yet out of nowhere, there I was, as if thrown back into a dream that I'd forgotten about while I'd been awake.

As I made my way, I heard Miles bark a few times. I'd gotten to know his barks pretty good over the years, and I could tell that he was just having fun, probably taunting the birds, I figured. Or maybe he was barking at the moonrise sitting just like a tear from God's own eye, right there over the summit of Mount Baldy.

It sure is strange how once in a while you can see that big old moon in the middle of the afternoon. But out in the Sangres, damned near anything can happen. I knew that better than most.

I finally made it over to the village area and could spy the mess hall and the ranger station too. There was an ice machine on the side of the building. That was a relief, since I figured that I'd need to refill the thermos before too long.

As I instinctively turned towards the area that I'd last made camp, I heard a voice that sounded strangely familiar.

"A good afternoon to you, my friend," said a man with a deep voice. Even though I was certain I'd never met him, I somehow felt like I had.

Maybe it was his look that seemed so familiar. He stood about seven feet tall, wore beat-up old cowboy boots, large tarnished belt buckle, button-down denim shirt, and sported a full beard and mustache and a huge ten-gallon black hat. Hell, it could've been a twenty-gallon hat, as big as it was. But it seemed to fit him just fine.

"Good afternoon to you too," I responded respectfully.

"What can I do *you* for?" he asked me with a chuckle. He had a sweet way about him. He really did.

"I have a friend that says that all the time." I looked up at him and smiled.

"Now you have two that do, I reckon," he said, holding out his baseball mitt of a hand.

"Name's Paul, But they call me Pappy 'round here."

I shook his hand feeling like I should have used both of mine to do so. This bastard was as strong as an ox, but his hand shake was gentler than I would've thought that it'd be.

"Pappy, huh? My name's Jack Wolfe, Troop 61," I said out of habit, one that had long ago been set aside and forgotten.

"Nice to see ya again, Jack," he said like he knew me, even though I knew that he didn't.

He peered up towards the sky from left to right. It was almost like he was trying to figure something out. So, I looked up too. It was only courteous after all. I sure as shit wasn't gonna just stand there checking out his belt buckle or anything.

So together we stood there saying nothing, not a goddamn word, for a good sixty seconds or so—just looking up in the air for God knows what.

And then it hit me. I did remember this guy. Sure as shit, his name *was* Pappy.

Pappy finally broke the silence. "You spending the night, Jack Wolfe?"

"Uh. Yeah, Pappy," I told him, as if it had been in the cards all along. Even though it hadn't.

"You're more than welcome to, old friend," he said warmly. "It's good to have ya back."

Just then Miles darted right up on us all outta breath. I figured he'd been running non-stop for the past 20 minutes or so. He had a bunch of burrs in the fur right under his chin, but he didn't seem to notice. He ran right up to old Pappy and started saying hello. Pappy, of course, obliged.

"Hey there, little fella," Pappy said real jolly like. He sounded like Santa Claus for a second it seemed.

"What's *your* name?" he asked, reaching down from far above to scratch his little head.

"That's Miles," I told him. "He's a terrier."

"He sure is," Pappy said laughing. "He's a terrier if I've ever seen one."

Miles took to him really good. Pappy grabbed the fur under his chin where the burrs were, real playfully, and Miles darted back and forth just like a puppy.

I could tell that Pappy was a good guy. And Miles could too, it seemed.

Miles grabbed some sort of a stick that had been lying on the ground and brought it over. I figured that he wanted Pappy to throw it around with him a bit.

The stick was sort of funny looking though. It had holes in it and resembled a loofa or something that my Mom would've had in the bathtub when I was a kid. I'd remembered seeing branches like that before, but I couldn't recall where.

Pappy reached down and played a little tug of war with Miles before he let go. They were really hitting it off the way that old friends do. Or at least the way that I'd imagine old friends do.

"What kind of a branch is that?" I asked Pappy, as though he had all of the answers for all the questions that there ever were.

"That's cholla," he said, handing it to me.

Miles sat there panting, waiting to fetch the way that I'd taught him to. That was way back when I was doing what I thought I should to domesticate the little bugger.

"Cholla?" I asked. Squinting through the holes, up towards the sky.

"It's a type of cactus, Jack Wolfe. Now are you gonna throw that for your little guy, or are you gonna just stand there looking at it?" he said warmly. I peered up at him as if he'd given me permission for something that I needed. I couldn't put my finger on it, but it felt good.

I hurled that cholla, or whatever the hell you call that stick, as far as I could, and Miles scampered off as fast as when he ran towards that mountain.

"Look at him go!" Pappy laughed. "Go get 'em, Miles!"

"I haven't seen him run like that in years. Yeah . . . go get 'em Miles," I muttered softly, smiling and just watching him run.

"A terrier's gotta run, you know," Pappy said as if there was some sorta life lesson in that.

"I guess you're right, Pappy." I looked up at the sky again. "A terrier's gotta run."

There was more wisdom in those few damned words than much of anything else that anybody'd ever said. And with that, Pappy called Miles over, cholla branch and all.

Pappy just let me be. He threw that cholla this way and that, and each time Miles would bring the cholla back to Pappy, who'd wrestle him and egg him on before tossing it again.

"Oh, you're not so strong," Pappy would say to Miles while pulling that old stick from his jaws. "You're not such a tough guy."

It reminded me of the way that my old man used to bust my chops, always telling me that I wasn't good enough. But I knew all the while that he thought I was the cat's ass. The apple of his eye. A chip off the old block.

I just watched the two of them and smiled. It took almost fifteen minutes for Miles to show any signs of tiring.

"You had enough, buddy?" Pappy asked as Miles stood there panting. "Let's get you some water."

There was an old hand pump about a hundred feet away, and we headed there without saying a word. To be honest, it felt a little awkward not saying anything.

I thought to break the silence by offering something up, but nothing was coming to me. And that was damn strange too, because there really was a whole hell of a lot on my mind.

We got to the pump and I saw an aluminum bucket hanging from the spigot. Instinctively, I grabbed that handle with both hands, pulled her up to my chest, and then leaned in with all my might to bring her down again. I hadn't used an old well like that in twenty years or more, but I had it down like it was something I did every goddamn day of my life.

It took five or six strokes before I got a trickle. But once I did, it was coming out like I'd opened a hydrant. I just kept pumping like I was trying to put out a fire, and once the bucket was full, Pappy set it on the ground for Miles.

"Keep it going there, Jack Wolfe," Pappy said as he threw his ten-gallon hat on the ground and leaned in with his hands cupped. It seemed like he was drinking the cold water and washing the grime off his face and beard all at the same time.

He must've been down there for a minute or more, just taking care of his personal needs and what not. He even shoved his head under the spigot like he was getting all washed up for a hot date.

Pumping that old well was just like riding a bike. I mean, it all comes back to you. It really does. Just like they say. Somehow, in a strange sorta way, it felt like being back home again too.

I thought back to all the things that had happened to me since I last pumped a godforsaken well. All the ways that the world took care of me, and all the ways that it had shit on me too. I thought about Jenny right then and there and all the un-selfish ways that she loved Miles and me. The way that she'd let him run in the park like he'd just been doing, playing fetch with a tennis ball or some stupid play toy. Just the way I hardly ever did with him.

And that made me feel like shit. Just plum awful. So, I pumped harder.

Before I knew it, I had that pump going like Niagara Falls. I was pumping so fast and furious that I lost track of damn near everything. My mind went sort of blank, almost like it was numb or something. Like I'd gone over the edge.

And that water was just pouring outta that spigot like it was trying to wash the whole goddamn world clean.

"You trying to get this place rezoned as a flood plain or something there, Jack?" Pappy asked with a chuckle.

I just kept pumping away. I was laughing as I did like a school kid or something.

"Maybe, Pappy," I said. "Let's see how fast we can get this old girl going!"

Pappy grabbed the end of the handle with his left hand facing me, and I scooted up a foot or so. I suddenly felt myself sweating like a pig, but it felt great.

"Okay, Jack Wolfe," Pappy exclaimed. "Give her all you've got!"

I pumped that darned pump like my whole life depended on it, and it seemed like Pappy did too. Miles was running around and around us, sticking his little head under the spigot every third or fourth pass, jumping up and down like a puppy, while Pappy and I did our best to drown the world together.

"Whoohoo!" I exclaimed to the universe.

"Yeeee haaaw!" Pappy followed suit. "Keep it going Jack Wolfe!"

My T-shirt was drenched with perspiration, but I didn't much care. It had been forever or longer since I felt as free as I did out there in Cimarron, New Mexico. And I knew that I didn't want it to end.

I could sense that Pappy was petering out on me just a bit, so a scooted down the handle where I could get a little more torque on that old pump. I still tried to keep up the pace, but it was getting difficult. The salty sweat was getting in my eyes and it stung like a mother. The muscles in my arms were starting to cramp, especially my right bicep. And my left hand was stinging from being in that mess the night before. But I still gave it all I had.

I knew that Pappy was done, but I wanted to keep going all night if I could. Something had taken over in that moment, and it seemed like my whole life could have some meaning again, if only I could just keep the water flowing.

Finally, I couldn't go on anymore. I gave that handle one last push downward with all my weight on it and fell to my knees at the head of the spigot. It was all that I could do to turn my hands upward and cup that water. But it sure as heck was worth it.

I stuck my head right under that old spigot, drenching myself in that cold mountain agua for a nearly a minute before she stopped flowing. It was cold as ice, and I cherished every drop of it, like it was a shower head for the fountain of youth or something. And right then and there, it was. It was for me, at least.

I sensed that the last drops were coming from the faucet head. I laid on my back up under her, closed my eyes and opened my mouth. I stretched out like I was on a king-size bed at the Four Seasons and took in those sweet last droplets like it was gonna quench every thirst that I'd ever had.

I kept my eyes closed as I lied there in the mud, never having felt so clean. All my senses were so alive, but there wasn't anything to sense in that moment. I heard that rusty pump make an old, tired squeak, but other than that, I didn't hear a damn thing. The sun tried to creep through my tightly sealed eyelids, but at most it just warmed my skin. Really, all I sensed was the peaceful place that I was in.

The funny thing about being at peace is that it's just like riding a bike or pumping a well. You never quite forget what it's like, no matter how much time you go without it.

Just then Miles stuck his snoot in my face and started licking me.

"Okay, Milo!" I said laughing. "That's enough!" I shooed him off and jumped to my feet. "Where's your buddy at?" I asked him. He just stared at me.

I looked around and realized that the sun was setting, and its reflection was making the mountains all kinds of colors that I'd forgotten even existed.

"Yo, Pappy!" I hollered. "Pappy?"

I figured that he'd gone to take a dump or something. But when I saw a bedroll and some firewood along with a roll of T.P., I knew I was wrong. Pappy was gone.

Although it stung for a minute, knowing he was gone, me being alone there with Miles was just perfect the way that it was. Just like that the moment under the pump and the one with Jessie next to the Woody Guthrie statue. Just like being with Jenny on the side of that mountain and the day I said goodbye to my old man.

Just like the night I lost my virginity and the time that I beat the bejesus out of old Mitch Moran. Just like the day I shut the doors for the last time to the brokerage. Just like three days before, when I threw the keys in the mail box.

Even that time when I sprang forth from my mother's womb against my will into this godforsaken place—that moment was perfect too. They were all perfect. Those moments were all the exact goddamn way that they were supposed to be, and I'd all but driven myself crazy trying to find all the ways that they weren't.

We spent the next couple of hours just being together, Miles and me.

We took a walk around the grounds, and got the thermos all set up like we needed to. I reminisced about all the good times that we'd had together that I'd all but forgotten about.

I started a fire in the pit and laid the bedroll out beside it. I washed my jeans and T-shirt as best I could and laid them next to that fire to dry out. And then I sat there in my skivvies without a care in the world.

We looked up at the stars and made up stories about the constellations. Miles took his insulin like a good boy, and we had our meager meal together under the stars, kibble for Miles and an old granola bar for me.

I knew that we could've driven into town. We could *always* drive into town. But we couldn't always have this time together. And I don't think either of us wanted to be anywhere else.

I kept that fire going really well with the stash of wood Pappy left us, and I could've sworn I felt him keeping an eye on us, just like a guardian angel ought to do.

Finally, I felt myself dozing and heard Miles' little snoot let out a snore. I was trying to stay awake for him, not wanting our night to end. But when I rolled over to pet his little head, he'd already gone off to dreamland.

We both slept like rocks that night, lying there right beside each other. We were where we belonged, and it doesn't get much better than that.

Living in a high rise on Lake Michigan can spoil a guy when it comes to seeing the sunrise. Like I've told ya, I don't get too sentimental about all that crap. But I've gotta tell you that seeing it come up in the middle of all those skyscrapers has got nothing on seeing it come up in the Sangres. Not a damn thing.

Miles caught it first and sort of nuzzled up next to my ear, waking me up. What a sight. It was like nothing we'd ever seen. The sun was the size of a basketball up there in the sky, and it burned with a blazing, hot orange. Not some normal kind of orange. Far from it. It was all the colors of fire, if that makes any sense, and they shimmered and shifted, some darker and some brighter than the rest of the ball.

Altogther they made an orange that was alive. I almost thought that I could see the solar flares but figured that it was just my eyes playing tricks on me. It was pretty damn stupid to look at it dead on, but it was worth it.

After laying there for a good twenty minutes, we hopped to it, seemingly out of instinct. I threw my clothes back on, all warm and toasty from lying by that fire all night. Then I rolled the bedroll up real tight, like I was in the Army or something.

The ashes were still smoldering a touch, so I got a bucket of water and lapped up a few mouthfuls while I washed the sleep up outta my eyes. I found that cholla branch lying by the pump and thought it best to leave our friend a note. Scraping the stick into the dirt, I wrote *Thanks, Pappy!* on the spot where we'd made camp.

With that, I slowly extinguished what was still going in the pit. As the embers hissed farewell and the steam began to rise, we made our way to the 911, ready for a full day. Come what may. Come what might. Just like Gene and Roy, ropin' and ridin'.

CHAPTER 13

We were on the road for the better part of an hour or so before the light came on telling me the tank was getting low. I think we were both just enamored with where we were, being up in the Blood of Christ Mountains and all. We didn't have on any music, and I really didn't even notice.

Pulling off on the Taos exit, I spied a Shell station and pulled on in.

"Come on, buddy," I said to Miles. "Get out there and take care of business." He looked at me like I was nuts.

"Okay . . . okay . . ." I told him. "Let's get a move on." I rubbed him right behind the ears where it feels best until he slowly got up and crawled over the console onto my lap. I picked him up and set him on the blacktop, and he looked back at me before eyeing his surroundings. "It's okay, Milo," I assured him. "It's all right."

He ambled over to the grass just to the left of the car, and I put my Visa in the pump. It went through all the usual crap that those things will put ya through, asking you this and that about your zip code and all, when suddenly it made my heart fall to my knees.

See Attendant, the pump instructed me. And that Randall knife that had been in my gut seemed to find some new virgin flesh to dig into. A new organ or artery to torture.

I took a deep breath and headed over to Miles. He was just sniffing around, and I figured that he'd either done what he needed to do or didn't need to do anything at all. I picked him up and set him in the car before heading inside to the attendant. I began planning my story, rehearsing my lines like it was a high school play or something.

The guy behind the counter was probably about my age, but he didn't seem to take a lot of pride in himself, at least it didn't look that way. He'd obviously not shaved in a few days, but I could tell that it wasn't officially a beard or anything. His hair was disheveled, and his belly stuck out about a foot in front of the rest of him. Still, none of that stopped him from flirting with the older redhead that was seemingly a regular at the station.

I didn't want to come across like an asshole or anything, so I thought it best to just mind my P's and Q's while he talked her ear off about some buck he'd just shot. Plus, I figured that throwing him a little respect in front of a gal might go a long way.

Finally, I guess he figured that he oughta address me. Either that or he didn't want me hanging around, listening to his line of bullshit any longer.

"Yes, sir," I said really respectful and all. "The pump said to see the attendant?" I looked back towards the car.

"Which pump you on?"

"I don't know," I answered. "I'm the silver car over there."

He peered out, and I could see his eyes kinda light up.

"The reader doesn't work on that one," he said in a real matter-of-fact way, not wanting to let on that he was impressed in front of his gal, I guessed. "How much ya want?"

I reached in my wallet and handed him my Visa. "Sixty, I guess?" I said.

He ran it through, and damned if it didn't work like a charm. My heart found its right place again for the most part, but my hand was shaking like a goddamn leaf pumping that gas.

All filled up, I put on "In a Silent Way," and we headed west. At least it felt like west to me.

It wasn't until we got to Santa Fe that my stomach started to settle down and I figured out how damned hungry I was. It was right about then that I realized that Miles hadn't gotten his insulin yet and needed some grub in his system too, so I pulled into a Burger King that had been advertising itself for the last ten or fifteen miles.

Miles was snoozing, so I let him be, pulled into a space, and quietly turned the engine off. He just laid there, opening his eyes a sliver, but not moving an inch.

"I'll be right back, buddy," I told him. "Just gonna get us something to eat."

You'd think that the Burger King was the only place in Santa Fe to grab breakfast by the line that they had in there, but it didn't take long for me to figure out that the hold-up was mostly the people working there. There must've been three or four people that came back to the counter while I was waiting because their order was messed up. The gal behind the counter was real apologetic about it, and I kinda felt bad for her.

Finally, I got up to her and could sense how stressed out she was. The poor kid couldn't even look me in the eye.

"Good morning, Maritza," I said while looking at her name tag. "You doing all right, today?" I asked more genuinely than she ever would have expected.

She just looked up, as if she didn't know how to answer me.

"You look like you're having one of those days," I offered up warmly.

"Yeah, I kinda am," she said as she started to well up. "I don't know if I'm cut out for this job," she stammered.

I knew she was on the brink, and I didn't want to be the one to push her over the edge.

"Hey . . . it's all right, kiddo. Just take a deep breath," I said. "It'll help. I promise."

She looked at me like I was nuts, which I probably was. But still, I stuck by my guns.

"Breath in," I said as I sucked in my stomach and stuck my chest out.

She looked from left to right as though she was worried about other people watching her. But there wasn't anybody else in line anymore, and the rest of the staff seemed to be in back.

She inhaled deeply, realizing that nobody was paying us any mind. And as I exhaled, I told her to relax. "Close your eyes," I instructed.

We did that three or four times before I could tell that her nerves were back where they needed to be.

"Do you feel better now?"

"I guess so," she said sheepishly.

"You just guess so?" I teased.

"Naw. I know so." She gave a big old grin. "That's a great trick, mister. Thanks a lot."

I just smiled.

"So, what can I get for you, sir?" Maritza asked.

"Is that breakfast burrito spicy?"

"Not really," she said. "I can leave the salsa on the side if you want."

I ordered the burrito for Miles and I got myself a couple of Whoppers—which I was kinda surprised that they served at nine in the morning—an order of fries, chocolate milk and two waters.

"That's a lot of food, mister," Maritza said real shyly.

"My buddy's sleeping in the car. I didn't wanna wake him."

Maritza smiled and took her time to check our order carefully. When she finally called our number, there were about six more people up at the counter, but she didn't seem so frazzled anymore.

"Thanks, Maritza," I said as I grabbed the two bags from her.

"Thanks again, mister." She smiled, looking me right in the eye.

I just winked and headed out the double doors.

As I approached the 911, I could see Miles standing on his hind legs pawing at the window. I knew that he must have been starving and probably felt a little out of sorts because of his sugar levels and all. When I opened the door, he jumped right out and started running around my legs.

"Okay, pal. Okay," I said. "Let's go over to the table." I put his leash on him, and we headed across the lot to a picnic table sitting under a big oak tree.

His sugar levels must've been way off because he pretty much ripped the bag open as I set it down. I grabbed the torpedo-shaped container and opened it up.

Sure as shit, there was enough salsa to burn a hole through a prison wall. I just laughed and scraped it off.

While Miles chowed down on his breakfast, I walked back to the car to get the thermos and a needle. I filled it up to the line, put it in the scruff of his neck and pushed the hammer down.

With that, I gobbled down my grub quicker than I should have. And before we knew it, we were back on the road with our bellies full and our thoughts racing.

I must've gotten her up over a hundred five or six times that drive, most of those times on a straightaway or downhill. Once or twice I could've sworn that I spied a cop hiding behind an underpass or embankment, but nobody bothered us at all. I've gotta say, that the Porsche sure hugged the road nicely.

I saw signs for Lake Powell and figured that would be as good of a spot as any to take a load off, so we turned off 89 and followed the road to the canyon.

It was simply amazing. It really was.

For the third or fourth time in that trip, you could just feel that something was electric in the air. I know that Miles could feel it too because he woke up and was leaning on the dashboard with his front paws, his hind legs on the seat.

"How do ya like that, buddy?" I asked him as I pulled onto the embankment above the chasm. I leaned over and scooted the seat forward so the space wasn't so big for him to straddle.

"Is that better for ya?" I asked him. He just stood there panting while taking it all in.

We weaved in and out of those curvy canyon roads for a while. The reflection of the sun off that glass lake was really something special. It was so different than the view over Lake Michigan. Though we were there just a few days before, it seemed more like a million. It almost felt like we were on another planet, nowhere close to where we'd been. It was kinda surreal to be sure, and pretty damn humbling too.

Finally, I saw a sign of life: an arrow pointing to Wahweap Marina. I followed it.

We pulled into a spot by the cliff, and before I could put it in park, Miles was on my lap reaching for the door. I grabbed him by his collar and pulled him back gently.

"Slow down there, pal," I said sternly.

I put the car in park and opened the door as he tried to dart out. It seemed safe, so I cradled his belly with my right hand while still holding firmly to his collar with my left.

His legs were motoring a mile a minute as I held him up, and it made me laugh. Since there weren't any other cars around, I figured it was okay to let him go. I set him down on the concrete, and he scampered off to the nearby boulders.

The mid-day sun kinda took me by surprise. It was a hell of a lot hotter than I thought it was gonna be, so I figured that before I'd turn the engine off, I'd put the fan on high and let that cold air hit my face for a few. It felt good, and I just watched in wonder as Miles discovered the world for the very first time all over again.

He ran this way and that, charging up steep slopes for about ten or fifteen feet before looking over at me and heading back down. He must've done that about twenty times before he finally got up the courage to just go up all the way. And I let him.

We didn't have a whole lot of rules anymore out on the road. As strange as it sounds, seeing him so free made me feel like I was too. Sometimes, that's all it takes.

I watched him head about forty feet up the cliff. I'd lose sight of him for ten or twenty seconds, but he'd always make it a point to find a spot to look down at me so that I knew he was all right. Once I'd wave at him or shout his name, he'd run off on whatever trail he'd found and do his thing for a bit.

Now I've already told you that I'm not one of those soft, sentimental types, but I've gotta say that seeing him so free like that really did choke me up. I can't really tell you why. I mean, I always gave him a damned good life, but somehow I felt like I'd really deprived him of something on the twentieth floor, especially for the past year or two.

Sure, we had a good thing going. Let's face it. A guy can get used to a life like that. Those fireworks going off every couple of nights right outside your window. Egyptian cotton, and a cleaning lady twice a week to do the dishes and scrub the toilet. Cable TV and satellite radio. Anything we ever wanted for breakfast lunch and dinner.

But what I didn't recognize, was that there's a cost for being free. I mean *really* free. The kinda freedom that only comes from letting go of everything.

Like I said earlier, all those things are encumbrances of one kind or another. Even a guy's friends and family are a nuisance to an extent. Responsibilities and obligations. People he's gotta answer to about this and that. At least that's the way that I see it.

I figure that a fellow can't *really* be free the way that the world is set up these days. And that's just the way that it is.

All the benchmarks that we set up for measuring our success become the very shackles of our own enslavement. We set out to conquer the world and in doing so become its indentured servants. The more a guy achieves, the deeper down into the goddamn quicksand he sinks. The higher he jumps, the bigger the pile of shit he lands in.

But we'd somehow done what nobody else I'd ever known had. We'd gotten the hell out of the race. We didn't owe anybody the time of day anymore, and that felt about as good as anything I'd ever felt. I didn't want that feeling to end. Ever.

But like feelings usually do, it did.

Up in the sky I saw two big birds circling, and I knew enough to realize that we weren't in Chicago anymore. I peered up the cliff and could tell that Miles had no idea at all that he was being sized up for lunch.

"Miles!" I hollered. "Come on back, buddy!" I jumped up outta the car.

His ears perked up and his little snoot caught a whiff of something. He looked down at me as if to tell me that he wasn't ready to stop exploring. But that wasn't an option anymore. I could tell that those vultures were fixated on his every move.

"Now!" I told him sternly, pointing to the ground. "Come here!"

I think that he could sense that there was something wrong, because he didn't mess around anymore. He started in my direction but was having trouble navigating the rocks to come back down.

I could see his hesitation, but my eyes kept going back to those goddamn birds. Their circles became more defined. They weren't making the same broad sweeps that they had been when I first spotted them. It almost seemed like they were getting ready to make a move, I thought.

I grabbed a rock and threw it as hard as I could up in their direction. Although it didn't come close, it caught their attention. I pointed my finger and yelled as loud as I could so that they knew that we saw them.

"Stay the hell away from him!" I hollered, my heart racing.

I grabbed a smaller stone and hurled it at them, once again not coming close. Miles looked briefly at the birds before eyeing up another step.

I started up the hill but soon realized that there weren't any real paths. Instead I just kept my eyes on the vultures and threw a rock every few seconds. It seemed that they were moving in closer and were maneuvering in tighter and tighter circles. And that scared the crap out of me.

At one point the smaller bird seemed to swoop down towards the cliff, but when I threw a rock, it retreated. All I could do was make a lot of noise and keep the artillery flying until Miles finally made it down to safety.

Suddenly, with talons fully extended, the larger vulture came out of nowhere and did what seemed like a dive-bomb in Miles direction. As it did, I sent a fastball his way with everything I had. And damned if I didn't come close.

Miles lept a good 12 feet down that embankment, and as he did, I heard a distinct whimper. One that I hadn't recalled hearing in a very long time.

Although he was still a ways off, he was getting out of harms way. But not quite. I couldn't see him in the bushes and he didn't make a peep to let me know he was OK.

And then, without warning, that smaller hawk came up outta nowhere and swooped down looking like a kamikaze.

I heard a thud, and ran full speed up that hill. Not giving a thought to the brush and bramble that stood between us. That bird flew off in a cloud of dust and feathers, and my heart skipped 2 beats out of blind fear at what might have happened. Rushing over, I picked Miles up frantically and then cradled him in my arms. "That's my guy." I said calmly to him.

I held him as tightly as I could for a moment or two, and he didn't seem to mind one bit. In fact, it sorta felt like he was hugging me back. And I liked that.

I set him down, and to my relief, he didn't seem any worse for wear. He hobbled for a split-second, but quickly started heading back towards the car without any difficulty. And we walked together down that cliff with our heads held high.

"Okay, okay . . . let's get a leash on ya," I said as I grabbed it from the back seat and put it on without a peep from him.

I looked up at the circles in the sky. Only now they didn't seem so menacing. I flipped them off with a smile, believing that it was gonna rattle them.

"Nice try, bastards!" I hollered.

Miles looked up too. And together, we marched confidently towards the waters edge as if we'd won a battle of some sort.

As we walked over to the marina, a loud bullhorn went off that scared the bejesus out of us. It was some sort of sightseeing boat returning to shore with a few dozen people on board.

Taking our time walking around, we passed a make-shift gift shop and a bait and tackle place that smelled like hell. Finally, I spied a little café with outdoor seating. I reckoned that was as good an invitation as any, so I sidled up to the empty counter and claimed a stool, Miles curling up underneath.

I must've sat there for a good ten minutes before anybody saw me. That would've bugged the shit outta me pretty much any other time, but it didn't then and there. It didn't bother me one bit. The sun on my face and that slight breeze off the lake felt pretty perfect.

About when I figured they should just charge me rent for sitting there, a kid who looked really pale and had super thin strawberry blonde hair came over.

"Sorry, sir," he said politely. "I didn't see ya there."

"No problem, pal. I'm just soaking it all up."

"Yeah?" He looked at me kinda puzzled. "What can I get you?" I could tell he wasn't the conversational kind, so I didn't force it on him.

"I'll take a light," I told him. "Whatever kind you've got is fine. Are you able to serve it to me?" I asked him genuinely. I figured he was probably about fourteen years old or so.

"Um, yea," he responded sorta bashfully. "My dad owns the place."

I just smiled. I knew that the kid had no idea what I was asking. And if it was okay with his old man, it sure as shit was fine with me. Things were sure different in the Wild West, at least compared to Chicago anyway.

"Can you bring some water for my buddy too?", I asked the kid. He just nodded.

He brought me a bottle with a label that I'd never seen before, but whatever was inside was cold and wet and tasted like champagne to me.

I could hear Miles snoring as I set the plastic bowl of water next to his snoot. I damn near fell asleep sitting there in a trance, with the sun shining right down on my noggin like that.

I must've sat there for a good forty-five minutes or more before the kid came back. "Would you like something else, sir?"

"I'll take another one of these. That's a darned good beer," I told him as if my approval meant something.

"It's a local one. A lot of people like it." Then a sheepish smile crossed his face. "Do you mind if I close you out now?" he said kinda nervously. "We're gonna be shutting down soon."

"Sure, kid. What do I owe ya?"

"Eight, for the two beers."

I reached in my pocket and handed him a ten. "Just keep it," I told him.

"Thank you, mister," he said without looking me in the eye. It was almost like he wasn't used to getting a tip or something and seemed strange about it.

"You're welcome," I responded as he started to slink away into the kitchen.

"Hey, junior," I said, interrupting his getaway. He stopped in his tracks as if someone had shoved a six-shooter into his ribcage.

"Yes, sir?"

"Are they going out anymore today?" I asked while pointing to the ferry at the waters edge.

"Um . . . yeah," he answered. "They've got one more at four o'clock."

Then he just stood there, half in the kitchen, half out. It was like he wanted me to release him. I felt like I should say "At ease" or something to him. He reminded me of someone I used to know a long time before. So goddamn green. So innocent and all.

"Thanks, kid" was all I said.

Sure, I could've busted his chops a little, like they used to do to me back when I was his age. But instead I just let him be. I guess maybe I felt bad for that little ginger bastard or something. Maybe I was just getting soft. Either way, I left him alone.

I looked at my watch. It was a quarter of four, so I chugged my beer and we headed down to the dock. Miles was a little droopy when I woke him, but once we started walking, he got a kick back in his step.

We made it down to the boat with time to spare, although it didn't seem like it mattered all that much. It looked like there were a few people seated up top, but nobody was lining up for the last cruise of the day, that was for certain.

A guy that looked about as much like a captain as any fellow could was standing at the landing. He had a full grey beard and a blue cap on. His belly was big, and he seemed like a jolly old fart. And I don't use the word jolly all that much. But with this guy it just seemed to fit.

"Permission to come aboard?" I asked real military-like, raising my hand in a salute.

"Permission granted, Ensign," he smiled.

"That's Ensign Wolfe, Captain," I continued. "And this is my first mate, Miles," I said, saluting the old codger.

He looked down and kinda shrugged his shoulders. Then he leaned in. "I hate to tell ya Ensign Wolfe, but first mates aren't allowed on board," he said. "Maritime rules, I'm afraid."

He folded his arms, peering down at Miles almost like he was sizing him up for duty or something. Miles looked up, panting and out of breath from the walk over. Then the captain crouched down and caressed his head.

"Yeah, that's a good boy," he muttered. Miles closed his eyes and rubbed his chin against the captain's strong fingers.

"You know," the captain finally said. "He looks more like a chief petty officer than a first mate to me."

"Yep, Captain," I smiled. "I suppose you might be right. Those Naval ranks tend to mess me up more often than not," I said real tongue in cheek.

"Provided Chief Petty Officer Miles is also some sort of service assistant to his Ensign, well the maritime rules don't much apply," he said warmly, smiling up at me.

"I don't think I'd be here today if it weren't for his dutiful assistance," I mused.

"Whelp, as long as you've got all the necessary paperwork in order, then I suppose his presence will be permissible," he said formally.

My heart dropped for a moment. I clearly didn't have anything to prove Miles was a service dog, because he wasn't. I must have worn my worry on my face more than I planned because the captain seemed to catch on.

"I don't need to see the papers, Ensign," he said quickly. "I trust that all of your affairs are in order."

With that, he winked and saluted me. He even looked down and saluted Miles as well. "Permission to come aboard," he said formally. "That'll be twenty dollars, Ensign," he said, holding out his left hand.

I handed him a twenty, and he directed us up ahead of the bridge where nobody else was sitting. That suited me just fine. They were the best seats in the house anyway, and I knew that the captain didn't want us where all the other fussbudgets could be bothered by a dog.

We maneuvered our way down the small walkway to the side of the bridge and found the bow. It was sunny as hell since it didn't have an overhang the way that the rest of the boat did. There were a few folding chairs and a large white chest for the life preservers sitting alongside the bridge. Seeing that the wall of the bridge was right behind the chest, it seemed like the best spot for two young cowboys to hang their hats. I sat myself right down and took a good look at everything that surrounded us.

It was like something out of a picture book. It really was.

There was a tap on the glass over my head. When I looked up, the captain did a fist pump, the kind you'd make to get eighteen-wheelers to blow their horns. Then he took his hands, and put them over his ears, gesturing for me to do the same. So, I did. But nothing happened.

I sat there for ten or twenty seconds covering my ears before he came out of the cabin and stood in front of me with his arms crossed.

"I'm more concerned about the petty officer than I am about you, Ensign," he said sternly.

I smiled and nodded, as he headed briskly back to the bridge. With that, I picked up Petty Officer Miles Wolfe and put him on my lap, where I held him tightly and covered his ears. Then the loudest goddamn bullhorn I've ever heard pierced through the canyon like a freight train in a tunnel.

Miles squirmed a little but calmed as I held him closer, keeping him safe in my arms. It did feel safe up there on that box, sitting on top of the life vests with my spine nestled up against the cabin and that warm sunshine smiling down upon us.

When the noise subsided, we headed off into the canyon. Miles stuck his snoot up in the air, the wind whipping about his hair and ears. I just rubbed his head and got a sideways, tongue-out smile from that little guy.

I found myself soothed by the sun again, right in the spot where it could hit me square in the kisser. It felt good, and with the rocking of the water, I sorta drifted off for a spell.

My thoughts wandered all over. Half in a haze of memory. Half right there where we were sitting. There was no place else I wanted to be. With the sun shining down, it was almost like what I imagined going to heaven would be like, if I believed in going to heaven, that is.

It made me think of Jenny's smile for a moment. And as crazy as it is, I wondered if it was her looking down on us from up there, smiling at seeing her two guys taking the world by the tail, finally.

I started thinking back to the last time that my old man and I went to Vegas. It had been etched in my mind like a tattoo, even though I hadn't thought of it in awhile. It was one of those bittersweet moments, sort of like the rest of this shit that I'd been going through. The sweet with the sour, and all.

I remembered how one spring weekend Pops surprised me with a ticket to meet him out at the MGM for his birthday. I'd only been there a time or two before, so I was really jazzed up about it the way a young tenderfoot would be—especially because I'd always heard the stories about all the antics that he and his buddies would get into out there. His tales were almost like scripture to me, and I was excited to finally be a part of the Pack for a weekend.

Naturally, I was a bit surprised when I got to the hotel and found out that it was just gonna be the two of us. I'd be lying if I didn't tell you that I was a little bummed at first. Still, I felt like shit for feeling that way. I still do.

After washing up from the flight, I headed down to meet my old man at the craps table where he was holding court. He handed me the bones before blowing on my hand. It felt a little off to me at the time, but everybody was cheering. Ten minutes later, we were up a few thousand bucks. We made our getaway to the lounge a couple hundred feet away or so.

"You saved my ass back there, Butch," he said like he was Dean Martin or something. "I was down fifteen hundred bucks when you rolled up. Those dice were cold as ice."

He gestured to the bartender, who obviously recognized him from times before. The next thing I knew, we each had a shot of iced Grey Goose in front of our noses. Almost like it was a race, we raised to one another and downed them like chocolate milk.

I felt a little rush, when another two mysteriously appeared. We downed those just as quickly, celebrating in full force, embracing the moment like two old pals, not a father and his son. I'll never forget that feeling.

"There's something I've been meaning to tell you," he said more sincerely than I figured anything should've been right then and there. I just peered in his direction, waiting expectantly.

But the seriousness of the moment went away as three of the hottest gals I'd ever seen showed up at the bar next to us. Two of them were blonde, and the other had a more exotic flair. None of them could've been more than twenty-four and my old man didn't need a sales pitch.

With that, he shoved some bills down one of the blondes' blouses and ordered another round of shooters for the group.

"To the fall of the Empire!" he shouted laughingly while raising his glass.

"To the fall of the Empire!" we all replied, raising ours to his as if it were well-rehearsed cheer or something.

"Wait a minute, wait a minute," I interjected laughingly, stuttering a bit over my words. I was already a little buzzed, and I was quite certain that they could tell.

"What the heck is that supposed to mean?" I slurred with a grin. "The fall of the Empire?"

"It means what it means, Butch," he smirked. "You don't question a toast, you just take it!" he insisted.

"Isn't that right girls?" he bellowed, raising the glass to his lips.

The other blonde grabbed my leg and winked at me, and all of us fired that shot down our gullets like our lives depended upon it.

"Nastrovia!" my old man belted out slamming his glass on the table. "Nastrovia!" we yelled back at the tops of our lungs.

We had another one or two before we split. I headed up to my room with one of the blondes, leaving the birthday boy at the craps table with the other two.

I was damned close to heaven for the next forty-five minutes or so. She was about as close to a professional as anyone I'd ever been with before or since. Afterwards, she dove into the mini-bar. At first, I thought to stop her, but figured I'd let it slide. I had a hunch that my old man had us covered anyway. Her slender hands reached right down instinctively to the bottom of the fridge, where she grabbed a little bottle of Chivas. She nabbed a Snickers before closing the door and headed back towards the bed.

"I figured you wouldn't mind," she smiled warmly. "A girl's gotta keep up her energy," she said as she kissed me gently on the nose.

I laid there exhausted as she sat beside me and opened the Chivas. "To the best you'll ever have," she grinned, raising the bottle. I just smiled. I couldn't argue with her about it even if I wanted to. And she sure as shootin' knew it.

She chugged about half of the little thing, and I finished the rest. Then she kissed me on the forehead like I was a little kid or something, put her clothes on, and left. Just like I always figured a hooker would do. Still, I never knew how empty it could leave a guy feeling.

For a moment, I wished for a fond farewell and a sentimental exchange of a few Ben Franklins. It's not like I expected her digits or anything.

Still, it somehow felt cheap just watching her walk on out that door. But I tried not to let it get to me. I appreciated my old man for letting me think that she came up to the room on her own. I really did. It was a pretty stand-up thing to do, I thought.

I washed my face, threw my threads back on, and headed downstairs, having caught a second wind. I did about two sweeps of the casino before I finally gave up on looking for him and found myself an end spot at one of the poker bars.

"A cup of coffee and an Amstel light," I directed the bartender. Within twenty seconds they were in front of me, almost as if she'd known my order before I ever showed up.

I threw a twenty in the machine and watched the credits kick in. I set my sights on the progressive payout that had inched its way up over sixteen hundred dollars.

The girl to my left kept looking over at me from the corner of her eye. I could tell right away that she wanted some small talk. She seemed like a sweet girl, and I figured I'd chat her up a little.

After about five minutes of telling me about the Mary Kay convention that she was in town for, she hit four of a kind. I thought the world was gonna end.

"Oh, my God! Did you see that? I can't believe it!" she started yelling like a high school girl on the pom pom squad. The truth is, I was excited for her. I really was. It was kinda cute.

I ordered another Amstel and a shot of Beam. I re-dealt my hand as the bartender was getting them, so that she knew I was playing max bet. The machine gave me four diamonds and a spade. The diamonds were all face cards, so it didn't take a whole lot of thinking to throw away the spade. Sure, as shit. The ten of diamonds. I hit the progressive royal, just the way I'd been picturing it in my mind for as long as I could remember.

Now I'll tell ya that I think that the gal next to me must've shit herself. She appeared to be more excited than I had been half an hour earlier up on the seventeenth floor. She was screaming like a goddamn hyena, and all I could do, was take a deep breath and smile.

The bartender didn't seem to give two shits. It was all business to her. I duked her a quarter anyways and slithered off into the night, almost seventeen hundred dollars richer.

I really wanted to tell my old man about my hit, so I dodged in and out of the pits looking for him. I think I was so jazzed up to find him because I felt like I was finally playing in his league. And I wanted more than anything to show him that.

But no matter where I looked, I couldn't find the old man. I even hit the damn slot machines, thinking that was the last place he'd be. Eventually I figured he was in his room. And I sure as hell wasn't gonna bother him if he was with one of the gals, or both.

I sauntered over to the lounge that we'd been at earlier and caught the bartender's eye.

"He hasn't been back," she said, shrugging her shoulders.

They never give you any real information anyways in these joints, especially when a guy leaves with a working girl. I just nodded to the bartender and headed back to the tables.

There was one spot open at a ten-dollar table, so I jumped on it. I glanced around, and it felt like the casino was more sophisticated. It was probably just the time of the evening, being late on a Friday night, but I knew that I wanted to fit in more than I had earlier.

Two seats down sat a young Asian gal drinking some sort of highball on the rocks and wearing a diamond bezel watch. It looked like a Cartier or a Piaget—something fancy and French. I noticed that she wasn't wearing a ring, and being as high as I was on everything right then, I kinda figured that she was going to be my mark. I can be pretty cocky like that once in a while, especially after a few snorts of good whiskey.

The dealer dealt to the full table, and I scored a blackjack right outta the box. I caught my girl's eye just as the ace of clubs graced the queen I'd been dealt, and for a few fleeting moments I thought that this one was in the bag.

About a half hour and a couple of Beam and Cokes later, I counted my chips and saw that I was pretty close to even. The couple at first base had gone, and a sharp-dressed, middle-aged guy rolled up. He was wearing white slacks with some expensive suede loafers and a pinstriped blazer, but what struck me as cool were the tinted blue sunglasses and his slicked back hair. I half expected him to order a martini, shaken not stirred. But he didn't order anything. Not a goddamn thing.

Instead, that Sonofabitch threw a purple chip on the table. He lost it with a soft seventeen against a twenty from the other side. Without thinking twice, he pulled out another one and lost it too.

I looked over at my girl, and she didn't seem to flinch. But somehow I could still tell that she was impressed with this bastard.

Much to everyone's surprise, a third purple chip appeared on the green, and the dealer threw him two aces. I spied the pit boss peering over his shoulder, checking out the action. It almost felt like you could hear a pin drop.

"Split 'em," the hot shot said indifferently. Throwing another chip up without a goddamn hint of emotion.

The first one got kissed with a queen, and another ace landed square on top of the second card. The dealer looked at him with either immense respect or pity. I couldn't tell which one.

"Again?" the dealer asked politely. The guy just nodded and gestured with his index finger, while throwing another purple on the line.

Out of the shoe came a nine and then another face card. I really don't recall which one, but I do remember how the dealer stayed on his hard seventeen, while Slick Willy took his six thousand bucks and disappeared into the crowd like Houdini.

Most of all, I recall how I wanted to be just like that bastard. Come to think of it, I still do. Damned if I don't still wanna be just like that guy from time to time.

Twenty minutes later I was down about sixty or eighty bucks. To be honest, that was big money to me back then, despite the score at the poker machine.

I could tell that the Asian gal had lost a little interest, although I could still catch her looking at my cards here and there. I figured that it was time to make my move since I had a deep pocket after the poker heist.

Without batting an eyelash, I threw twelve red chips on the green, looking to get even with one hit. I was picturing myself just like the guy who'd walked away. Calm, cool and collected.

Out came a bunch of decent hands against the dealer's face card. Mine wasn't one of them though, and I saw her take my money as I drew and busted.

I looked around the table. Not catching anybody's eye but the dealer's. "Tough one," she said sympathetically, not knowing my strategy.

"That's okay," I said with confidence. "I'm the man with the plan." She just smiled.

I set some hundreds on the table and told her to give me green. She didn't hesitate, and swiftly exchanged them.

"Color out," she said looking over her shoulder. The boss just gave her a customary nod.

"Okay!" she said, counting out my quarters. "Let's do some good here!" she said and slapped the green felt.

I put five chips down on my spot, folded my arms and took a deep breath. "Good luck," the doll two seats down mouthed to me. I winked at her like a cocky prick and sat back and watched.

I stayed on a hard seventeen against the dealer's seven. She drew an eight, and I figured it was in the bag. But she whipped a four out right after and pulled my chips into the bank with a sigh.

"Sorry, kid," she said. I could tell that she really felt bad about it too. But I didn't let it phase me. It was gonna work out all right. I just knew it.

You see, I was imagining that I could feel the eyes of the whole damn table on me. And being the punk that I was, I wanted so badly to impress them. Sure, I was down over two hundred and fifty bucks, but that was no big deal. I was a high roller for Christ's sake. I looked down at my stack and counted 'em out, knowing that this hit would set me right.

The dealer flung an ace in my direction, and I just had a hunch it was all good again. Then a five found its way on top of it, leaving me with a soft sixteen. I hit and got a face card. Then I hit again and got another.

It felt like my heart was gonna come right out of my chest. But I dug in my pocket and threw another five hundred out there anyways.

"Money plays," I said confidently.

Now I'm not gonna lie to you. I don't know what the hell I got or what anybody else at that godforsaken table got. All I know is that I walked away from that spot with my ass handed to me.

I didn't look back. I knew that they were either laughing at me or pitying my sorry ass. And the truth is that I didn't really give two shits which it was. I just wanted to disappear into the crowd the way that six-thousand-dollar big shot had done.

And I did, but not like I planned. I walked those lonely streets for probably four or five hours, thinking that every Asian hottie I saw was the one at the table, and that every hot shot in a sport coat and loafers was that high roller. But I didn't see my Pops anywhere that night. No matter where the heck I went looking for him.

The next day I stumbled down to the coffee shop to meet the old man for breakfast. We didn't discuss either of our conquests from the night before, and I sure as hell didn't tell him about the shellacking I took.

It seemed like something was on his mind. Somehow, I could feel his energy from across the table. The music was a little too loud for a breakfast joint I thought, with the bass vibrating the tables. But this was his place, in his town. I wasn't gonna second guess him on it.

After a few moments of catching up and saying the usual crap, we ordered from an older, overweight waitress who'd probably been a cocktail gal thirty years earlier. It seemed like she still had that swagger. A sort of confidence that you might not expect.

My old man ordered what he always did. I used to rib him and call it a heart-attack on a plate. Eggs Benedict with corned beef hash. "Burn 'em up" was how he'd always tell them to make the hash.

I just ordered a cinnamon roll, which the menu said was a house specialty. I'm not much of a breakfast guy. She filled our cups with some Joe and headed off with our orders.

It was kinda nice, those next few minutes. It really was. It seemed like the first time in ages that I got to catch up with him. We really didn't talk about shit. At least nothing that mattered all that much. He asked me about the chicks that I was banging, the way he always did, and about work too. But it was nothing heavy. Just small talk. Just two regular guys catching up with one another. And that felt just right.

You see, my relationship with my old man had always been like that. At least as long as I could remember.

Sure, he'd bust my chops from time to time, back when I'd be doing all the kind of crap that young punks do. I figured that he always saw it as some sort of a half-assed responsibility that he took on, but for the most part, we'd always been pals more than anything else. That was the way he'd wanted it, and I'd be lying if I said that it wasn't the way I wanted it too.

The truth is that he never was much of a father to me in the traditional sense. But I wasn't much of a conventional son to him either.

I always kept my end of the deal by never asking him for anything. Not a goddamn thing. He appreciated it. He'd even brag about it to his buddies once in a while. I know because they'd tell me how damned proud he was of me for being so darned independent. Hearing that always put a smile on my mug.

"Keno?" I heard a gal's voice ask faintly through the thumping bass.

"Yeah!" Pops said as he grabbed a sheet from her and scribbled seven or eight Xs on it. "Can I still get in on this one?" he asked her.

"Yes, sir," she responded. "Plenty of time."

What a looker she was, dressed like a Vegas showgirl and all. Skirt up to her ass and those stockings with the line up the back. My old man handed her the sheet and a fin, and she pranced off shouting "Keno? Keno?" through the rest of the coffee shop.

Just then our food arrived, and it looked better than I expected. Even the stupid cinnamon roll looked incredible, and I was glad that it brought my appetite back.

"Looks pretty good, Pops," I nodded.

"Why do you think I come here, Butch? The music?" he smiled at me.

He always loved busting my chops, and I'd be full of shit if I told ya that I didn't get a rise out of it too. Of course, I did. He was my old man after all.

"Best breakfast on the strip," he said while salting his hash as though it actually needed it.

I put some of the fresh whipped butter on the roll and watched it melt almost instantly. The smell of the gooey sugar did get me back on track. It was either that or the coffee. Either way, there wasn't a hint of a hangover at the table.

Pops had already jumped in before I took my first bite, and it was as good as I thought it was gonna be. That doesn't often happen, but this time it did. It was probably the best goddamn cinnamon roll I'd ever tasted.

He took a swig of coffee and cleared his throat. I didn't think anything of it. I swear to Christ I didn't. Then he peered intently in my direction.

"It's really no big deal . . ." he started. Staring at me kinda deadpan. ". . . but there's something I've been meaning to tell you."

"Sure," I said real matter-of-factly, not thinking much of his sudden sincerity. "Can you speak up? The music is kinda loud in here, Pops."

"Yeah, I know," he said. "It's always that way in here. I guess that they wanna get you all pumped up to go out and lose your money or something," he chuckled.

"So, what gives?" I said louder than I needed to, just to make my point about how frickin' noisy the place was. He just sat there discerningly.

"What's up, Pops?" I asked kinda pointedly but not as loudly this time. I could tell something heavy was on his mind, and I wasn't ready for whatever it was.

He cleared his throat again. "The doc says I've got something," he said seriously, staring a hole through me.

He raised his voice so I could hear him good and clear. "He says it's pretty serious."

My old man looked down at the table and then up at me. I sat there feeling the bass pounding through the bench seat.

"It's some sort of a cross between Parkinson's and Alzheimer's," he went on. "And it sounds like it's a pretty fast mover."

My eyes started to well up a little bit, although I did my best to keep my cool. I didn't want to show it, since he obviously wasn't. Nonetheless, I started to feel like I was gonna hurl.

"But I don't know, Butch. I'm sure I can beat it."

I sat there as if my world had just been yanked out from under me. I wondered how the hell he could've been so high the night before. I didn't wanna eat a thing, but I took another bite of that cinnamon roll anyways just because it was sitting there.

He spent the next ten minutes telling me all the details of the prognosis and the stages of his condition. I just listened, not believing any of it. Not a goddamn word.

Whatever that disease was that he was talking about, I didn't want to give it a shred of credibility. I just wanted to dismiss it like some drunken asshole at the end of the bar or some sad ten-o'clock news story about a family far away that I'd never met.

I wanted to make the story go away so we could get back to our weekend together. And in some small juvenile way, it worked for a moment or two. But the truth is, the feeling didn't stick.

I couldn't picture my old man using a walker. I couldn't see him stopping every twenty feet or so to catch his breath and gain his balance. I couldn't imagine cutting his food into little pieces and feeding it to him like a baby or something. I just couldn't.

"It's sure gonna be tough for you to get laid with me pushing your sorry ass around in a wheelchair," I said for levity. Shit. It was the only way that I knew how to deal with the situation. These were unchartered waters.

"Oh, you'd be surprised," he laughed back.

All we could do was try to hit that godforsaken curveball.

"This isn't the first mountain I've had to climb, and I'll be damned if it's gonna be my last," he said with a smile, clearing his throat again.

I leaned over the table to hear his words over the background, turning my ear towards him. Although maybe it was just to avoid looking him in the eyes.

"I never could've learned how to have a successful business if I hadn't fallen on my face once or twice," he said as I sat there silent. "I never would've had any good loves either if I hadn't had my share of screwed up ones first. I can tell you that for sure."

I didn't say anything.

He leaned over and grabbed my hands firmly and he forced me to look him right square in the face, the last place I wanted to be staring. The very last.

"And I know that I couldn't have known how to be a good friend if I hadn't been a bad one my share of times too, Butch."

I think that was the first time that I felt that Randall knife in my gut, now that I think about it. The first time ever. Right there and then. And I can tell ya that it hurt like a son of a bitch. Like a real mother.

"Can you turn the goddamn music down for Christ's sake!" I yelled back towards the kitchen as people looked over at me like I was nuts. My eyes started to well up.

"What's the matter?" I stood up and turned around.

"Is that a problem for you guys?" I bellowed, like the tough guy that I wasn't.

Everybody just turned away and went back to whatever they were doing before my outburst.

"Calm down," my old man pleaded sternly. "Sit your ass back down in that booth." he said.

I hesitantly lowered myself into my seat.

"I know you're upset, Butch. But we've gotta see this for what it's worth. It all comes out in the wash."

He tried to grab my hands, but I pulled them back, pretending like I was taking another bite of the cinnamon roll. All the time trying to blink in order to keep the tears from rolling down my mug.

"I'm not going anywhere," he said firmly. "Neither are you. That much I know."

He was calm. Calmer than I'd ever seen him before.

He half stood up and leaned over the table. He grabbed my right shoulder firmly. I could feel his stare going right through me. All I could do was look up at him. It was like I had no choice.

"But it took me a lot of living to learn that," he said affectionately.

"So, what exactly are you trying to say?" I asked. "Are you telling me that it took a lot of living for you to learn how to kick the bucket?"

I felt the tears coming down, feeling pathetic and weak, and I grabbed a napkin to stop them. I snorted like I had a cold or allergies or something just in case somebody was watching. But nobody was. Nobody gave two shits.

"Seriously, Pops," I said quietly, in as calm a voice as I could, considering the situation. "What can this thing possibly teach us?" I asked again.

"I guess we'll know when the lesson is over," he somehow managed a smile. "Maybe it's meant to show us how to live."

I just sat there staring down into my cup of coffee, thinking that I'd never noticed how goddamn black something could be. So entirely empty.

Finally, I looked up at him eating his eggs benedict and hash browns as if it were a day like any other. Just like it was nothing.

"You gonna eat or what?" he asked with a chuckle. I couldn't believe how unfazed he was.

"How can you be filling your belly like nothing's wrong?"

"What else am I gonna do?" he smiled. "Starve to death?"

"But Pops," I stuttered. "No matter how you play this, it just seems like you've been dealt a losing hand," I said as those tears made their way down my cheeks.

"Unfortunately, Butch," he said while taking another mouthful, "it happens to be the only game in town."

The shiv twisted in my belly, and my Adam's apple turned into a pineapple.

"But if you're up for it . . ." he grinned warmly, "maybe we can play this hand together."

Just then that bullhorn went off from the stern of the ship, and the passengers behind us cheered.

I peered over my shoulder and could see that some poor guy was putting a ring on his girl. It seemed as though he was screwing his life up pretty good, although everybody seemed really happy about it. I figured that it was better him than me. She was all teary eyed, and I suppose it was a beautiful place to do it. If you were gonna do it, that is.

The sun was getting lower in the distance, but it still had a way to go. They were pouring champagne, and I figured I'd oblige and toast the happy couple.

I took Miles from my lap and set him down on the deck of the ship. I think he'd dozed off along with me, because he really jumped when the horn went off and his hind claws dug into my thighs pretty good. I could faintly hear the captain going on about all the times that people had shared special moments on his ship, but the truth was that nobody seemed to care.

It didn't seem like Miles much liked walking on board that ship, so I let him crawl back up on my lap where he felt more at ease. I decided that I didn't need any champagne anyways. Champagne always gave me a headache, and seeing as I was out on the water rocking back and forth, the combination probably had the potential to not go so well together.

"What's the matter buddy?" I asked him. "Your sea legs not working too good?" I smiled and scratched his head. He pushed his little noggin right into the crook of my arm. I petted him really good, in and out around the ears, right in the sweet spot.

We spent the better part of the next hour simply being together. Together, alone.

By the time we made it back to the dock the sun was just a sliver. Things had died down behind us quite a bit, not that I really paid it any mind.

The captain eased her back into the landing real smooth, just like he'd probably done ten thousand times before. The lake was smooth as glass, the way that old Lake Geneva used to become in the middle of January. That was back when my old man would scare the bejesus outta me by driving on it. No matter how comforting the old coot was, all that I wanted was to get back to shore, back to where I knew the bottom couldn't fall out on me. Back to where I had some control.

Even though I know he didn't like it, I carried Miles in my arms as I slithered off that ship with the rest of them. I was feeling kinda spacey, and I wasn't in the mood for any more banter with the captain, even though I had a hunch he was looking forward to it.

Once we got to the dock, I set Miles down. He led me instinctively all the way to the 911. With that, I opened his door and he jumped right up to the co-pilot seat while I closed it behind him.

As I walked around to my side, I looked back at the magnificent sunset. And as I gazed from one end of the horizon to the other, I could see our friend the captain folding the chairs and getting his best girl ready for the night.

I could've sworn that he caught my eye as I looked in his direction, but when I waved, he didn't wave back. I popped the trunk and filled Miles bowl with some kibble for the road.

"Here ya go, buddy," I said as I opened my side and set his food on the floor.

He jumped down and started scarfing it up like he hadn't eaten in weeks. I just smiled and fixed his syringe right up to that eighth line. And before he knew it, we were done. Good to go. Just like Batman and Robin. We were already gone.

CHAPTER 14

We got to Vegas just before four a.m. and were jazzed up as all get-out. It's amazing how three or four hours shut-eye is really all you need when you're in the zone. We managed to catch a few winks in some rest stop off of 89 on the north rim of the Grand Canyon.

As much as I was kinda deflated that we didn't get to see the sunrise there, I figured we had a whole lifetime of sunrises ahead of us for that. Besides, I felt like I'd been standing on the edge of the Grand Canyon for the last couple of years anyways, not knowing which step to take. And I sure as shit didn't need a cliff staring at me with a two-thousand-foot drop—not that I'd ever do anything like that. Still, it's a hell of long way down.

It must've been my twentieth time in that city. I was up at four a.m. on most of those nights, so being there then shouldn't have hit me funny at all. But it did. The skyline took me completely by surprise as we rolled in, and I felt like my heart was gonna pop clear up outta my chest.

It must've been something that Miles could sense too, because he woke up out of his coma just like he knew something was different there. Like we were on the brink of something. On a precipice of sorts.

We passed Sam's Town, and I started to feel my throat swell up again. My heart was pounding, and Miles sat right beside me, panting at the horizon going by the windshield. It seemed like an hour or more passed before we got to the boulevard, even though I knew it wasn't.

Vegas had an eerie quality to it that I had never really experienced before. I drove by the Stratosphere and the Riv. Petting Miles, I felt his heart racing too. Like I said, something was way different, but I couldn't put my finger on it. The euphoria that always accompanied a ride down the strip seemed a million miles away from me then and there.

There were a few people out and about, so I knew I wasn't in the midst of a dream. But nobody seemed to be acting as I expected, here at the nexus of the universe. Nobody was laughing like a fool. I didn't see any new love on the streets or any big shots out celebrating a hot night at the craps table.

There were a few people holding hands out of what seemed like obligation, but what the hell do I know?

But I didn't feel like such an orphan while driving down Las Vegas Boulevard in that moment. I still felt alone—don't get me wrong—but I didn't feel abandoned.

I knew that without Miles, I wouldn't have even made it this far. Strangely, it didn't seem like it was *us against them* right there, though. We were a part of something again, it seemed. We weren't just deserted out on the end of a pier somewhere.

I think that the warm and fuzzy feeling in my chest going down the road, as inexplicable as it was, seemed to be telling me that I was on the brink of a new chapter, or at least the end of one.

That can be scary, ending a chapter, that is. Sometimes the end of something can seem like a beginning, even when it's not. They can get all intertwined and mixed together. And that can mess with a fellow's mind pretty good. That is, if he's alone in it and all.

But I wasn't alone in it. Not by a long shot. And I'd guess that's why I was feeling like everything was finally working itself out, right there on the corner of Las Vegas Boulevard and Sands.

Still, I knew that I was at the end of something. The culmination of an episode. That pivotal plot twist of the movie. Somehow, in some strange way, I could just feel it.

I used to have this dream every couple of weeks or so when I was a kid. It all started sophomore year around the time that Professor Bialek had us watch *Cosmos* in science class.

Those were always the best days at the Academy. The days when they would wheel in the big old TV with a VCR, and you'd get to spend the better part of an hour catching some Zs.

But with this show, I kinda got caught up in it. *Cosmos* was different than the other crap that they used to throw at us back then. I really got into it.

It was the *pièce de résistance* of this guy Carl Sagan. I've gotta say, I always sorta dug him. He'd wear a turtleneck with a sports coat, and have his hair cut like a bowl around his noggin. He would talk about *billions of stars*, or *billions of asteroids,* or whatever. Everything was measured out in billions. That was this guy's unit of measurement, it seemed. Today when I think back, he sounds like a goof, but back then he sure didn't. I mean, I really thought that he was the shit.

Anyway, I used to have these dreams that I was falling through a black hole in the middle of some galaxy or something. And of course, everybody knows that a black hole is billions and billions of light years from end to end.

But in my dream, where matter had become antimatter, and where light was sucked up by everything around it, I still always knew exactly when I was getting to the end of that damn black hole. I could always feel when it was right there.

I recall trying to fight it with everything that I had. Flailing my arms this way and that just to keep from getting sucked into that damned abyss. Sticking my legs out as far as I could just to try to slow my descent.

Then I would wake up, of course, so I never *really* knew if there was anything on the other side.

But that feeling, where you know you are on the cusp of something, that was the same feeling I had with the brokerage. It was the same when Pops kicked the bucket too. Shit. When I think about it, I guess that it was even like that before Jenny died. Something inside had sorta prepared me for the end.

It's almost as though there's a setting in our internal compass that gets us ready for the heavy stuff, so that it isn't quite so heavy. So that we're prepared for it.

Maybe I just felt that way because I wasn't hopped up on something. It must've been my millionth time on the strip, watching the sun come up, but it was probably my first not being lit up on free drinks from the long night before.

Now, if you've made it this far in my B.S. story, I've gotta figure that you know me pretty well. But if you're thinking that I've been feeling sorry for myself, then I've gotta ask you to stop reading right now and go screw yourself. One thing I don't ever do is sit around looking for pity from anyone. Over my dead body.

I hate those bastards that force-feed that crap to the people around 'em. And if I ever become one of those assholes, I'm putting a bullet in my brain or giving you permission to do it for me.

Even though I knew that a lot of guys were going through a tough time with this economy and all, I didn't share my problems with them, and they didn't share theirs with me. That was the deal that we made. Or at least the one that I did.

But I felt different there. I could tell that I needed a drink or two, or I was gonna go over the edge.

Everybody seemed to be walking around in a trance or something. Just like the zombies back on Navy Pier.

I saw a group of older fellows that must've been there on some sort of business trip. I was fairly certain that they were walking from Olympic Gardens, their ties all undone and really just looking like death warmed over.

As I drove by 'em, something came over me. I had that dumb old Stones song in my head and yelled out the sunroof at the top of my lungs, "What's da matter witchew, boy?"

They didn't even turn, and Miles looked down his snout at me like I was crazy. He was probably right.

I saw the sign for Circus Circus and pulled into the lot. The entrance to Slot's O' Fun was wide open like the front of a mechanic's garage on a nice summer day. I parked the car near the RV area so I could get Miles out to take a leak without anybody getting too riled up about it.

I opened my door, and he hopped right over the console to get out. For a moment, I'd forgotten that this was all so new to him. And as stupid as it sounds, I was enjoying seeing it through his eyes. I barely remembered my first time in this city, and sharing it with Miles was about as close as I was going to get to that feeling.

As soon as he hit the pavement, he scampered over to a light pole, and then another. I've gotta tell you that I have never seen that little guy pee so goddamn much in all my life. When he ran out, he crouched down and took a crap right there on the side of the Slots O' Fun wall.

All I could do was chuckle at that little shit. I guess I was laughing at the thought that I finally got even with 'em. All of 'em.

I found a Subway bag lying on the ground, cleaned up his mess, and threw it in a can that already reeked of shit from somebody else's four-legged friend. There was probably a diaper or two in there also, I was pretty damned sure.

We walked around to the front of the casino. I didn't know whether or not they were going to have a hard time with Miles, so I dodged in under the canopy. Even though Miles heeled right next to me, making it less obvious that I had a dog, the hawker who was standing at the door saw him. But for whatever reason, she didn't say anything.

After that we were pretty much scot-free. There were only a few tables open, maybe three blackjack tables and just one of each of the other novelty games. There couldn't have been more than fifteen guys in there, and ten of them were at the bar playing video poker.

As we were making our way to the counter, I noticed a rather stocky lady slowly making her way into our path. She looked familiar. I had a feeling that I'd seen her before.

"You're not supposed to bring dogs in here, sonny," she said. "I'm sorry."

"Oh. Well, he's a good boy," I explained. "We just got into town after a few days on the road. We're hoping to grab a bite to eat and maybe stretch our legs a little," I went on, hoping my story would get her to warm up to us.

"Really? Where did you boys come from?" she inquired, sounding like she cared.

"Chicago."

I swear that every goddamn person in Sin City has some experience with Chicago, especially in the dive bars. This was no exception.

Sure as shit, she grew up on 63rd Street and moved out to Vegas ten years earlier. She asked where we lived, but I didn't much feel like telling her. I just said we lived on the north side, not needing her thinking that I was a big shot or anything. It didn't much matter anymore anyways.

Her name was Renae, and she damn near talked my ear off, but I didn't mind. I ordered three hotdogs, and a beer once I realized that she was gonna go easy on us.

Miles scarfed his down like a wild animal. Renae laughed like she had never seen anything like it before. He liked it so much that I gave him half of my second one after I scraped the onions off of it. After that, he just curled up under my barstool and nodded off to sleep.

Renae and I talked for at least an hour, mostly about home. We discussed the Bears and how much she hated the Cubs. We talked about the White Sox and Michigan Avenue. She said that she had gotten to a point that she actually missed the snow. I told her that I didn't believe her.

"Really, Jack," she began. "You get to a point where all the things that you used to hate become the things that you miss the most. And sometimes, the things that you used to love become the things that no longer mean much of anything anymore."

I told her she was nucking futz, and she laughed. But part of me still knew that there was some truth to what she was saying.

I used to hate cutting the grass once a week when I was a kid. I hated it more than most anything. Now I would jump at the chance to yank some old ripcord, giving it everything I had just to hear that old muffled roar of a four-cycle engine.

When Pops was sick, I used to dread visiting him in that stinky old nursing home. He didn't belong there, and I hated like hell seeing him lying in that bed dying. But I would do anything to be driving out there one last time. I'd take a bullet to have a good old cry with him. I'd take a state audit again in a heartbeat and answer all their bullshit questions about CAP rates, loads, and disclosures. I'd be just fine sitting on that shitter, realizing that Jenny had taken my last roll of TP too. Damned if that wouldn't be all right with me.

I guess that there were a lot of things that I used to despise that I would trade my eye-teeth for. Maybe Renae was right.

A bunch of rowdy guys walked in at the end of the bar and started giving the cute young bartender a hard time. She appeared to be taking it in stride. She probably had to, working the morning shift at Slots O' Fun. But still, they were pushing it.

I could tell that Renae was keeping an eye on the action like a pit-bull getting ready for a fight. It was sort of strange, the way she flipped the switch like that. She was so sweet and kind, not at all how I'd imagined when she first came walking up to us over an hour earlier. But she had a job to do, and her job was to keep this place in order.

I could see myself in a few of those guy's eyes too. God knows that I sure as heck used to come on to the cuties after I'd been overserved. And I definitely came on too strong a time or two.

One of the guys in particular was a real asshole, and I sensed that Renae had him marked.

His buddies were joking back and forth about his manhood, chiding him about not being able to get it up. The bartender seemed to be taking it like a trooper. But when that stupid son of a bitch whipped his pants wide open, all hell broke loose.

A big fellow I hadn't even seen came running out from a room behind the casino cage, and Renae gestured my way. "You boys best get outta here," she said abruptly. "Don't worry about that. Just go."

I didn't even have time to leave a fin on the counter for the bartender, but I reckoned that was fine. I knew we'd be back anyways.

Plus, I figured that Renae stood to get into a little bit of heat if that big guy had seen her talking to us. I had a hunch that he didn't like dogs all that much, and I sure didn't wanna get Renae into any trouble. We scooted out a side door and didn't look back.

It already felt like at least a-hundred degrees on the strip, and the sun was bright as hell. I was worried that Miles' feet would be burning on the pavement, but he seemed all right.

We doubled back around to the front of Slots, not making eye contact with any of them inside. I reckoned that they weren't looking in our direction either. It sounded like the hotheaded guy hadn't lost any of his charm, and I smiled at the thought of how many nights before I might have been that jerk.

I knew that we didn't want to get too far from the car, and I wasn't sure if The Deuce bus let dogs on or not. Instead, we walked for about a half hour til we got to Treasure Island.

Some goofy pirate guy came up to us with a parrot on his shoulder. I don't think that he planned on talking to me, until he saw Miles.

"Ahoy, mateys!" he said with that Scottish brogue that everyone seems to think pirates have. "What brings ye to the Island of Treasures?"

Normally I would have just kept walking, but I recognized that this was his job. Maybe he was some out-of-work actor who was looking for a break or even one of the Cirque du Soleil guys doing his day gig. He could have been a bartender or a dealer that was cut loose because of the economy. Hell, I didn't know.

But when I looked at him with his curly shoulder length hair and eyepatch, trying to act like somebody he wasn't, I realized that he kinda looked a lot like me. And I guess I took pity on him.

"Just passing through my friend," I said to him. "If you and your mate would be so kind as to oblige us."

"And who be your companion?" he asked, leaning over to pet Miles.

"Well, my companion be Miles Lucifer Wolfe the Turd," I said with a chuckle.

Well this son of a bitch laughed like he'd never heard anything so goddamn funny before in his life. Damned if we didn't make this guy's day. And it wasn't one of those deep, pirate-like laughs like you would expect to hear if he was singing "Yo, Ho, Ho, and a Bottle of Rum" or something. This was the real guy—the bartender or actor or dealer or mortgage broker—laughing like this was the funniest damned thing he'd ever heard. I think even his parrot thought that he was nuts.

Part of me wanted to stick around and get this guy's story, but a bigger part just wanted to keep on heading down the strip. I wasn't there to make friends. And even though that was what Miles and I did best, I simply wasn't in the mood. I patted our new pirate friend on the shoulder as he was bellowing, and we kept heading up towards Caesars.

I felt good. I was a part of the world again. Miles and I were in Vegas together. And as long as we still had a dollar in our pocket, we still had a chance.

We got to The Mirage, and Miles was eyeing the water everywhere and panting a whole lot. I realized that he was getting dry.

I'd forgotten how old he was, and he couldn't keep up like he used to. The diabetes had taken its toll, and I knew I needed to keep him hydrated.

I was lucky that there was some guy selling water for a dollar out of a cooler, so I got one. We sat down on the little patch of grass near the pond in front by the volcano. I put the rim of the plastic bottle low enough that he knew what I was doing. I started to slowly pour it out near his snoot so that he could tell that it was for him.

I watched that parched little tongue licking a million times a minute as the water slowly dribbled out of the bottle. As he was drinking, I rubbed his head real gently. The way that I used to when he was so much younger. The way that Hope would do to me. The way that Pops did it when I was a young punk, the way that I'd do to him near the end.

Finally, the quench of the water seemed to be overwhelmed by the massage that he was getting, so I knew he'd had enough. He polished off two-thirds of the bottle, and I downed the last gulp.

Then I just laid down on that green grass. I kept rubbing Miles' head and looking up at that clear blue sky, doing whatever I could to forget why I was there.

I dozed off. Miles didn't move a peep, so I figure that he did too. Shit. We must've needed it. I was sure that we did. We really hadn't gotten much shut-eye since we'd left home.

Nobody bothered us either, which really kind of blew my mind. No cops came to shoo us away, and no homeless people came begging for a buck. Even the guy who sold us the water left us alone and moved to the other corner. I almost felt invisible.

I was at the center of the universe. And yet I was just a small part of it. I'd never felt that way before in this town. Nobody seemed to want nothing from me. I wasn't the object of anybody's con. I wasn't someone's mark.

I was just a blade of grass along with *billions and billions* in that little patch. I was alone, and yet I was connected in a strange sort of way.

I yanked a handful of turf outta that bed of earth and tossed it in the air. The breeze took it away almost straight in the direction of Caesars. Miles nipped at the wind as the grass blew by, and we got up and headed in that direction, looking for a sign of something. Looking for a sign of anything, really.

We got to the Caesars entrance that led into the Forum Shops and headed in. As usual, it was mobbed. That was just fine by me. It allowed us to blend right in.

We saw the classiest old dame walking with a black standard poodle. She wore giant sunglasses that cracked me up a bit, and her poodle had a collar of real diamonds it seemed. Sure, we were inside of Caesars Palace, but she acted like she was strutting down some Paris runway with her mascot in tow. I spotted her watch too. It was a Rolex Masterpiece with rocks all around the bezel. But no ring.

Damn. She really was something, all wrapped up in her little world. For a moment I wondered how much better her pretty little planet was than mine. But the truth is that I probably didn't really want to know.

We wound up the staircase, and I could see that Miles was having a tough time navigating the steps. They were just a bit too wide for his short little legs.

There were a few people behind us heading up to the third floor, and I didn't wanna hold anybody up who could be upset about it. I leaned over to pick him up, and although he usually always lets me have my way with him, today he didn't. He wriggled and fought me a bit, so I let him be. It seemed like this was important to him in an odd way. To do this on his own. I smiled at the people to let them know to just pass us, and they nodded and grinned at Miles as they walked by.

I knew better than to make it obvious that I had a dog with me. I figured that they had rules about that sort of stuff. And I didn't want to bring any unnecessary attention to us.

I knew that for people like Princess Pussycat with the big sunglasses and the French poodle, the rules were there to be broken. I mean, most of those people walk around thinking that the rules don't apply to them anyways.

But I never was somebody to make waves. Even when I had all that dough, I didn't flaunt it the way some people do. Now that I had hardly anything, I figured the world sorta owed me something, outta karma or whatever.

So far the deal was working all right, but I knew that my luck could turn on a dime. Especially in this town.

Everyone seemed to be in a really good mood for a Monday in Las Vegas. Most everybody that I made eye contact with smiled right back at me, and most all of them really warmed up to Miles. You could tell that he was loving it too.

I had a bug to put a few bucks on the table after a while, but first I wanted to get a decent buzz on. So we headed over to a little Mexican joint where I knew I could find one of those giant margaritas with all the chips and salsa I could eat.

By the time we got there, though, it was clear the place had moved since I'd visited last. It took a few minutes before I saw some underage hottie drinking one of the giant margaritas near the City of Atlantis.

"Hey, beautiful," I leaned in. "Where'd you get that?"

"Oh! A puppy! What's his name?" she asked, obviously a little buzzed. She leaned over to pet him, and he kinda shied away behind me. I think he could tell that she was a little unpredictable.

"Oh, that's Lucifer," I said, real matter-of-factly.

She must've been super religious or something because she sobered up in an instant. She obviously thought that I was serious, and seeing as she suddenly seemed a little too goofy, I recognized that I didn't wanna get into any sort of a conversation with her afterall, so I just let her keep thinking that he was named after the devil.

"Down that a way," she said pointing. "Near the entrance."

"Thanks a lot," I smiled and headed off in that direction.

Damn, how Vegas had changed. The corridor was bright marble and all, just the way you'd expect it to be at Caesars, but the neon everywhere kinda took me by surprise. The energy really made me feel like I was a part of something larger than myself.

But not at the Mexican place.

It was dead in there, despite all the signs they had pointing in its direction. It was all too easy to find a spot at the bar.

"What up, man?" the bartender rattled off in my direction. He was a big, burly guy with tattooed sleeves covering his forearms and piercings all over his face.

"Just wanted to get a marg," I said coolly.

I was sorta taken aback by how low key this big dude was. I'd expected him to at least start out somewhat professional and then work his way down to the casual B.S. two guys usually throw around. But not him. In fact, it seemed a little strange to have him on the front line for this over-the-top neon joint.

"You can't stay here with it though," he said seriously.

I looked back at his beady eyes. "The dog?" I asked, feeling a bit dejected.

I was kinda jazzed up about having some chips and salsa. I remembered pigging out on far too many of them in the past, and it was a nice memory that had been chipping away at me for a while. Plus, I figured that if I was gonna be dropping all that dough for a margarita, at least I should be able to eat my weight in fried tortillas.

"Hey, brother," he said smoothly. "I'm really sorry. I have a Rott at home myself, but they are really pissy around here about that sort of stuff."

Now I think he could tell right about then that I wasn't one of those confrontational guys. A lot of times people don't realize that right away with me. I know that I look like I could be trouble once in a while, and I have a real sharp tongue when I need it. But I'm not usually looking for a quarrel.

Truth is, all and all I'm a pretty passive fellow. It's one of the things that I kinda cherish about myself. It helps me get on most people's good side right away. I mean, I'm not Mahatma Gandhi or Pope John Paul the Deuce, but for the most part, people like me.

"If you want some chips and salsa for the road, I'll put some in a bag for ya, pal" he said.

"You make those big ones strong?" I asked him.

"I can.", He retorted.

I ordered the cheapest margarita that they had. I figured that he knew I was down on my luck, but I could tell he wasn't judging me for it. It almost seemed like he had a softer spot because of it.

I sensed that he really was a dog lover too. Just something about the way that he looked down at Miles. I knew that it wasn't up to him to boot us. It was just the way that they were around this place.

He sure made me a strong one too. I took a big swig out of that giant pink straw and just about gagged. For a second I even thought that I was going to puke it right back up all over this guy's goddamn neon countertop. I tried not to let on that it went down rough, but I was sure he could tell. And I had a hunch that he got a kick out of it too.

"I threw an extra shot of Silver in there for ya," he said as he smiled down at Miles and handed me a bag of chips and a side container of salsa. I tossed the salsa in the warm, grease-stained bag, and the bartender acted like he was doing some calculations in his head.

"Twelve fifty," he said as he walked away.

I knew it was a deal, so I didn't even give him the customary raised eye-brow thing. Hell, we were at the Forum Shops. Seeing as this would probably get me moving in the right direction, I reckoned that even at fifteen buck's I was ahead of the game.

I reached in my front pocket for some cash. The bartender was washing some glasses, but I could tell that he had half an eye on me. I knew I had a ten in there with some other bills from the trip. Sure enough, I had a ten with four singles. And since I didn't really wanna converse with Shakespeare much more than I wanted to leave him a twenty, I just threw fourteen dollars on the counter and gestured down to him.

"Stay between the lines, guy's" he said loudly.

"We're gonna do our best," I hollered back. And Miles and I headed out to the boulevard.

We must've walked five miles that day, looking at all the ways that town had changed. Down past the Bellagio there was a whole new city it seemed. At first, my heart started to race like it did the first time Pops and I went there together. But then I got that feeling in my gut that I get from time to time. And as usual, it cut right through me.

"Come on buddy, let's keep walking," I said as we crossed the street in front of a Bentley that seemed to think that it had the right of way. Shit. Maybe it did. I didn't really notice the walk indicator on the light. The guy inside didn't honk his horn, and I didn't make eye contact. I guess we both figured we were better off that way.

By the time we made it back to Slots, the sun was sitting at about four o'clock. I was due for a drink and could tell that Miles was too. But I also wanted to start heading downtown to get situated for the night, so we hopped in the 911 and took a left down Las Vegas Boulevard.

It took about fifteen minutes to find my bearings before we made it downtown. We passed a few wedding chapels, City Hall, and some other landmarks that I'd remembered from before. They helped guide me.

I took a right turn onto Fremont once I hit it, realizing that we were down in the shadier part of town. But it didn't look as bad as I remembered, and it seemed like they'd cleaned it up pretty good since the last time I'd been there.

I kept my eyes out for a place to grab a beer, and The Western seemed like the right call. I pulled in the lot and found us a spot right in front.

We headed inside, where the AC greeted us with the biggest blast of cold air I'd ever felt. It just about scared the shit out of Miles too.

I knew that I didn't wanna drag him through the whole goddamn casino, and we got lucky. The corner seat was open at the bar next to the waitress station, so I sidled up like I do, and Miles laid down beneath me with his head rested at the base of the brass stool.

It was kinda slow I thought. But then again, it was a Monday afternoon. There were a few gals working behind the bar, and I'd guess that the median age between them must've been about a hundred and ten.

It made me kinda sad in a strange way, thinking they had to dress in those ridiculous uniforms each day just to pay the rent. Hell, they weren't really even uniforms. They were more like costumes. The skirts were so damn short that you could see the tops of their support hose anytime they leaned down to grab a beer out of the cooler.

But those dames had it pretty locked up in this joint. Rollers didn't come in for the most part, and the regulars weren't looking for anything more than cheap drinks and a place to throw a few bucks around. There wasn't a volcano or pyramid or pirate show. This was the shithole, and that was the appeal of the place. While other casinos had their cutesy little themes, the shtick at The Western was that it was a dump. I felt like I fit right in.

The bartender named Millie came down and smiled an old wrinkly smile at me on the way. It felt real, yet you could tell she knew what it meant to be stuck working in a place like that. I threw a grin back her way.

"What'll ya have?" she said warmly.

"Let me grab one of the Heinekens and a shrimp cocktail," I said like I owned the place. "Oh, and can I get a glass of water too?"

"You want one glass or two?" she smirked and batted her big old false eyelashes downward.

"Two would be wonderful, Millie," I said. "Thanks." She just winked at me.

She reached down to grab my beer, and I saw more than any fellow ought to. It reminded me of the time that I walked in on my grandmother taking a shower. You sure don't forget a thing like that. And if you ask any guy, he's got a story like that. We all do.

By the grace of God, she snapped right back up, and threw my beer on the counter before she popped the top. No small talk. Not a word about Miles being there. I liked that.

I looked around, but the scene seemed sort of eerie. People were milling about, but there didn't seem to be a peep. You could almost hear a pin drop. Nobody was winning, and nobody was losing. It didn't feel a bit like Vegas to me.

Millie brought back a glass of water for me and filled a soup bowl and added a few ice cubes for Miles.

"I fixed this up for your little friend," she said. Before I could even thank her, she was gone.

I didn't wanna bring a whole lot of attention to either of us, although it didn't seem like I could if I set myself on fire. So, I crouched down after scoping everything out, and set the bowl beside his snoot. I think he was snoozing, which I figured he oughta be after the hike we'd just had. When I rubbed his head he perked up and started slurping down the cold water.

I couldn't help but get lost in the moment with him there. He was getting old. But he was still a puppy to me. I rubbed behind his ears while he drank his fill, and when he was done, he looked up at me like he'd done a million times before. But this time it kinda stung for some reason.

"My little guy . . ." I muttered under my breath, peering down at him.

And then I felt those pangs in my gullet and tried to swallow them down

I was sure getting sick and tired of that samurai sword inside me, but it didn't seem like there was much that I could do right then.

I got back up on that old red leather barstool like it was a saddle, and I figured I'd get that thing checked out as soon as we got settled somewhere. It seemed to be getting worse each time, and it was taking longer to go away too.

My shrimp cocktail was right in front of me, but I chugged three quarters of that Heineken instead. It helped. It really did. But I still wanted to just sit there and get my breath before I took a bite.

I took one of those really deep breaths that I do when I'm getting worked up about something, even though I wasn't really thinking about much of anything right there and then. Still, something was sticking that Bowie knife in my gut.

I stabbed two or three of the sea monkeys with the plastic fork and took a bite. Yeah, they tasted just like I'd always remembered. And I didn't care how tiny they were. It was still the best damned shrimp cocktail that I could recall. For the life of me, I didn't know why it tasted so good. I figured it had something to do with just being there.

I thought back to the time that Jenny and I stumbled into The Western in the middle of the night. We'd just seen that nut job the Dice Man somewhere, and we were still riding kinda high from the show. I don't think that either of us had ever laughed so goddamn hard in all our lives. Man, he was a pig. But he was funny as hell.

I remember we were laughing so hard from a joke he'd told that he'd gone through two or three more one-liners before we took a breath. I can see how he made his dough. You'd have to go back a few times just to catch everything. It was one after another, and it took a special gal to appreciate it and look past the fact that he was such a pig.

I recall meeting a couple of local guys who had seen his show a hundred times or more. They would hang at the bar outside of the theater, just waiting for the couples that'd leave a few minutes into the show offended at Dice's routine. They said that they never had to wait more than ten minutes to get a pair of tickets for nothing.

What a lot of people didn't understand was that the appeal of the show was Dice being that pig. He was the pig inside all of us guys. And Jenny was one of the few people that got that. I remember how our guts were hurting like they were gonna split wide open. But still we couldn't stop laughing.

We stumbled into The Western at what must've been four in the morning, reciting those damned nursery rhymes for each other. Man, did we make a scene. Not that either of us gave a shit. We were doing shots of gobble juice one after another, just laughing our asses off while playing red dog. I must've thrown away a fortune in this dump.

I'd forgotten all about that night, and it made me feel like crap because I had a hunch that she hadn't. I knew that she deserved better memories than she wound up taking with her. And I should've remembered this one more often than I had. But that's the way it goes, I figure, and that's all there is to it.

I finished that five-star shrimp cocktail before Millie made it back down by us. I thought I heard Miles snoring, but it could've been the dishwasher rumbling the bar. Millie spotted the empty bottle in front of me and instinctively grabbed me another. I guess she could tell that I wasn't going anywhere.

"Can I grab a shot of Maker's Mark too?" I asked her.

"That's a premium shot," she responded.

"What's the house here again, Millie?" I tilted my head and shrugged.

"Wild Turkey is the well, if that's what you're wondering."

"That's right. "I'll take one of those chilled, if you can," I asked nicely. "In fact, make it two."

Old Millie filled a shaker with ice and turned that bottle upside down. Then she shook it for a good thirty seconds before heading back down towards us, slow and steady all the way.

Now, a place like The Western has shot glasses behind the bar. Probably thousands of 'em. But old Millie sidled down our way with two highball glasses and that stainless-steel shaker.

"Were all outta shot glasses today," she smiled with a wink as she began to pour.

"I've got your other shot when you're ready," she said as she turned that second highball glass upside down and set it on the bar. I've gotta believe she thought that I was gonna shoot the first. Instead, I smiled.

"Can I get 'em both up front, Millie?" I asked politely and all, knowing she probably thought I was crazy.

"I can back ya up, but I'm not really supposed to do that," she explained.

I looked at her kinda sheepishly, and I have a hunch that she thought I had a screw loose. Hell, she was probably thinking that the second shot was for Miles or something.

Either way, she did it. She looked down to the end of the bar as if she was scoping out the scene. But damned if old Millie didn't pour that second shot nice and neat, just like she'd done the first.

I fumbled through my front pocket and found a twenty that I threw in the machine. I tell ya, it's like riding a bike. You never forget how to play those darned poker hands no matter how long it's been.

I took a sip of that gobble juice and set it on the counter to my left. Then I placed the other one to my right for good old Jenny.

I guess that in some pricky way, I pretended like she was right there with me. Well, more like right there with us. She'd get a kick outta me being at The Western with Miles. A real kick. She'd be cackling louder than she was the last time she was in this dump. Sure as shit, I'd be cackling just as loud right there beside her.

I think I zoned out there for a bit, just going through the motions on that darned machine. I don't think I hit anything better than two pair or maybe three of a kind. Either way, I didn't hit anything worth talking about and got cleaned out pretty quick.

My heart wasn't in it anyway. And if there's one thing I've learned about gambling, it's that if your heart isn't feeling lucky, none of you will. I just sat there with that shot in my hand, sipping it like it was brandy or something worth drinking slow.

I must've been there for an hour or more. And when I finally looked outside, the sun was all but gone. Millie hadn't come around to pay me any mind, but I figured it was because she probably guessed that I didn't much wanna be bothered. She would've been right.

I didn't want nothing to do with nobody, so I grabbed another twenty from my pocket and threw it on the bar. I took one last sip of that Wild Turkey and left Jenny's on the counter.

And with that, we got up and headed outside to the getaway car, just like the two cowboys that we were.

CHAPTER 15

When we got to the Porsche, Miles found the light pole right beside it and did his thing while I looked the other way. I didn't know if somebody would mind a little guy taking a leak in a public place like this, so I thought it best to keep my eyes peeled.

I reckoned that we should probably find a place to crash. He was gonna need his shot soon, and dinner too. I figured that I'd find us a place downtown since we were already there, and I knew that if our luck could change anywhere, that's where it would happen.

I took a left out of the lot and then a right onto Las Vegas. I wanted to wind around all the action. Not much in this area of town had changed since the last time I was there, but everything else in my life sure as hell had.

To be honest, I thought it was kinda funny. Either that or it was sad as hell. Given the two choices, I figured I'd just laugh.

Miles was staring out the window as we drove past Siegel Suites. I smiled and rubbed his head right behind his ears, but I don't think he much noticed. I realized that I wasn't really doing it for him anyway.

I led us through downtown, thinking that I knew where I was going. But I was wrong. Hell, I realized I had never driven these streets before. It was a million miles from Chicago, and I'd never been behind the wheel in Vegas until now.

I had an idea of where Main Street was, and for the time being, that was just fine. Miles sure didn't care. I think he liked checking out the hookers and the bums hanging out by some of the cheap motels. Some chick in stilettos saw him panting her way while we were stopped at a light. She waved at him and mouthed "Hey, little fella," real sexy like.

He panted harder and tried to scramble out the window to her. I swear that I've never seen that little guy get so excited. And over a hooker no less!

I did my best to not make eye contact, holding him back so he wouldn't go airborne. Finally the light changed, and we headed off.

Eventually we found Main and took a left. I felt like I was in Vegas for the first time all over again and my heart kinda raced. I saw a sign for thirty-nine-dollar rooms at the Plaza, and that seemed all right to me. I didn't want to be screwing around all night, and Miles needed to get settled in and all.

I pulled into the rotunda with all the flashing lights. I vaguely remembered this place because Jenny and I had dinner in the dome above it once. It was a dumpy steak joint, but I remembered that the food was damn good. I turned in the drive, and the valet guy came over to my door.

"Are you staying with us tonight, sir?" he asked real professional and all.

"Yeah . . . I think so," I said. "Do you guys have thirty-nine-dollar rooms?" I asked in order to make sure it wasn't a feeder just to get you in the door.

He looked at me, and I think he could tell that I was a regular guy and all because his demeanor changed a bit. Not in a bad way, but it did change completely.

"Yeah, buddy, I think we still have a few . . . but they don't allow dogs," he said. "No place down here does, I don't think."

I looked up at him, feeling stupid. Damn. I didn't even think of that.

I turned over at Miles, and he was panting up a strorm. There was no hiding him now, that was for sure.

"Where can I go that'll let us two cowboys hang our hats, Brandon?" I asked him, trying to sound folksy while noting his name tag.

He smiled a quirky smile, and I figured that he sorta liked us. Not that I should give a shit one way or the other. But still, I did.

"All I know is that some of the motels don't care, but most of them are pretty shady," he suggested. "Sam's Town is all right with pets, but that's about twenty minutes away."

I could tell that he was a stand-up dude, and I figured he'd steer me in the right direction if he could.

"Hey there, little guy . . ." he said as he leaned in a bit towards Miles. "Listen, man. I've got a shepherd at home."

There was a certain slyness in his voice now.

"Go around and park in the side lot," he explained. "Come back up to the front with your suitcase like you just took a cab in from the airport. From there, just step up to counter and get a room. Leave your little guy in the car and use the side door to get him. After eight, the security guys check keys by the elevators, but I'm pretty sure that you'll be fine as long as you get him to your room before then."

As he was giving me the scoop, I was digging in my pocket for whatever I had left to give him, but I had nothing. I knew I had some change in the ashtray, probably at least a few dollar's worth. When he was done, I reached in and grabbed what was there and handed it to him.

"No thanks, man. We're all good," Brandon said while standing back up straight like the corporate guy he was supposed to be.

"Are you sure?" I asked. "I mean, I wanna take care of you."

"Let the fat cats take care of me, man," he said with a slightly cocky grin. "For now, you can take care of me by just forgetting my name, all right?" he peered down at me as though looking for affirmation. "You *didn't try* to valet your car with me, right?"

"What car?" I chuckled. "I just flew in from LaGuardia!"

I stuck out my hand to shake his, but he was already gone. I looked in the side view to see him mucking it up with some bald guy in an Escalade behind me. I figured I'd catch up with him soon anyway. He seemed like a good guy. And I'd been feeling as though there had been a shortage of good guys around lately.

I turned out of the drive and headed down the way that Brandon told me to go. Sure enough, a block down Main there was an empty lot. I pulled in and said to Miles, "I'll be back in a minute, pal."

I opened the trunk and slung the little tote that I had over my shoulder before making my way towards the entrance. On the way I must've passed six or seven locals begging for whatever a guy could throw 'em.

"I've got nothin' for ya, buddy," I said to a couple right on the corner.

"That's all right, man," one guy said. "Maybe next time," It didn't much seem like they expected a handout from anyone anyhow.

I got to the front door of the Plaza and headed towards the casino. I thought to make eye contact with my new buddy Brandon, but he must've been parking that big Escalade or something. I walked right past everyone and didn't make eyes with anybody, the way that Hank or Waylon would've done. Just like I was some stranger rambling' into town. Kinda like I was, I supposed.

That's how I handled the check in with the fella running the desk too. It seemed like it worked. I didn't get the usual upsell shit. He checked me in at thirty-nine dollars for the night and didn't say more than a sentence or two while doing it.

Sure, he read me the script about not smoking or conducting illegal activities in the room and all. But he didn't say nothing about pets. I mean, I've gotta figure that he thought that I was just some cowboy in town with nothing but his overnight bag. Plus, I gave him my address on Lake Shore Drive, so he had to figure I'd just flown in. Still, I was glad that he didn't make me lie about nothing.

I walked through the casino in the direction that the check-in guy had told me to head. I thought to run out and get Miles before I headed up to the room since Brandon told me I had until eight o'clock. I peeked at my watch, and seeing that I had at least a half hour, I decided to scope out the scene first.

I headed up to the ninth floor and slid the key in the slot. It was a cheap room all right, but it suited us just fine. We were close enough to the elevator and the ice maker and even had a view down at the pool. Hell, the room had a mini-fridge in it. As far as I was concerned, it was perfect.

It seemed like the elevator hadn't moved since I'd gotten off it a minute before because as soon as I pushed the button, it opened. That was a good sign. I didn't want to have to be waiting down there with Miles if it were stuck on the seventy-first floor or something.

When I got about a hundred yards from the car, I decided to go real slow and quiet to try and sneak up on my little guy. I'd always wondered what he did when I wasn't around, and I liked to try to catch him when he didn't expect it. Nine times outta ten he'd just be sleeping.

Right about then I heard him start yipping at me. I guess this was the one outta ten because he saw me plain as day. It was no use. He was too riled up and excited. He wasn't gonna miss a thing.

I hit the button on the remote and unlocked the door. I popped the trunk first and grabbed my big duffle. When I opened the driver door, he jumped right out. I shoved his thermos in the duffle and grabbed the carrier from the backseat.

Okay, buddy. Let's go," I told him as I scooted him into the carrier.

I carried him beside me, with the duffle bag draped over the top of the carrier. Just like two cowboys heading off into the night. Roping and riding. Well,maybe not quite.

I took the back way to stay off the main drag where the bums were for a more direct route to the side door.

And then, out of nowhere, the strangest thing happened. Miles' twin came out from behind a green dumpster about twenty feet from the door. I mean, it wasn't his twin. But it was a damn doppelganger.

Miles saw him first and did something he never does. He started growling.

"Come here, buddy," I said. Gently holding my hand out. The dog just stared at me with the blackest eyes I'd ever seen. It was uncanny how dark this dog's eyes were. That's all that kept him from being Miles' body double.

"It's okay, guy," I tried to persuade him. "See. I've got your brother in here," I held the carrier out so that he could see Miles.

But all this dog did was look at us intently. He barely moved, just staring through us with those deep, black eyes.

Then Miles did something that he'd never done before. He snarled loudly and started to bark. To be honest, it scared the shit out of me.

"Miles!" I exclaimed. "Cool down, buddy! It's all okay."

But he would have none of it. He was riled, and it didn't seem like I could calm his nerves.

He just kept growling and snarling, yet the other dog remained calm. This only seemed to incite Miles further. He started barking and flailing in the carrier, trying to wrestle it open it seemed. And that other dog just stood there. Staring. Peering a black hole right through us.

Finally, a crazy gust of wind came out of nowhere and blew my duffle right off the carrier. With that, the other dog darted around the building, off to God knows where. Still, Miles seemed on edge, and I can't tell you why. He'd always gotten along well with other dogs, but I figured that it was all the uncertainty going on right then and there. It probably spooked him a bit.

I walked a good twenty feet over to grab my duffle and glanced at my watch. I saw that we were cutting it just a little close with only fifteen minutes, but I felt pretty certain that there wasn't a single security guard at the Plaza that was gonna start his shift early.

I was still a little unsettled, and Miles was too. But I hit the button on the elevator without making eye contact with anybody. And Miles didn't make another peep.

The elevator door didn't open right away like I'd hoped, but it still got there pretty quick. We got in with an older lady on an electric scooter.

"Is that a dog that you've got there?" she asked me. Miles was silent in the carrier.

"Um . . . yeah," I responded. "His name is Miles."

"Well hello, Miles," she said sweetly. I figured that she was fine with him and wouldn't make any trouble.

"I didn't know that they allowed dogs in the hotel," she said as if she might have brought hers had she known. Since I didn't want her checking with the front desk about it, I came up with something quick.

"He's actually a service animal, Ma'am," I said really sincere.

Just then the elevator opened on nine, and we scooted out. I could tell that she wanted to sit there and chat all night, but I sure didn't feel like I'd want a part of that conversation knowing I was gonna have to come up with all kinds of bullshit to feed her.

"Have a nice night," I said hurriedly as I dodged out the elevator door. It was probably a little too abrupt to come off as polite, but I didn't really give a crap.

I opened our door and took Miles right out. He really was so well behaved when he was in his crate normally. Miles started sniffing all around the place, and I was glad to see that he had recovered from whatever it was that spooked him about that black-eyed dog in the lot.

I unpacked the little bit that I had and put it in a dresser that seemed right out of the nineteen-seventies. We were going to be there for at least a couple of nights, so I figured it best to settle in. It was the closest thing to home that we were gonna have for a while I reckoned.

I threw the TV on and had to shuffle through the stations before I found one that wasn't advertising something a tourist could waste money on. I suddenly had to piss really bad, so I just settled on an infomercial about some exercise bike that cost fifteen thousand dollars and headed to the shitter.

Now, I don't know if I already told you this or not, but a lot of guys would think I was a real pansy in the John. I sit down no matter what I'm doing. I get some of my best thinking done there. Plus, it doesn't make a mess that way. So, I'd prefer to sit down no matter what's on my agenda at that moment.

I mean, not when I'm out or anything. When I'm at a bar or restaurant or whatever, I won't sit down to save my soul. But other than that, I'll cop a squat. So I did. And damned if that wasn't the exact moment that I heard my phone vibrating on the dresser where I'd laid it.

It seemed like it had been days since I'd talked to anybody that I really knew, and for the life of me I couldn't recall when I had ever gone so long. As a first reaction, I wanted to jump up with my dick in my hand and talk to anybody that gave shit about me. But instead I just sat there and listened to that buzz until it stopped.

I had a hunch that it was Hope that had called. And that made me feel good that she was thinking about me, wherever the hell she was.

I'd guessed that she had just gotten home. She was probably about to settle in to a good movie or a book or something and wanted to hear my voice before she did.

I'd call her back as soon as I finished up. That was right about the time that I half passed out on the shitter from just plain exhaustion, I supposed. So, when Miles came sniffing in, it kinda took me by surprise.

I shook and pulled my jeans back up before walking out to my phone to see who it had been, but it was a blocked call.

I knew that it wasn't like Hope to block a call. So, I guessed that it could have been a bill collector or the mortgage company saying that they'd gotten the keys for all I knew.

Not sure why, but my heart kinda sank. As much as I didn't want to give a shit, I started to get that pain in my gut.

There was no message or nothing. Just some goddamn private call that could have been a wrong number.

All I knew was that whoever the hell it was wasn't calling to make sure that I was still alive, or they would've left something there for me. That's what people do when they give a shit. And, obviously, whoever called didn't.

I was gonna call Hope anyhow. Even if it wasn't her.

I'd been meaning to ring her for a long enough time anyways, and she deserved to know that I was doing all right. Then suddenly the house phone rang, and I knew that couldn't be good.

The only thing that made any sense was that my credit card didn't work. Then I worried that maybe the woman in the elevator had spilled the beans on me about Miles or something. Either way, it freaked me out, and I knew I didn't wanna deal with it.

My first thought was to answer the phone the way that any schmuck would have. But I let my common sense talk me out of it.

I let it ring for what seemed like fifteen minutes before it stopped. Meanwhile, I unpacked Miles' insulin and slipped it in the fridge so it could stay cold without me needing to worry about it. Then I took whatever clothes I had left in the small tote and threw them in the top dresser drawer. I grabbed the bag with my toothbrush, deodorant, razor, and all and tossed it on the bathroom counter.

I wanted to brush my teeth, but I wanted to get the hell out of the room even more. I grabbed my wallet and slapped the "Do Not Disturb" sign on the knob before heading out.

If somebody was coming up to give me heck about something, I knew I'd be golden if I was in the casino or on Fremont.

Not wanting to chance anything, I took the stairs, knowing it was only nine flights. As I opened the stairwell door, I heard the bell for the elevator go off. I darted in and gently closed the stairwell door behind me, all the time knowing that the odds were a million to one that it was anybody worth dodging.

Still, it made me feel like I was a real clever guy. Whether I was or not, I felt that way, so, I went with it as I headed down those nine flights of stairs.

The place was hopping pretty good. I knew that it wasn't in full force yet or anything, but for a school night, things were on their way.

It was funny. I always knew that the Plaza was a dive. I'd seen drifters hang out in dumps like this and drunks cash their welfare checks at the casino cage and all. But somehow, I didn't see a single one of them this night.

Sure, there were a couple of guys that could've used a shower hanging around, but they seemed all right to me. I figured they were just having a guy's weekend that lasted a day longer than they'd thought it would.

There were a handful of people that were obviously overserved stumbling around too, but they didn't bother me any either. They seemed happy enough, and if you can't get good and drunk in Vegas, then where the hell can you?

I suppose there were more old people walking around with walkers than you'd see on the strip. And, sure, they weren't wearing Prada or Gucci or nothing. But they seemed just fine by me.

All in all, it appeared that things had cleaned up a bit since I'd last been downtown. Or maybe it was just me. Either way, I decided that I'd head over to that dome and splurge on a snort or two for old time's sake.

On the way over, I passed a couple of fast food places that I thought might seem good to grab a bite for Miles. I knew I wanted to get back to the room before too long in order to feed him and give him his shot.

I'd forgotten that there was an escalator to the dome. I don't know how I forgot since Jenny and I almost got our asses thrown in jail one night for running up and down them the wrong way. I remembered laughing about how a fellow can do almost anything he damn well wants to in this town except go up a godforsaken escalator the wrong way.

I got up to the dome, and it had changed. I've gotta say that it was a helluva lot nicer. They'd classed it up a bit to say the least.

I remembered that they used to have all sorts of corny black-and-white pictures on the walls of every celeb that had ever accidently walked into the place, but they'd taken them down and dimmed the lights real nice and romantic like.

I've gotta tell ya, it made all the difference in the world too. The bar must've had twenty-five seats stretching down it, and most of them were filled with couples, leaving only a few open spots in between.

I didn't grab the first one or even the second. I never do. Not at a place like this anyways. I'd always rather scope out the scene and get a feel for what's going on. I walked down the bar and did my best to see if there was anyone worth talking to.

I wound up grabbing a seat about three quarters of the way down, next to a pretty classy looking couple. The guy must've been seventy, but the gal couldn't have been more than forty. She had a great bobb cut—blonde, but not bright platinum like some of those dye jobs. I didn't see a ring on her finger, but I couldn't be sure the way that she was holding her glass of red wine.

He looked grey but still had a decent head of hair on him. He was wearing a polo-style yellow shirt and a Yachtmaster on his wrist and had some sort of a highball on ice in front of him. It seemed like he was a little buzzed, but what the hell did I know from a two-second glance?

The gal behind the bar was right on me. I think she might have caught me checking this guy's gal out, but I couldn't be sure. Either way, I looked away as if I hadn't even noticed the two of them.

"What's it gonna be, cowboy?" she smiled and winked as if we had our own little secret.

"Have you got any specials?" I asked.

She seemed a little miffed and gestured to me as if saying *Look around you idiot. Do you think you're at Hooters or something?*

"The prime rib is twenty-nine ninety-five tonight, while supplies last," she said with a smirk. I thought to chuckle, but then wondered if maybe she was being sincere.

"I'll take a shot of Makers Mark and an Amstel Light," I told her coolly.

She didn't say anything and just turned to the fridge and grabbed my beer. I took a deep breath and looked around. I was starting to feel alive in a way, and I wanted to get things going.

"You know what?" I kinda yelled to get her attention. "Forget the Makers. Give me a shot of Wild Turkey."

"Wild Turkey?" she said kinda miffed again. She probably thought I was a kook ordering that poison in a place like this.

"Yeah," I smiled back. "For old time's sake."

She rolled her eyes and stuck her index finger in her mouth like she was making herself puke or something. I think her boss might've caught it because she stopped really quick and got serious again. But still, it made me laugh.

She was cute. I'm not gonna lie. I hadn't caught it at first. And I usually do with bartenders and waitresses. Most times that's who I'd wind up with, but this one caught me off guard.

It was probably because her hair was short, or maybe it was the tattoo that anybody could see creeping out of her cleavage. She had a ring on, and I didn't think that she was all that interested anyways until she started busting my balls for ordering gobble juice. If that isn't a sign that a gal's into you, then I don't know what is. Still, I wasn't there to pick up a chick, and I needed to get back to Miles soon anyhow.

Now, as I've already told you, every place in town has shot glasses behind the bar, but she poured about three fingers into the bottom of a highball glass and set it next to the Amstel in front of me.

"For old time's sake," she said with a smile and a nod. The truth is that I think there was a wink in there too. But since I'm not certain, I'm not gonna say that there was, just in case there wasn't. But I'd bet my bottom dollar that it was there.

I shot more than half of that rocks glass and took a swig of the beer. It went down rough. Really rough. And I'd be lying if I didn't mention that it almost came right back up.

But I covered it well and downed two or three swigs of that beer to overcome the urge to hurl all over the classy couple to my right.

Like I said, I was starting to feel alive. And it felt good. I sorta felt like I was in the game again. Almost like I was home after a long lonely trip somewhere.

I glanced around. It didn't feel like I was in a room full of strangers. It had been awhile since I'd felt that way in a classy place like this. It sure wasn't the saloon at the old Fink Building. And I liked it.

I took another half swig of the gobble juice and shot it down with a gulp of Amstel. That time, I couldn't taste a thing.

The gal next to me seemed to be leaning in and whispering to her man, and although it could have been about anything, I sort of figured it might be about me. I didn't think that it was my ego talking, but I wasn't entirely certain.

I peered down to the other end of the bar and saw that four seats had just opened up. I thought to head down but changed my mind. I didn't want these people thinking that they were bothering me, because they weren't. Plus, I worried that I might stumble a bit right then and there since that shot had hit me a little hard right off the bat. So, I decided to stay put.

The bartender was hanging out by the waitress station, talking to the person that I figured to be the manager. He was probably forty and dressed pretty sharp. Even though I wasn't trying to catch her eye, I kinda was. But she didn't look in my direction at all, which I figured was probably just as well.

The room suddenly went sort of dark. It was pretty dimly lit before that, but for a split second it got even darker until some lights started flickering outside. I turned around on the barstool, looking out of the domed ceiling. I could see the flash of lights coming from Fremont and realized it was the light show. The sound of pounding bass from outside was rattling the room really good.

A few people crowded around the window to see how much they could see, but it mustn't have been much since they soon came back. I stared off into the flickering, sipped my Wild Turkey, and thought about nothing at all for a few minutes.

"Excuse me," a sexy, high-pitched voice interjected. "Are you with the tournament?" Sure as shit, it was the classy blonde with the rich, old fart.

I was really taken aback at first. I wasn't even a hundred percent certain that she was talking to me. I was in a Wild Turkey haze after all. But she was staring me right in the eyes, and her guy was looking at me too.

"Um no," I said like the frickin linguist that I am. "I'm not sure what you're talking about."

"Yes, you are!" she insisted. "I've seen you. What's your name again?" she said with a big grin while her guy rolled his eyes.

"Really?" I chuckled. "I have no idea what tournament you're talking about. I just got into town today."

"What brings you to town then?" she asked as if she was interrogating me or something.

"Nothing in particular," I said like a real dodo.

You see on a different day I would've played along with these two. I would've had them thinking that I was somebody that I wasn't, even if I didn't know who that somebody was supposed to be. I'd be signing autographs all scribbled so they couldn't be read, and I'd have had that couple eating right outta my hand.

But I wasn't much up for it right then and there. The truth is, I was having a hard enough time just being me at that domed steak house at the Plaza.

"Well, you sure look like one of those guys," she chirped as she hugged her old geezer. He just smiled and seemed a man of few words. As it turned out, that assumption was wrong.

"What tournament are you talking about?" I asked, completely oblivious.

"That WWF or whatever it is," she exclaimed. "We saw a sign for it at the airport."

I laughed. I knew that she sure wouldn't mistake me for one of those animals if she'd seen me out by the pool. But I recognized that I hadn't shaved in a few days, and between that and my hair, I could probably fool a lady after a few glasses of wine.

"Nope. Not me," I smiled. "I'm no tough guy," I said. "But then again, the night is still young," I mused.

She giggled. And her old man actually acknowledged me for a second.

"Are you sure you're not one of them?" she asked as if she wouldn't tell a soul if I had been.

"Yep, I'm pretty sure," I smiled, trying to catch her gaze. Her old guy wasn't paying much attention to me anyways, so I figured it couldn't hurt.

She spent that extra tenth of second that we're all shooting for, looking me in the eye and smiling. But I couldn't go anywhere with it anyway and wondered why the hell I was even trying.

It may have been that interaction that caused some awkwardness in the moment. I really don't think that he caught it, as small as it was.

She and I were at that fork in the road that I'd come to know all too well in a conversation, the fork where it can either turn into one of those nights or just slip away. And to be honest, at that very moment I really wasn't sure which direction I was headed.

I'd gotten really good at this sort of thing. I just smiled. Knowing that the ball was in my court to say something funny, interesting or at least somewhat conversational.

But I was drawing blanks, and it felt like I was running on autopilot right there. So, I decided to just let it slide.

I just let it go and polished off the finger and a half that was left in my glass while looking at the flashing of the lights coming in from Fremont. After that, they pretty much left me alone.

Warm gobble juice always goes down smoother after the first snort. I don't know why it works that way. It just does, especially with a few swigs of Amstel left to chase it. I was feeling no pain at all, sitting there all alone high above the corner of Main and Fremont.

My head was a little bigger than it probably should have been at that bar. And as stupid as it sounds, it felt kinda good to be mistaken for a minor celebrity, even if he was some meathead.

I don't really know what it was, but like I said, I was really feeling alive again. The way that I'd hoped I would when I decided to head out to this city.

The light show seemed to end as the bass thrusts died down, so you could hear people hooting and hollering out on the street.

It was odd because you could feel the energy change in the bar too. Not that anybody was cheering or anything like that, but it felt like the show was over, even though there really wasn't any kind of a show going on in there anyways.

The blonde got up to go to the bathroom I figured, but I didn't watch her walk away the way I wanted to. I just sat there enjoying the buzz of the Wild Turkey mixed with the vibe in the room. Still, it felt like the old guy with the Rolex Yachtmaster was sucking up all the juju in there.

Out of the corner of my eye, I could see that he was sitting up tall like a goddamn rooster or something. Although he hadn't said anything yet, I could tell that he had a lot that he wanted to get off that big old chest he was sticking out. I also had a hunch that I was just the kind of guy that he wanted to say it to.

"So, what's your story there, punk?" he asked with an attitude.

He was drunk, but the truth was that I didn't care. It didn't even bother me that he called me a punk. I probably looked like one anyways.

"No story, pal," I said without hesitating.

I figured that calling him *pal* would smooth out any chip that he had on his shoulder.

"You a musician or something?" he asked while looking me up and down. It was apparent that he didn't much approve of my shoulder-length hair. I could tell by that damned sour-puss expression on his face. For some strange reason I was glad about it. I was just buzzed enough to play ball with him.

"Nope. I'm a screenwriter," I said confidently. "I write screenplays" I told him as if he wouldn't know what a screenwriter did by the job title. "Why? What's your story, old man?" I asked him as cocky as a young punk could.

"My story?"

I could tell that he didn't give a shit about anybody else's gig. He'd been waiting patiently to shove his life down my throat, the way that so many of these washed up old farts like to do.

"I'm just living the dream, kid," he said leaning back in his stool. "Just living the dream."

Now, it's not like me to form judgments, usually. But I've gotta tell ya that I hated this old prick.

I knew that back in the day I would have stood toe to toe with him. Sitting up, dressed to the nines with Hope or any one of a hundred gals.

I would've had this guy kissing my ass, looking for pointers. And I'll be honest. That bugged the shit out of me.

Sure, my head was telling me not to give a crap about this guy's opinion and all, but I didn't care what my head had to say. I needed this old bastard to know that I wasn't some washed-up punk who was all out of cash and uncertain if his credit card was gonna work at some cheesy old steak house in Vegas.

Even if there wasn't an ounce of truth to it. I needed this dinosaur to buy it.

"So, you write screenplays?" he said arrogantly. "Figures."

"Yeah. Now that I shut my brokerage down," I told him while choking back all of the bullshit.

He didn't bat an eyelash at that, and it kinda surprised me after the way he'd seemingly been analyzing my every move.

Yeah, he was arrogant all right. But I was suddenly getting a rise out of it. I felt up to the challenge.

"Oh yeah?" he slurred at me. "Banking, brokering, or investments?" He obviously knew something about the industry and talked like he was above it all.

"All of them."

"Well I guess the bottom fell out on ya, huh?" he stammered smugly. "But you had to know it was going to. You were just living on borrowed time."

I hated him *before* he opened his mouth, rubbing his sexy girlfriend in everybody's face like a trophy or something. But now I *really hated* this creep. Having him all up in my face, hopped up on cognac or whatever, judging me for having the balls to think that I deserved to be at the same bar with him, made me wanna cold cock him.

But I don't cold cock people. Never have, never will. Over my dead body.

"Actually, I did just fine," I said without flinching. "I had a great run and don't regret a thing. I got out at the right time, and I haven't looked back." I kept my voice even and stuck my chest out a bit, puffing up to hide that the words made me sick.

I don't much think he believed me, not that I really gave a shit one way or the other. But then something happened, and sometimes, that one thing is all that it takes to change everything.

You see, what I hadn't noticed was that behind the bar was a mirror on the wall. Come to think of it, most places like this are set up that way. I'd guess that it makes the room look bigger and the booze all the more abundant.

Anyway, I was doing just fine until I looked across the bar and saw myself looking back. Sure enough, the old codger was right as rain. That kid jabber-jawing about being a screenwriter *was* a punk: hair down past his shoulders, unshaven, shirt open with a smarmy grin on his face. Yeah. That old son of a bitch had me dead to rights. I was a goddamn punk whether I liked it or not.

Well, I'd like to tell you that I didn't give a shit what that old guy thought. The truth is, I hadn't until I saw that empty face staring at me from the other side of the bar.

But I'm not gonna lie. It bothered me that this guy saw through me, and I realized that trying to convince him otherwise felt like too much for me then and there.

"You know, old man, I had a good thing going there for a while," I told him. "I worked my ass off and built a heck of a company."

I looked down to the bartender to get her attention, but she was too involved with her conversation to notice. I just wanted to have my thoughts somewhere other than this old bastard. But it didn't much work.

"I had a million-dollar place, twenty floors up on Lake Shore Drive," I continued. "I drove a Porsche and had all the gals that come along with it. I had season tickets to Wrigley and a cleaning lady come over twice a week. There wasn't much that I wanted that I didn't have. Not much at all. And I'll tell ya, with God as my witness, if it meant shit to me, I'd still have it all today."

I had found some confidence again, and as I spun my yarn, it seemed almost as if it was true.

"It's nothing I couldn't have again in heartbeat if I set my mind to it," I insisted. "But I'd rather be free."

I felt like I was giving a goddamn sermon or something, maybe even exocising some demons.

"You see, old man, I don't answer to anyone anymore, so maybe you oughta order another one before your boss gets back and cuts you off." I smirked, nodding towards the restrooms.

I looked back at that damn mirror behind the whiskey bottles and prepared for the worst. But he just sat there, calm and collected, not giving in to any of it. No veins bulged from his temple, and there was no gritting of teeth. Cool as a cucumber, that son of a bitch leaned back and took a sip from his highball glass as I stared at his reflection in the mirror.

"So, you really think that you earned all of that, kid?" he asked rhetorically. "You must've thought you were the chosen one. The Christ Child. Did you think all of that was your destiny? That somebody picked you out of a lineup and said, 'Hey, give this punk a break'?"

I didn't move a muscle. I just kept my gaze straight ahead.

"I bet you believed that there was some divine intervention in it all. That the universe had some sort of a plan that chose you above all the other brats out there," he chided further.

I took a deep breath and didn't answer the asshole. Instead, I just kept staring straight ahead so he couldn't get to me. I couldn't let him see the nerve he'd struck and just looked forward into the face of the punk in front of me on that wall.

"You didn't get anything more than what we gave you, junior," he said sternly. "And when it was time for it to end, *we* pulled the plug. Not you."

I imagined him as some kind of a puppet master, an evil Geppetto.

"You got it?" he went on, demanding I understand. "That's all it was kid. You never had control of the game. We made the rules, and you followed them. You dug the trenches where we showed you to, and it was us who told you how far to go and how deep to dig."

I started to get that feeling in my gut again. I took a deep breath to stifle the pain a bit, my eyes going glassy and staring straight ahead.

I finally caught the bartender's eye and gestured for another shot of courage and beer. I looked at my adversary, doing my best to hide my contempt for him.

"What are you drinking, pal?" I asked like nothing he said had fazed me, as if I simply wanted to buy an old friend a drink.

He'd chewed me up and spit me out. He'd tried to take away everything that I ever had. But even after trying to ignore the question, he made it clear he wasn't done.

"Who the hell did you think you were? Magellan? Columbus?" he laughed loudly. "Did you really think that you were rediscovering the world? Reinventing the wheel?" I began to wonder if this guy knew when the hell to stop or not.

But then I remembered how drunk he was when I sat down half an hour earlier, and I reckoned his sense of right and wrong had left the building long before I ever got there.

"It was our money, you brat!" he spewed. "It was our world that we shared with you. Forget all the bullshit you told yourself each night before bed."

I think that the bartender could tell that the air had gotten a lot little thicker over by us and just set my drinks on the bar without making a peep. I was looking straight ahead and didn't even catch hide or hair of her. All I knew was that out of nowhere my drinks were right in front of me, just like I'd asked for them.

I picked up the shot in my right hand. I don't think it was as big as the last one, but it was still far more than a typical shooter.

I eyed the orangish-yellow liquor reflect and bend the dim light shining in the barroom. How clear and unassuming this poison was among the fingerprints and the left-over lipstick on the rocks glass.

"Your generation makes me sick, kid," his noxious voice cut through the room. "It's not just you, so don't start boo-hooing and shitting in your diaper."

I held that glass up as if I was making a toast before putting it to my mouth. I took in about three quarters of it and just let it sit there in limbo, knowing the burn of the swallow that I was never quite ready for.

"You're damn right that you had it good, junior," he slurred some more. "That's the way that we handed it to you."

I turned to him with all the rage of the world in my eyes. And I knew he could feel it too.

"But you screwed that up too, didn't you?" he fired off at me like some loose cannon. "Just like everything else that we ever handed you on a silver platter."

I burnt a hole right through that bastard with my gaze. And I swallowed that swill just like it was water.

I felt my eyes start to fill.

It felt like kerosene or something was burning its way down my esophagus. And that son of a bitch loved every moment of it.

Then that shiv in my gullet came back worse than ever. For a split-second I almost wondered if that crazy bastard had pulled out a switch-blade and stabbed me in the belly or something.

I clenched my teeth to try to fight it, but it was no use. It was too much to bear. I grabbed my stomach to try to hold back the inevitable, but that whiskey was burning like hell, and I knew that I had to get to the head.

I jumped up and darted back towards the entrance. I saw the arrow and headed off in that direction.

As I began running, I started to feel the acid burn. I put both my hands to my mouth to try to keep it in, knowing damn well that there wasn't a whole hell of a lot that I could do.

God only knows how I made it to the shitter and stumbled into a stall with a working toilet. As any fellow will tell ya, it's not puking up your lunch that sucks. That's a walk in the park. It's trying to hurl when you've got nothing left that'll kill ya. And those dry heaves accounted for about four-and-a-half minutes of the five that I was down there on my hands and knees beside the porcelain.

Finally, the urge subsided, and I just laid there with my forehead up against the cool clammy toilet. I was a bowl of Jell-O lying in somebody else's piss.

I couldn't much tell if it was tears or sweat that was stinging my eyes. Hell, it could have been backsplash. All I knew was that I was a mess there on that floor. I just kept hearing that bastard's voice rattling through my head, and I regretted not punching him right in the brain. I knew I could've taken him too. Hell, he was pushing a hundred years old and drunk to boot.

For a moment, I thought to run back out there and straighten shit out, but my senses got the better of me. I stayed there, just thinking about things. All kinds of things.

I knew that it wasn't really the old son of a bitch that got to me. I'm usually quite good at just ignoring people when they're blabbing about this and that.

The truth is that most people are gonna talk your ear off about whatever's on their mind, and nine times outta ten you're not gonna agree with them anyway. I know that most everybody is full of shit about one thing or the other.

But this guy struck a chord. Lying there in that mess, I realized that it really bothered me that he'd gotten me so riled.

And then it hit me like three fingers of Wild Turkey will do. He was right. And I hated every bone in his body for it.

Everything I'd had was just on loan. I lied there and thought about it.

Every goddamn thing we have is just temporary, no matter what they try to tell you. The whole goddamn American Dream is just that: a godforsaken dream. You know what happens with dreams, don't ya? You wake up. At least ninety-nine times out of a hundred you do. That made me chuckle. Until I felt the heaves coming on again.

Hanging over the bowl, my mind wandered to Geronimo and Cochise. I remembered reading *Bury My Heart at Wounded Knee* when I was a kid, and it kinda stuck with me.

We'd spent the last hundred fifty years trying to convince ourselves of something different than the truth. The Indians couldn't comprehend what the hell us stupid white people were talking about when we traded them a pouch of shit for their land. They knew that we can't own the grass, the air, the stone or the dirt. They understood that it's only there on loan for our fifty, sixty, seventy years or whatever.

They couldn't comprehend the concept of taking something that was there millions of years before your sorry ass came out of your mama's womb and calling it yours. And then we slaughtered them like sheep for it. I pitied those poor bastards. They got it, you know?

I finally did what I'd learned to do so well as of late. I took a deep breath, jumped to my feet, brushed myself off and got the hell outta that stall. And when I walked up to the sink to wash off my mug, I was surprised at something. I didn't look all that bad standing there.

Sure, I had some puke on my chin, just like I figured I would. But that wasn't a problem. I turned the knob for the hot and got nothing, so I turned on the cold, cupped my hands, and took a few splashes of icy water to the kisser.

A few seconds later, I dried myself off and walked out with my shoulders arched back and my head held high like nothing had happened. And as far as anybody else could possibly know out there on Fremont, nothing had.

By the time I got back to the bar, I was glad to see that those two were gone. With the exception of the bartender, I didn't really recognize anyone else. I couldn't spot my ticket on the bar, so I gestured for my check.

"Oh . . . your friends picked it up," she said. "You know, the nice couple sitting next to you?"

"Really?" I said. "How much was it?" I asked.

"I dunno" she shrugged. "Twenty-two or so? He insisted. Said you guys were old friends or something."

I reached in my pocket and pulled out two tens and a twenty. I threw down the twenty along with one of the tens and didn't say nothing. Not a goddamn thing. I just turned around and walked the hell outta that place. With God as my witness, I'll say I don't ever see myself going back.

CHAPTER 16

I started to walk down the up escalator for a step or two. You know, for old time's sake. Just to see what would happen. Nobody stopped me. I figured it was probably too early for that old pricky security guard to be keeping tabs anyways, so I ran for it.

About half way down, it dawned on me that I'd just gotten done puking my guts out, and this probably wasn't the smartest thing a guy could be doing. But at that point, I just kept on going. Just like riding a bike or puking your guts out, it all comes back to you.

I figured that somebody would be scolding me for screwing around by the time I got to the bottom, and I was almost disappointed when nobody gave a crap.

The place had picked up even more, and I could feel the vibe. I walked past one of the bars and people were cheering like crazy. I popped my head in and saw that they were doing karaoke. There was some skinny guy up on stage singing the Sonny Bono lines of *I've Got You Babe* to an empty chair beside him.

What a sorry son of a bitch, I thought to myself. But with all the cheering and whatnot going on, I reckoned he'd probably wind up scoring with somebody that night.

There was one of those Chinese buffet places in the lobby that looked like they were closing for the night. I knew that whatever was left had probably been lying around for a few hours, but sometimes it's better that way.

Nobody was up at the register, with everyone cleaning up and all behind the kitchen area.

"Can I grab something to go?" I shouted.

"Fo' here o' to go?" a guy asked. "We closing."

I wasn't gonna bust his chops. I figured he'd been there all day. "To go," I said again.

"Okay. No pwoblem. What you wan'?" he asked me.

There was about a spoonful and a half in a couple of the pans. A little more or less in others. I knew that I wasn't really that hungry, but I needed to get something for Miles. He should have had his insulin at least an hour earlier.

I pointed to the sweet and sour chicken. You can always tell which one that is when you're at one of these fast food Chinese joints because the sauce looks like the raspberry syrup you'd see at an IHOP. Still, I'd always kinda liked it.

"Wice, noodles, or wegetables?"

"Rice would be great," I said politely.

"What else you like?" he asked.

Judging by the wrinkles around his eyes, I figured he owned the joint. He'd probably come to live the American Dream some twenty or thirty years earlier and wound up working doubles at the Plaza Hotel, dealing with drunk's day in and day out. But he didn't seem to mind.

I pointed to the beef with broccoli. "Not too much broccoli," I said respectfully. "It's actually for my dog."

He smiled and did what I asked. I could tell that he didn't know what the hell I was talking about. I'd guessed that it was probably about the millionth time that day that somebody had said something to him that he didn't understand.

But for him, smiling and nodding in the affirmative was a skill he'd perfected. Just like every other skill that any of us pick up, to make our lives work. So, I did what I do. I smiled right back and nodded. Just the way that I'd learned a lifetime before.

I weaved right through that crowd with that bag of grub dangling from my wrist just like a professional delivery guy on Wentworth would've done.

I slid the key card in the door and was surprised that Miles didn't greet me. Sure enough, he was beat. That little bugger was snoozing in the center of the bed with his head on the pillow.

"Hey, buddy. You hungry?" I asked softly. I figured that his sugar was probably off too.

He looked up at me and yawned one of his yawns. One of the big ones where you can see all the way down the esophagus. Then he smiled at me, sacked out on the bed, or at least that's the way I saw it.

"Come on, Miles. Gotcha some Chinese." Seeing the food, he jumped right up and hopped off the bed.

Before the diabetes, there wasn't anything he'd choose to do besides breakfast or dinner. He could be in the middle of taking a dump, and if somebody walked by with a treat, he'd cut it off and run over.

But he'd gotten older and probably figured out that his dinner wasn't going anywhere. I wasn't gonna give it away.

Tonight though, he must've been starving, or else his levels were off the charts. He didn't screw around at all once the beef-and-rice container was open.

I realized that he shouldn't over do it on the Chinese. I'd learned long before that too much *people food* isn't a good thing, especially with his condition and all. Still, I wanted him to enjoy his meal as best he could.

I still felt rather buzzed from the Wild Turkey and wavered a bit as I set the fortune cookie on the dresser with the carryout bag, which still held my chicken.

I grabbed a syringe and opened the fridge for the insulin. It was nice and cold, and I was glad as hell that I didn't need to fiddle around filling a thermos with ice all the time.

I rubbed the vial back and forth in my palms in order to get it to the right temperature while Miles inhaled his supper. In those twenty seconds, my eyes locked on to that fortune cookie sitting there on the dresser.

I laughed to myself. There was no time in my whole life that I needed to know my future more than then. I took a step over to grab it, and as I did, I heard Miles yelp.

As I stumbled, I instinctively jumped out of the way so that I didn't land on him. But in doing so, I landed sideways on my right ankle.

Off balance, I impulsively threw my hands out like any normal fellow would do to break my fall and to prevent myself from knocking all my teeth out as I hit the floor.

But I didn't hit the floor and instead fell right on that dresser with all my weight. All One-hundred-seventy-five pounds of my sorry ass collided with that cheap wood veneer like a sack of potatoes. The only thing between me and that dresser was the ten- milliliter glass vial of insulin in my left hand.

"Shit!" I yelled loud enough that I was certain they could hear me down at the craps table. "Shit! Shit! Shit!" I hollered as I marched around the room, not wanting to look at my hand.

Miles scooted under the bed, and I ran into the bathroom, grabbed one of the large bath towels, and tried my best to not look down.

I figured that I'd really done it pretty good to myself, but I didn't want to know. I held pressure on it with my right hand and paced around the room, trying to fight off the sting that I knew must be on its way.

"You're an idiot!" I bellowed, hobbling around the room. "What are you going to do now?" I scolded myself.

I hollered a lot of stupid stuff while I was raging. But that all stopped when the house phone started ringing again.

It was then that I knew that I'd better simmer down. The last thing that I needed was security coming up to a blood-soaked room that was beginning to reek.

The truth is, it didn't really hurt that much anyways, so I decided that I'd finally take a peek at the damage. Although it wasn't pretty, it didn't look all that bad enough to go to the ER for stitches, assuming I paid attention to it.

Still, there was a lot of blood. So, I slowly unlatched the safety clasp on my Sub to maneuver it around the wound. It took a little patience. But I got it off without aggravating the cut or getting too much blood on my watch.

It sure did stink though. It's amazing how potent that insulin can be. It reminded me of those cold winter days when I'd jump outta my car to put five bucks in the tank so I didn't run out on the way to school. I'd put on my Dollar Store wool gloves, run into the old Chevron, and throw a fin on the counter before running back and carefully squeezing exactly three and a half gallons, or whatever five bucks put in your tank back then. Then I'd hop back in the car, pull off those cheap gloves, and take one whiff. Man, you could smell all the fumes on them.

That's exactly how the entire room smelled from that insulin. Just like my cheap wool gloves did back on a cold Chicago day. Damn near a lifetime ago.

After about five minutes, the bleeding had pretty much stopped, but there were a few pieces of glass in there. They weren't in deep though, which I was plenty glad about. I sure didn't want to go to the hospital, and stitches were about the last thing I needed. Slowly, I pulled the little bladelike shards out with a pair of tweezers from my toothpaste bag. It stung like the dickens, probably from the insulin that was still burning in the wound.

I finally got everything out that I could find and washed it off really good with warm water. By then I couldn't feel much of anything unless I made a fist, which I reckoned I wouldn't need to unless I saw that old fart from the bar playing pai gow with a stack of black chips.

By the time I came out of the bathroom, Miles was back eating his beef with broccoli. He really seemed to be enjoying it, and I couldn't much blame him. He had to be thinking how much better the food is on the road.

So as much as I had the weight of the world on my shoulders right then, I just lay there with my head on that stiff hotel room pillow, watching him enjoy his supper like he didn't have a care in the world. Despite all interfering logic, nothing else mattered all that much. Not even the fact that Miles didn't get his insulin.

In that moment, it didn't matter that we didn't have a real home anymore. It didn't matter that we were almost out of dough. It didn't even matter that I'd missed another call from Hope, which I'd noticed when I glanced at my phone lying next to the bed.

I knew that I was gonna call her the very second that I felt like talking, and I was gonna get Miles his refill in the morning. We would surely find a home again, probably a nicer one with a yard and a pool too.

Just like always, we'd make ends meet. I knew it. And he knew it too.

So I just watched him enjoy the shit out of that Chinese, and I didn't let myself think about anything else. Not a goddamn thing.

CHAPTER 17

"**S**hit!" I hollered, waking from a deep sleep. "No, no, come back later, please!"

I simultaneously ripped the sheets off the bed and lunged toward the door to make sure she wasn't going to open it.

"No neccesito, por favor," I said as if I knew what the hell I was talking about. Fortunately, the housekeeper figured out what I was trying to say and left us alone.

Miles was pacing back and forth, and I recognized that I darned well better get my wits about me. I worried about his blood sugar, and I realized that I had to try to keep him as level as possible until I could get his refill. I couldn't remember the last time he'd missed a dose, and by now his little body was so accustomed to counting on it. He'd already missed one, and missing another could be a serious problem.

In the meantime, I figured that the most pressing issue was him needing to take care of business. I splashed some cold water on my face and smoothed my hair back as best I could.

"Come on, buddy," I said like always. "No shot right now, but I'm gonna get you taken care of."

I looked at the Styrofoam and there wasn't a damn thing left in there. His sugar must've been out of control, and I recognized that I needed to get his prescription filled as soon as I could.

I grabbed my phone and saw that it was just after nine a.m. I presumed that the Walgreens down the street would be open, and with some luck, I could have his prescription back within the hour. He could surely wait until ten o'clock for breakfast. Everything was gonna be all right. If I could just get him walked and back, everything was going to be just fine.

I got Miles in the carrier without any issues. That was never a problem with him, and even though he was probably feeling way out of sorts, he cooperated just fine. I grabbed the half full duffle bag and draped it over the carrier as a kind of urban camouflage. Security probably wouldn't be down by the side door, but any other employee could be a potential problem.

Miles didn't make a peep as we made our way down the hall into the stairwell and down through the casino. He didn't whimper or bark or pant, though I know he couldn't see anything since the duffle was pulled over the gated door of the carrier.

I was used to carrying him with my left arm but needed to carry him righty because of the cut. It was awkward and likely drew some people's eyes, but we got out to the lot with no problem. I took him over by the car and used it as cover, being paranoid that somebody at the hotel might be watching.

I was able to get him out of the carrier, but not without a struggle. He seemed more tired than usual, and his legs didn't appear to be working the way they should. He still did his business real good, and then stumbled right back into the crate almost like he knew that we didn't have a whole lot of time to waste.

I cleaned it up but just left the tied bag sitting under my wheel well to get later. We had things that we needed to do, and time was not our friend in that moment. I packed him up, traversed that stairwell just like Sisyphus would've done, and got him back to the room safe and sound where any lingering scent of petrol had all but vanished.

It took me about a minute to put some kibble in the Styrofoam, refill his bowl with water, and make a half-assed attempt at brushing my teeth. Then I grabbed my wallet and headed out.

I headed out all right. Just like the Lone Ranger would have done in a time of crisis for Tonto. The same way Batman would've done for Robin. Gene for Roy. Clyde for Bonnie. Jenny for me. The way any good partner would when the cards were down.

It had been a while since I'd walked Fremont, but still everything felt the same. I passed the Golden Gate, the Las Vegas Club, the Nugget, and Sam Boyd's place too. Yep, they were all right there where they belonged. Right where I'd left them.

It was hot but dry. Despite the pace of my step, I didn't feel like I was working up much of a sweat.

About a half mile down on the right side of the street I spied the Walgreens. I blew past the air-conditioned barrier separating the store from the street and made a beeline to the back, where I expected the pharmacy to be. Sure enough, there it was, but the sign said that it didn't open until ten, a half hour from then.

"Excuse me, ma'am," I said to an employee restocking in an isle.

"Yes, how can I help you?" She seemed sincere, which surprised me a bit since I probably looked a little crazed, being unshowered, unshaved, and generally a flat-out mess.

"I've got a bit of an emergency, and I was hoping that somebody could help me out," I said while looking squarely in her eyes. I really needed a hand here, not just a sympathetic ear.

"My dog and I just got into town last night, and I accidently broke his bottle of insulin," I explained as genuinely as I could. "He's already missed two doses, you see, and I'm hoping that there's a way that I can just get a bottle even if the pharmacist isn't in right now."

I asked it so politely that I probably would've puked hearing it come out of my mouth on any other day. But it wasn't any other day. Not by a longshot. And wouldn't you know, it actually seemed like she gave it shit. It really did.

"Oh no. I am so sorry young man," she said maternally, just like my grandmother would've done. "Everything is locked up back there. You're going to have to wait till ten. Sundeep usually gets in a little early, but he won't open that window till it's ten o'clock on the nose. He's funny like that. What kind of dog do you have?"

"He's a terrier."

"Those are sweeties," she replied. I just smiled.

I didn't feel like getting into it with her. I had a lump in my throat that felt like a coconut, and that pain was flaring up again in my gut.

I knew that I didn't want to go back to the hotel, but I didn't know what the hell I was gonna do walking around a Walgreens for twenty minutes. I thought to grab some Rolaids to help with the damn pain but decided against it and headed back out to Fremont.

My head was buzzing. All I could think about was getting that damn medicine and getting it back to the room.

Nothing else seemed to mean anything right then. Not a goddamn thing.

I decided to just wander around the block once or twice. It was such a strange place to be before 10:00 a.m., Fremont Street was.

I saw a couple of trashy hookers just hanging out down by one of the bus stops. I have a hunch that they saw me and figured that I was pretty trashy too. That was sorta nice in a strange way because it made me forget about everything and just chuckle for a second or two. I did my best to not make eye contact, and it seemed to work fine since they let me be.

By the time I got to the El Cortez I had worked up a sweat. My heart was racing a mile a minute, and I was starting to feel a little queasy.

I didn't wanna puke again, especially since I was running on empty. Seeing that there wasn't a line at the coffee shop, I went up to the register and ordered my old standby.

"Just a large chocolate milk, please."

"That all?" she asked. I think she could tell that I was hurting a little bit.

"That's it," I told her perhaps a little too eagerly. I didn't wanna be rude, but I didn't want any conversation either. She just smiled.

I'd sat for a minute or two on the old leather couches, which had probably been there since Dean Martin passed through, when she came back with a large glass.

"Are you gambling with us today at the El Cortez?" she asked. The question bugged the shit out of me because I knew she could tell that I didn't wanna talk. I just looked at her and very seriously told her I wasn't so she'd get the hint.

Instead, she leaned right into me with a smile and said, "Yes, you are," handing me the glass. Then, real loud so that her boss could hear, she said, "Have a nice day now, and good luck!"

Well I'll tell ya that nothing tastes as good as a cold glass of chocolate milk when you're feeling under the weather. I drank about half of it right down in two gulps and then held the glass to my forehead to cool the sweats. I was damn near one hundred percent just thirty seconds after she handed me the chocolate milk, the best medicine in the world.

I wanted to be back at Walgreens at 9:59 a.m. I knew I still had a minute or two to kill, so I sat there and took a deep breath of that smoky casino air conditioning. The fake leather couch was sticking to my clammy legs inside my jeans, but it didn't gross me out the way that it would've most other times.

I felt the stare of the waitress, but did my best to not look in her direction. I probably owed her a tip, but the little bit of cash that I still had was back at the room. I knew that I wasn't gonna give her my card, so I just tried to find peace in the moment before it would be gone.

I got up and started to head out through the casino. I passed the slot and poker machines, then the blackjack, craps, and novelty games tables. By the time I'd made it to the other end of the place it was five till ten. I took that last swig of my glass, set it on the top of the bill breaker, and headed out to Fremont.

Things had picked up in the last fifteen minutes. Most of the newcomers were just the couples who hadn't been hitting it too hard the night before. You can always tell the kind. They holding hands, looking at everything like it's so damn taboo.

"Oh, a pawn shop!" they'd mutter. "Don't look over there, but I think that might be a real hooker."

The guys would be wearing Hawaiian shirts with leather sandals half the time, and the gals would be dressed all prude because they feared being confused with a working girl or whatever. You know the type.

I made it to Walgreens, and there were quite a few of those tourist types in there. It was one of the places that a couple of dopes would recognize from back home and feel comfortable walking into for a bottle of water or some Pepto-Bismol.

My phone said 10:02 a.m., so I knocked on the metal gate surrounding the pharmacy. It opened.

I'd expected to see some guy named Sundeep, who the lady had said earlier, but instead it was a well-groomed white kid with a name tag that said "Eric."

"How can I help you, sir?" he said, annoyed.

"Thanks for opening the cage, Eric. I saw the sign that says you guys open at ten." I sounded kinda pricky, but I didn't wanna piss him off, so I covered the delivery up with a smile. I figured he'd be guessing about whether I was being a smart ass or being sincere.

"What can I do for you, sir?" he asked like a jackass.

"I need to get a refill of insulin for my terrier. I accidently broke the bottle last night in our hotel room," I told him with all the sincerity, and bullshit respect, that I could muster in that moment.

"Do you have a prescription?"

"Well, no," I began. "Not with me. It was kind of an accident."

"I cannot fill any orders without a prescription, sir. Insulin is a controlled substance."

"Can you look in the system?" I asked nicely, trying to find a soft spot in him.

"Name?" he responded, peering down at his computer with fingers on the home row keys.

"Wolfe," I said. "Miles Wolfe. Canine." I knew the drill.

"You from Chicago? North Lake Shore Drive?" he asked.

"Yes, that's us," I said with relief.

"Shows here that the prescription is expired."

"You're kidding?"

"Nope," he went on. "It looks like it expired over six months ago. Are you sure it's in your name and not somebody else's?" he asked down his nose.

I was worried that shit was going to hit the fan, but I didn't let on. I know I can sometimes be wrong about things. Well, most of the time these days. But I wasn't going to get riled up over this. I knew that I needed to stay calm and collected for everything to work out.

"Listen, man," I said calmly. "Eric, right? I'm gonna level with you." I tried to catch his eyes because if I was ever going to have a sale that really mattered, this one was it.

"I had his prescription with you guys for ages," I went on. "I'm sure that you can see that in your system. But my buddy had a line on a pharmacy out of Canada that was getting his insulin for a third of the price. Plus they didn't need me to update the script every time I needed it. . . . I'm sure you can understand."

I hoped that he was a regular guy living paycheck to paycheck, and I figured that he was.

"It was saving me a over a hundred and fifty bucks a month, Eric."

"Sir, are you telling me, a licensed Pharmacist, that you were obtaining your dog's insulin by way of insurance fraud?" he asked pointedly.

"Well, not exactly," I responded. I knew I had to start backpedaling.

"I'll pretend like I never heard that," Eric said like the dick that I could tell he was. But I wasn't gonna get down to his level. I needed to remain cool.

"Thanks for understanding, Eric," I smiled as if using his name every other sentence was gonna get him to warm up to me. "Is there any way that I can buy a vial without you guys having an updated perscription?"

"Sir, there is absolutely no way that I can sell a controlled substance without having the proper documentation. That's entirely out of the question."

My gut was starting to cramp up, and those sweats were coming back, but I knew that I had to stay calm. At all costs, I had to remain in control.

"Okay, okay. So, what do I need to have in order for you to get me his medicine then? He's missed two doses already, and he can't miss a third, doc."

I think that little prick got a kick out of me calling him doc because he lightened up a touch. Not much, just a little bit.

Still, I knew that he wanted to get rid of me. Some classy-looking chick had come up behind me and was waiting for him, and I figured that he didn't wanna look like too much a jerk in front of her.

"I've got twenty bottles of insulin back in the refrigerator, Mr. Wolfe. I can assure you that we are not going to run out. If you can get your vet to fax me a perscription, you'll have it in your hands five minutes later," he explained. "But without one, I can't do a thing."

He handed me a business card with the store info on it. I looked for his name, but it wasn't there. I figured that he didn't have his own business cards, and that probably pissed him off pretty darned good too. Working the opening shift on a Tuesday at Walgreens. Wearing a lab coat like he was a doctor or a scientist. Not having his own cards. All those things probably contributed to him being a generally miserable son of a bitch.

He was nobody, and he knew it. Nothing but a two-bit order taker. And I could kinda see why he was such a prick right then and there. I really could.

So far the day wasn't what I'd planned, but then again, not much had been in quite a while. I just smiled and nodded.

"That's fine. Thanks, doc."

For a second, I started to panic. But I recognized that wouldn't do us any good. I had to keep my wits about me and knew from experience that if I did, we'd be all right. I made my way down the side street to find a quiet place to straighten shit out.

There was a parking lot that was all but empty, so I headed in there. Back in the corner was an open space that abutted the brick wall of one of the casinos. It seemed quiet enough, and I copped a squat on one of the parking blocks near the wall.

I rifled through my phone for the vet's number in Chicago but couldn't find it. Most people would have labeled it "Vet," "Vet Peter," or "Vet Mary" or whatever, so at least they could locate the number when they needed it. But once again I reminded myself that I wasn't most people.

Finally, I found it under "Peterson Vet," and I called.

It must've rung ten times before the machine went on, so I hung up and dialed again. A second time it rang and rang until the answering machine went on, and I freaked out thinking that they were closed. This time I listened to the message.

Good news. They were open until five, so I figured that they must just be busy. I hung up and called again. And for the third time I got the machine.

Finally, I got somebody on the sixth or seventh time. "Good afternoon, Hutchin's Animal Hospital. This is Natalie. How may I help you?" a young voice said.

"Hello, Natalie. Is Doctor Peterson in today?" I asked.

"Doctor Peterson is no longer with us, sir. How may I help you?"

"I'm sorry to hear that," I responded. "He was a wonderful man."

I sounded like a goddamn priest or something. I wanted her to think that I had a real rapport with Peterson, and that I must be a stand-up guy because of it. Not to mention, it was the truth.

"Yes, he was," she replied. "How can I help you, sir?"

"My name is Jack Wolfe and my terrier Miles is a patient with you guys."

As I was talking, I could tell that she was looking my file up. I could hear the clicking keys of her keyboard.

"We are actually out of town . . . Las Vegas, to be precise," I told her. "I need to refill his insulin. I was hoping that you could fax over a script to my friend Eric at the Walgreens here."

I could tell that she was only half listening to my story, and it took a moment for her voice to sound through the speaker.

"I see an outstanding invoice here, Mr. Wolfe, that's over a year old." I could tell that she wasn't surprised at this. I'd gathered that this wasn't the first time that a client called that had a past-due bill. Hell, with the economy the way that it was, it probably happened ten times a day.

I could hear a phone ringing in the background and a bunch of barking too. I remembered how busy it always was there, but I knew that I needed all her attention.

"You're kidding?" I said with feigned surprise. "How much do I owe you guys? I'll be happy to clear that up now." I barely noticed the giant, phony-ass smile on my face.

"It looks like two-hundred and eighty-one dollars for two visits," she said. "And the card we have on file doesn't work."

"Geez. I'm sorry about that. I wasn't aware," I told her. I could tell that she didn't buy what I was selling, but that was all right.

"Let me give you a new one," I said. "After that, can you fax over that script for Miles?" I asked, trying to not sound desperate.

"I'll need to transfer you to a doctor for that sir, but I need to get your information first."

"Can I speak to a doctor before I give you the credit card info?" I asked nicely. "It's kind of an emergency."

"Doctor Rickover is the only veterinarian here today, and he's in an exam. He'll have to call you back."

"Is it possible to hold for him?" I asked as genuinely as possible.

"I'm sorry, Mr. Wolfe," she said. "I can't tie up the line."

"I understand. "I've just gotta get Miles his insulin soon because he's already missed two doses.

"I'm very sorry to hear that," she said with a voice that had rehearsed those words a million times. "If you'd care to give me your credit card number, I'll be certain to have Doctor Rickover call you as soon as he's free."

I knew that I had to get on her good side. I needed to let her know what was going on without coming across like a jerk.

"Listen, Natalie. I know I owe you guys some money, and I'm really sorry about that," I began. "I can give you a new card number right now and make good on it. It really was just an oversight. But if I do, can you please, *please* have the doctor call me before his next appointment?"

My pleading had thrown her a curveball. I knew that she was thinking things through because she took her time answering me, but I wasn't certain if she thought that I was just some two-bit deadbeat or if indeed she believed me.

"I cannot make any promises about Doctor Rickover returning your call that quickly, sir," she said. "All I can do is give him the message and explain your urgency."

"Okay . . . that's fine," I conceded. "But please, tell him as soon as you can."

And just like I needed a hole in the head, I gave her my charge card numbers one at a time. I was getting to the end of the line of that rope, but I also knew that I didn't have much of a choice. I needed this guy to call me back.

I walked back and forth down Fremont about five times before I finally called again. Although it took six rings for her to answer, I was happy that it didn't go to voicemail. I figured it was a sign that things had slowed down.

"Yeah. Hey, Natalie. It's Jack again," I said like we were old friends. "Is the doctor free yet?"

"Mr. Wolfe?" she said inquistively. I had a hunch she didn't expect me to just use my first name, but I wanted her to warm up to me. You see, it's awfully hard to screw with somebody when you're on a first name basis with them. At least that's what I'd always thought.

"Yeah, Natalie. Jack Wolfe. Miles and Jack Wolfe. Is the doctor free?"

"Let me check Mr. Wolfe," she said as she put me on hold.

I sat there, and I sat there, and I sat there. But I sure as shit wasn't gonna hang up.

Finally, Natalie came back. "Doctor Rickover will be right with you, sir," she said calmly.

"Thanks, Natalie."

What seemed like an artificially deep voice came on the line.

"This is Doctor Rickover."

"Great. Hello, doctor. This is Jack Wolfe," I began. "I've been a client there for about ten years or so and was close with Doctor Peterson. I'm sorry to hear that he isn't there anymore."

"Doctor Peterson left this practice over a year ago, Mr. Wolfe. How can I help you?"

"Well," I started. "Miles and I are out of town and had a bit of a mishap. "I accidently broke his bottle of insulin, and we desperately need to get a refill," I explained calmly.

"Uh huh," Deep Throat replied.

"The pharmacist needs an updated prescription."

The line was silent after I finished. I mean, it couldn't have been more than ten seconds, but it felt like ten minutes. This jerk off knew damn well why I was calling but acted like he didn't. He just waited for me to say something.

"I was hoping that you could help me get his prescription faxed over, doc," I said, finally breaking the silence. "He's already missed two doses."

"I see that Miles hasn't been into the clinic for quite awhile, Mr. Wolfe," he accused, his voice stern. "And I see you just paid an overdue bill this morning. It wouldn't be ethical for me to issue any sort of a prescription for your dog without a proper examination."

I tried to stay calm, and I did a damn good job. I really did.

"Doc . . . I really don't know what to tell you." I went on.

I just wanted to fix this, and I didn't have a need to win. I just had to get this godforsaken prescription filled so that we could get on with our lives.

"I'll level with you, doc," I said respectfully. "It's been a rough couple of years."

I knew that I wanted to make it sound like I was sorta coming clean. Almost like confession or reconciliation, I'd suppose. I wanted him to know that I really was a stand-up guy, and that I wasn't a screw-up. There's something about showing a guy that you're vulnerable that makes 'em let down their cards. At least that's what I'd always found.

"But I swear to God that the invoice just slipped my mind," I tried to convince him. "He seems to be doing great with the eight units twice a day. I make sure that I give it to him like clockwork. I'm fairly certain that we've got his dosage down pat or else I would've been in there immediately."

I knew that I had to stay level and get this guy to know that I was responsible. And the truth is, I was. I mean, not with everything these days, but with Miles and his medicine, I sure as heck was. I was always on top of it, as much as anybody I know could've been.

"I've gotta tell you, Mr. Wolfe, that I am bound to certain ethical responsibilities. One of them is the administering of controlled substances. Insulin is a controlled medication."

All I could do was listen.

"I would guess that there are plenty of veterinarians out there that would gladly examine your dog and make a proper diagnosis and offer a prescription. But unfortunately, my hands are tied. There's nothing that I can do here."

Once I heard him refer to Miles as *my dog*, I knew it was over. He didn't give a shit.

I took a really deep breath, so deep that I am pretty sure that the jackass at the other end of the line could hear it. I was all ready for that knife in my gullet to do its thing and make me keel over and die.

"Mr. Wolfe?" he asked. "Mr. Wolfe?"

"Yeah . . . yeah. I'm here," I responded through that pineapple in my throat.

"Like I said, I am sure that you can find a vet there that can help you."

"In a strange town, without a home address, and no appointment?" I asked softly, defeated. "Do you really think I can find a vet that will give me a prescription before Miles goes into a coma or whatever?"

I raised my voice just a little.

"Is that the long and short of it, doc? Is that really what you are telling me?"

"Yes, Mr. Wolfe. I'm afraid so."

The lump in my throat felt like it would suffocate me. It was all I could do to not break out in a complete rage. But I came close.

"Did my payment on the credit card clear okay for you today, Dr. Jackoffer?" It came out snide and rude, more than it should have.

"The payment from over a year ago, Mr. Wolfe?" he replied, and I couldn't help but think he enjoyed putting me in my place. "Yes, I believe that it cleared just fine. Best of luck to you and your dog."

Within one thousandth of a second came the damn click of the phone. The hangup, to end all hangups.

"His name is Miles!" I yelled into the mouthpiece as goddamn loud as I could, my cry echoing off the nearby buildings.

I put the phone in my pocket and breathed in and out real slow. There wasn't a whole lot that I could do. And I knew it.

It was just past noon, and the sun was hot as hell out there on Fremont. I could feel my pits sweating, and I recognized that I'd found myself at a fork in the road. I needed to do something.

I began shaking feverishly. Panic was starting to set in, even though I knew I couldn't let it. My gullet starting doing its thing the way that I figured it would. And my eyes were welling up uncontrollably.

Hope. Hope would know what to do, I thought. I kept trying to breath in and out like I was meditating or something. But instead, it seemed like I was hyperventilating.

I knew that I had to get my thoughts together. I needed to be able to listen really carefully to whatever she'd tell me to do. Even if she didn't know, I knew she'd look it up online and figure things out.

As I walked, breathing deep with each step, I tried desperately to find some sort of peace. I even thought about how the tables had turned. It wasn't that long ago that Hope would come to me for everything, not that she ever really needed much. She was just a college kid when I met her, studying physics or something brainy like that. She wasn't that close with her folks, and for the most part, she had to pay her own way through school. I guess I sort of admired her for that. Still do. But she'd still seek my advice about this and that from time to time, never really being able to make a move without me.

Some guy wouldn't leave her alone once, and I remember needing to set him straight. Then there was a time or two that she couldn't pay her rent. She was scared silly that her landlord was gonna boot her. I got in between them and worked things out. I don't think that she was more than ten days behind, but she was still frightened as can be about it. She was so damn grateful, and it made me feel like a bit of a hero.

Truth is, when I look back, I kinda wonder if I really did it for her. Maybe it was really all for me.

She'd sure come a long way since those days. And thinking about that for a minute at least got my mind off things while I headed over to that old parking lot behind the casino.

I sat back down on that concrete parking block and dialed Hopes number. Before I could even hear a ring, it went to voicemail.

"Hi. It's me," her greeting said. "You know what to do and when to do it."

I hung up and dialed again. Right to voicemail a second time.

Those pangs came back like a shotgun blast to the belly, and I was so freaked that I didn't leave a message. All I could do was take the phone off vibrate and turn the volume up as loud as it would go, hoping I wouldn't miss her next call—if she called.

I tried to breathe to ease the pain in my gut, but I couldn't this time. While sitting on that block, I leaned over and put my head between my legs. It was so goddamn fierce that I thought for a second or two that I was a goner. I really did.

I screamed loud enough that I could hear the echo come back at me over the next few seconds. I crawled to where the two buildings met in a corner and lay there on my hands and knees.

My stomach started heaving, and I felt the acid burn my chest. I felt it rise to my throat and then my mouth.

Finally, that demon inside, or whatever the hell it was, spewed forth from me, right onto the concrete. I don't know if it was chocolate milk or an ulcer or one of my lungs. All I can tell you is that it burned like nothing's ever burned before. With a fricken blow torch in my stomach, I'd puked up a fireball.

After that eruption, all I could do was lie there with my face on that pavement about an inch from that vomit. It stunk like the dickens too. But I didn't much care. The crippling pain was finally fading away, for the moment. That's all I was worried about then and there. It'd give me the chance to do the only thing I could: get back to that hotel room on the double.

I picked myself up and started running through groups of people finally starting to show up. I knew that all I had to do was run until I ran out of real estate. To the end of that canopy. Where Fremont ends. The last hotel on the line. The Plaza Hotel and Casino.

I'm sure I was a hell of a sight for the tourists, my eyes watery and bloodshot, my shirt covered in puke. The hell if I cared. I didn't give two shits.

I made it as far as Glitter Gulch before I had to slow down and catch my breath. I kept walking at a fast pace, and when I got to the stoplight, I just ran between the cars flipping a cabbie off as he laid on his horn.

I took the stairs and got to the room. I was glad to see the housekeeper's cart about six doors down, so I knew that they weren't nearby. I slid my key in the door and felt the cold air hit me all at once, dry and cool. I took that cold blast in for a second or two before I even realized that Miles hadn't accosted me at the door the way that I'd hoped he would.

I could smell the scent of day-old Chinese food the moment I walked in, and I could see that he'd found his way to my sweet and sour chicken from the night before. The bag was torn, and pieces of rice lay strewn throughout the hotel room. That stiletto in my gullet somehow found even deeper flesh to inflict it's suffering.

"Hey, buddy. . . . How you doing?" I asked real fatherly, trying to not let on about the fear that was inside of me.

He just looked up, panting from under the table in the corner of the room. I could tell he was under the weather. Goddamnit, of course he was.

I looked lovingly in his direction and walked over to where he was lying. I crouched down on my knees and rubbed his little head. I got in real good too, around the ears the way that he likes. Right in sweet spot. He just looked up at me like it was all that he could do.

I could tell that it was taking a lot of effort, so I held his head for him. I was certain that the sugar was sending his system into a tailspin. But it seemed as though he wanted me to believe that everything was all right, as though it was a day like any other.

But I wasn't about to let him pretend that it was okay. Over my dead body. It wasn't. It wasn't okay by a longshot.

I thought to pick him up and put him on the bed, but that wouldn't have accomplished anything other than freak him out.

Being out of control was one of the few things that he could never handle, and I wasn't going to do that anymore than I already had. So, I set his head gently down and stroked along his backbone the way that he'd always enjoyed. To be honest, I didn't know who was getting the most out of that moment right then and there. I think that I needed it just as much as he did.

I could hear him snoring ever so quietly, and it broke my heart into a million pieces. I got up real slowly and grabbed my phone from my pocket to try Hope again.

For a second his snoring stopped, or at least I imagined that it did, and I jumped back to the tableside. I must've startled him, cause he sorta jumped right there. He just looked up, his eyes like slits, yawning like nothing was the matter. Just like *I was the one* making a big deal out of nothing.

I searched local veterinarians on my phone and mapped them out. There were about six that were all within a few miles, and I hoped that maybe I could offer them a few extra bucks to come to the hotel. My thinking was that the less that I dragged him around, the longer he'd be all right.

I started dialing and got mostly machines. Finally, I got a hold of a place called, of all things, Animal Lover's Clinic. *What a stupid-ass name*, I thought to myself.

But I didn't much give a shit. At the end of the day, the kind of goof who would name a place something like that was the one I wanted on my side anyways.

"Animal Lover's," a mild-mannered voice answered.

"Yes, hello," I began. "My name is Jack Wolfe, and I am in town on business with my terrier. We had a little mishap."

As I went through the story, I made it all sound completely above board, which really was the truth. Of course, I didn't tell him about the pissing match that I got into with that jackoff back in Chicago, the fact that I was behind on his bill, or anything like that. But for the most part, I came clean with the guy.

Even though he sounded a little flaky on the phone, he seemed to be a really good-natured fellow. I fessed up and told him that I'd been getting Miles' insulin from Canada the last year or more because it was cheaper. But he didn't seem to mind a bit. He even laughed about it, almost like he admired that I did what I had to in order to keep Miles healthy.

At the end of my story, he convinced me that everything was going to be fine. It really put my mind at ease. He appeared to be a gentle fellow, and that was exactly what I needed right then and there. Still, he made certain to let me know that due to Miles' age and the amount of insulin he was accustomed to, it was important that we took care of this right away. But that was pretty obvious to me anyways.

I told him that Miles was just lying there. I chuckled and said, "He's moving kinda slow today, doc," even though it was anything but a joke.

"It wouldn't be good for him to miss another dose," he said gravely, but I was glad that he was serious like that.

I have a tendency to make light of difficult situations, and his sincere demeanor kept me in check.

"I really can't come to the hotel, Jack," he finally said with both compassion and regret. "I would, but I've got clients coming in until 5:00 p.m. today. I was actually just grabbing a bite to eat between patients when you called. I'm glad I was there or else it would've gone to the answering service."

"Tell me about it," I said with a slight smile. "Is there any shot of you just writing the script over the phone?" I asked like I was sitting on Santa's knee.

"I'm sorry, man," he said coolly. "If I'd seen him before, maybe I could. But I'd be putting my license on the line otherwise."

I understood. There was nothing I could do about it.

I told him that I'd be down as soon as possible, and he said that I didn't need an appointment. I could sense that he was all right, and for the first time in a while, my gut wasn't on fire.

I took a deep breath and filled the bottom of the Styrofoam with some kibble and placed it by Miles' snoot. He just laid there but finally took a few bites of dry food as I stroked along his backbone. I got up to splash some water on my face, but by the time I got back to him, he was snoozing again.

I got the carrier set up and put a couple of towels in it to make it a little cozier. Once he knew what was going on, he got up on his own and didn't need my help getting in.

"That's a good boy," I said as I gently picked up the crate and headed out the door to the elevator. This time the cleaning lady saw me, but she didn't say anything. That was the best I could hope for, I supposed.

Off the elevator, I walked with purpose past what seemed like a hundred slot machines, a fully-staffed bar, and even a security guard. Nobody said a word. Not a goddamn thing.

I'm guessing that they could all tell that I wasn't in the mood for discussing much of anything. So, they left me alone, and I did the same as I headed out to the 911 with my best friend, just like Butch and Sundance would've done. Pancho and Lefty too. Loop and Lil.

I put the crate next to me in the passenger's seat but didn't open it. He wasn't begging for me to and just looked through the holes at me, panting in the heat.

I plugged the address in the GPS and started up the car. Townes was somehow already queued up, right at the beginning of "If I Needed You."

I'd always loved that song, so I turned it up just a touch. It was a mellow song anyways. Sort of a lullaby. And Miles didn't seem to mind much. He just lay there, staring at me with his tongue out, doing pretty much everything that'd make me think nothing was the matter.

I must've been on another planet or something because I took about five or six wrong turns despite Matilda's instructions, but I finally got us there.

It was a tiny little storefront in the corner of a run-down strip mall. It certainly wasn't the Forum Shops or anything, but that didn't much matter. With any luck, we wouldn't be there more than a half hour.

There was a dumpy bar, some local joint, about a hundred yards down that advertised loose poker machines. I pulled up and parked four spaces away from a beat-up Pontiac with two guys inside. They weren't paying me any mind, but it was pretty obvious that they were smoking something. As I headed towards the storefront with Miles and locked the 911, I got a whiff of it. I couldn't help but peek into their old beater, and sure enough, they were checking me out too. I just smiled. One guy smiled back a half of a smile and nodded.

It felt to me like we were two cowboys meeting on the trail in the middle of the frickin' Sonoran. Neither of them knowing what the other guy is all about, wondering if the other son of a bitch is gonna shoot and rob him. But it's that moment when they both realize the other's just a regular guy, and all he wants is a little goddamn respect.

The nod that stoner gave me wasn't all that different. In fact, it was the same damn thing. Just a cowboy on the trail acknowledging my goddamn existence. My very right to be there. Nothing more, and nothing less. So sure as shit, I nodded back. You bet your bottom dollar I did.

We got inside the clinic, and it was obvious that they weren't even attempting to cover up the smell of piss and feces.

I didn't much care. We were there for one simple reason. Getting in and getting out was the only thing on my mind.

Nobody was up at the makeshift counter that was covered with all sorts of paperwork and print ads for flea collars and pet-sitting services. There was an older lady with what looked like a pit-bull mix or something on a leash beside her.

"He's in back with somebody," she said, implying that she was next and that I ought to just take a seat. Putting Miles' carrier beside me, on the opposite side of the muscular dog, I sat down.

"Oh," the lady said warmly. "Don't mind him," she smiled. "He's a lover boy."

I looked at her dog as he momentarily took his eyes off the carrier and looked up at me.

"Aren't you a lover boy, Brutus?" she mused as she massaged his neck and head.

"I can tell he is," I smiled back.

She looked real proud when I said that. Proud as a peacock. She rubbed Brutus' neck all the more enthusiastically, his jowls bouncing up and down, his tongue hanging out with saliva dangling about six inches from it. As if in slow motion, that slipping slobber lost its battle with gravity and fell to floor in a puddle the size of a silver dollar. She pretended not to notice, so I did the same.

"Okay, Margo . . . I'm all ready for Brutus," a familiar voice resonated, and out came a bumbling, middle-aged guy dressed like what I used to refer to as a schlub. His hair was tussled, and his pants seemed to be dragging below his ankles to the point that I wondered if he was gonna trip over them. He had an oversized lab coat on and looked like he hadn't shaved in a week or more.

"You must be . . ." he looked at me through thick, large rimmed glasses. "Mr—"

"Wolfe," I interjected. "But please call me Jack, doc."

"Sure thing. I'm Dr. Spinelli—well, Tony. Tony Spinelli. And this must be Miles. How are you feeling there, Miles?" he said as he kneeled down to his level.

I could tell that he really gave a shit. Miles stared back at him real sweetly through the grate. I think he could tell that the doc was a good guy. Dr. Spinelli stuck two fingers through the door on the carrier, and Miles leaned in for a scratch.

"I'll just be a few minutes, guys," he said like we were two buddies waiting to play a pick-up game of basketball or something.

"No problem, doc," I smiled. "We're not going anywhere."

He headed towards the exam room with Margo and Brutus, and I leaned back on that waiting room seat and gave a big sigh of relief. Everything was gonna be all right. Sure, as shit. Everything was going to be just fine. I just had a feeling.

I don't know if it was five minutes or fifty before Dr. Spinelli came back out because I'd totally crashed. I jumped up out of my coma when I heard him come bursting out of the back room.

"Okay, guys, I'm all set for you!" he said enthusiastically. "Thanks for being patient."

I don't think he had any clue that I'd been snoozing.

"No problem, doc," I said. "Thanks again for seeing us on short notice."

I set the carrier on the stainless-steel table in the examination room and opened the cage door. Miles just sort of lay there, looking out at us.

"You gonna come out on your own, pal, or am I going to have to give you a little help?" I asked him calmly. He just sorta stared at me. He was tuckered out. I could tell.

"Maybe we should help him out a little?" Dr. Spinelli suggested as he grabbed the back of the carrier. He held it in place, gesturing for me to reach in and pull him out.

I leaned in and patted his head softly so that he knew everything was okay. Grabbing him behind the shoulders, I pulled him out slowly, careful not to disrupt the open wound that was still throbbing on my left hand.

"That's a good boy," I said as if he really gave a shit right then. "Let Dr. Tony check you out, buddy."

I knew what my job was, was simple: to make him feel comfortable and safe. So, I rubbed his head, in and around the ears the way he liked. While I was doing my thing, the doc was doing his. He got the thermometer in Miles' ass and all. He even drew some blood from his leg and got it bandaged up before either of us knew what had happened.

"I'll be back in a minute," he said as he darted from the room. I heard a *ding* like a doorbell and presumed that it was somebody coming in for his next appointment. I just sat there rubbing Miles' head, and he just lay there taking it in as best he could.

It couldn't have been more than two minutes later that Doctor Spinelli came back in.

"Okay, guys," he said with a professional demeanor that clashed with the way that he looked. "Sugar levels are pretty high. Higher than I'd like to see."

My eyes started to well up. It's not like I didn't expect him to say it, but somehow hearing it from this guy really rattled me. I took a deep breath and listened intently.

"We're going to have to get it down, but we've gotta do it carefully," he began. "You can't just double up or anything like that," he explained.

"Just tell me what to do, doc. Just tell me what to do."

He grabbed a pad and began to write on it.

"You are going to want to give him eleven . . . no, make it twelve units as soon as you can. But I am also prescribing a bottle of glucose spray."

"Great . . . I know what that is," I told him, choking on my words.

"If he has a reaction, don't mess around. You've gotta be on top of it. You've gotta spray it in his mouth if he's struggling with the injection."

"Okay," I said through the pineapple lodged in my throat.

"After three hours, as long as he's doing all right, you're going to give him another four units. Just four. That should start getting him leveled off and back on a routine. Okay?"

"Yeah," I assured him. "After three hours, just another four units."

"Perfect. Then three hours after that, another four units. Three and then four. It's easy to remember, Jack," he said as serious as can be.

"Got it," I nodded.

"Make sure that he's eating too, and drinking lots of water. We've gotta keep him hydrated and eating on a regular schedule," he went on. "And no people food! At all costs, he needs to be clear of anything at all with sugar in it."

And that's when it hit me like the freight train that it was. The damn Chinese food was all sugar. And he polished it off like it was his last supper.

I started to feel the waterworks coming, and it took everything I had to keep them at bay. No wonder he was so bad. Because of me. It was all because of me and my selfish stupidity.

"I've got a few cans of Vet-RX soft food for him here," Doctor Spinelli told me as he handed them over. "If he's gonna eat anything, it'll be this. This ought to get his appetite back."

I grabbed them from him, but I couldn't stop thinking about how I'd left that bag of sweet and sour chicken right out there in the open. How hungry he must've been when I wasn't there to give him his kibble and insulin. None of this, not one little bit of it, was his fault. I did it. I damn near killed my little guy.

"Thanks, doc," I said after clearing my throat. "You're a lifesaver."

I held out my hand for his.

"What do I owe ya?" I asked as he shook my hand more firmly than I imagined a schlubby guy would.

"A hundred is good," he said kinda looking away.

"Sure . . . whatever," I responded. "Let me get you my Visa," I said as I reached for my wallet.

"I can only take cash," he told me. Not sternly. He just said it like it was. "It says so out front on the door as well as on the counter," he explained, pointing.

"Shoot," I muttered to him. "I don't have it on me," I said.

My head started spinning with all the things that I could do to get him paid, but before I could throw anything out there, he handed me the script and said "It's all right, Jack. Just get him taken care of, and you can throw a check in the mail."

"Shit!" I exclaimed. "I mean, thanks! Really, doc. I can't begin to tell you . . . we've had a few roadblocks, but we're on the home stretch."

"Just get him taken care of," the doc said. "He's a good dog, and life is short." He directed me out a side door that I didn't know was even there.

Before I could turn to thank him again, the door was three quarters of the way shut. I just kept walking with Miles in tow. He didn't make a peep as I popped him in the passenger seat and started up the engine.

CHAPTER 18

I figured I'd hit the Walgreens on Fremont since it was close to the hotel and I knew that they had plenty of insulin in stock. I turned the air conditioning on high. It didn't seem to do a whole lot of good, so I rolled down the windows.

I was coming up to a streetlight that was turning yellow about fifty feet before I got to it. I probably could've made it, but I didn't wanna do anything crazy. I knew that I was driving like an old man, but I reckoned that was all right considering the circumstances.

Since I figured that I had a minute or two to kill before the light changed, I opened one of the cans of food that the doc had given me and unlatched the carrier. The food stunk as much as I figured it would. I know that dogs really like it that way when they don't have much of an appetite. At least that's what Jenny once told me.

I swung the door aside and put the can next to the cage. He sniffed it a bit but didn't eat any. I figured his appetite was at about a zero based on all he was going through.

"You're not hungry, buddy?" I asked him. "It'll make you feel better." I said gently. He just laid there with his head on one of the towels. Even the stinkiest food in the goddamn world wasn't gonna make him feel much like eating until I got his levels back in check.

By the time I got back downtown, the air was finally kicking in. Still, it must've been twenty degrees warmer than I would've liked, and I figured it wasn't any better inside of the crate. To make matters worse, I could tell that Miles had peed himself in that darned carrier. I doubt he even knew it though. He was just sorta lying there with his eyes half shut, and I knew that I wasn't about to leave him in the car with the engine running.

"It's all right, buddy," I said as my eyes started to ache and my throat began to close. "It's gonna be okay."

I pulled into the lot where I'd puked my lung out. In fact, I even parked right in the same spot in the corner.

I got out of the 911, walked around to the passenger side and gently took him out of the crate. Sure enough, he'd pissed himself pretty good. I kissed his forehead and grabbed a T-shirt from the back to wipe him off. He just hung there in my arms and didn't fight me on it.

I pulled the carrier out to set it on the pavement so that I could put Miles down on the leather seat. I propped the crate on its side for a minute or two so the pee would drain out, and I wiped the inside out as best I could.

I looked over, and he was just lying there like a lump. All I could do was laugh. Well, laugh and cry. Kinda at the same time, like the pussy that I am. Laughing with tears rolling down. Just like a goddamn sissy.

I didn't have time, so I sucked it up and threw him in the carrier the way that Tonto would've done when all the cards were down.

We marched into the Walgreens, and it was mobbed. It took a few minutes to wade through the tourists to get to the back, and I was pleasantly surprised to see that there wasn't a wait at the pharmacy counter. Still, I had to stand there like a schmuck waiting for somebody to notice me.

I could see the back of a guy in a lab coat doing something feverishly around a corner. After about a minute,

I finally got his attention by yelling louder than I probably should have.

"Excuse me!"

Sure as shit, it was that prick from earlier, and I'd be lying if I told you that I wasn't sort of glad in a strange way that it was him.

"Okay, Eric," I said as I looked at his badge just to make sure that I'd remembered his name correctly. "Here's the prescription that you so diligently required earlier."

I was happy with the amount of snootiness I put into saying it.

"I'll also need the glucose spray that's on the prescription form as well as a package of your smallest-gauge, long-needle syringes."

I could tell that he felt vindicated, so proud that he'd done his job so goddamn well. He'd made certain that every rule had been followed to the letter, every *i* dotted, every *t* crossed.

"Certainly, Miles," he said arrogantly. "Do you have an ID?" he asked.

"Miles is my terrier, Eric. And he's right here," I said snidely, holding Miles up. "Would you like his ID too?" I mused snidely.

"Sir," he sounded alarmed as well as authoritative. "Only service animals are allowed in the store."

"Then get me the damn insulin so we can get the hell out of here, Eric," I said looking him dead in the eyes.

Now, I'm no tough guy. Never have been. I think I already told you that. But when push comes to shove, I know how to act like it. And this was one of those times.

"I'll be right back" is all he said as he went to the shelves behind the counter. Sure as shit, that little pansy came running back with his dick between his legs.

"Here's the vial," he said. "This needs to be refrigerated. This is the glucose spray and a twelve-pack of syringes."

I nodded but didn't break a smile. In charge now, I just watched him put everything in a bag and ring it up.

"Is there anything else that I can get for you and your dog?" he said politely.

"His name is Miles," I responded.

"Miles," he conceded.

"That'll do it, Eric."

I wanted to rip this jackass a new one, but it wasn't worth it. Right then and there, all I cared about was getting that medication for Miles and getting our lives back to normal—whatever the hell normal had become for us. Plus, I always knew where I could find this little piece of shit if I changed my mind.

"That'll be $186.70," he said. I gave him my Visa.

He didn't say a thing. I think that he thought that I was hanging on by a thread. He was torn between his ego, and his common sense. And fortunately for him, common sense took over.

Then I saw his forehead wrinkle, and I felt my stomach knot.

He grabbed the bag from the counter and handed me my card back.

"This card doesn't work, Jack," he said gruffly. "How would you like to pay for your items?" he asked me.

I was ready to start crying, but I wasn't gonna do that. Over my dead body.

I felt him looking at me the same way that Ali looked down at Frazier on the mat a million years ago. I fumbled through my wallet, knowing damn well that I didn't have anything else in there. The Plaza must've run through an extra hundred or two to guarantee incidentals or something. Still . . . I wasn't gonna let on.

"You're kidding?" I said with my voice shaking a touch, trying to sound baffled to conceal the panic I felt. But I was sure that this jerk could see through me because his arrogance was back as though it had never left.

"No. I'm afraid I'm not kidding, Mr. Wolfe," he ripped into me. "Now, as I told you, only service animals are allowed in the store. I'm going to have to ask you to leave or else I'll need to call security." He pointed towards the front door.

As much as it killed me to bow down to this piece of shit, I knew it was my only shot. Desperate men do desperate things. I did what I had to do. I said what I had to say.

"Listen, Eric," I retreated "Miles is going to die if I don't get him that insulin. Please. If not for me, can you at least help my dog out?" I pleaded to him like that pussy I hate to be. "He's my best friend, and he's all I've got."

Those were perhaps the truest words I'd ever said. I knew that Eric stood between me and keeping everything I had left.

"Give me till tomorrow," I begged. "I'll come back with twice that amount. You can keep the difference if you'll just front it for me. I swear to Christ, man. I won't leave you hanging. Please. What do you say?"

I held my hands together as if I was praying and tried to hold back the tears that I knew were inevitable. I looked him squarely in the eyes, awaiting his response.

"I say that if you don't leave the store with that dog within the next ten seconds, I am going to call the police," he warned, lording over me from behind that damn pharmacist's counter. "That's what I say, Mr. Wolfe."

I wanted to jump over that counter. You would too. But I didn't. It was all I could do, but I didn't. Instead I took that deep breath. In and then out. As deep as I could.

"Okay. We're going, Eric," I said without an ounce of confrontation left in my voice. "I'm gonna get you cash. I'll be back in just a little bit. Will you keep that order ready for me?" I asked as gently as I could in that moment.

"It'll be right here for you, Mr. Wolfe," he said as smug as can be.

I still wanted to slug him, but I knew that would be a death sentence, for Miles and for me. I smiled a big pricky smile and grabbed the carrier.

I started to walk to the Porsche, but my thoughts were going a mile a minute. I was feeling things that I hadn't felt for twenty years or more. Not since old Mitch Moran on the playground.

I wanted to strangle that son of a bitch. I felt this rage, for lack of better term, taking over me. Not just for Eric, the two-bit pharmacist, but also for that dick at the bar from the night before. Shit. I was starting to think that I was having a meltdown out there on the streets of Las Vegas. You see, it wasn't just those two that I was good and ready to go to blows with.

I started thinking about my mom. I could never make her happy no matter what the heck I did. Same with just about every girl I'd ever dated besides Hope. Even the people I most considered my closest friends never gave me a goddamn ounce of their approval.

Just Jenny. And I couldn't even do that right.

Still, I knew that I had to stop obsessing or I was gonna blow. I rubbed my eyes with the palms of my hands as I took another deep breath in and out when I remembered something. There was a pawn shop around the corner, and I was going to have to pawn the very last thing of value that I had. There was nothing left to do.

I buzzed, and the guy opened the door for me. He was sitting behind the thick bulletproof glass, and I presumed was Middle Eastern by the way he dressed with Al Jazeera on the TV.

"How can I help you?" he said through a speaker that made his accent seem even thicker.

"I'm in a bind," I said quickly. "I need some cash."

He took a quick glance at me, briefly pulling himself away from the day's news.

"I've got this . . ." I muttered to myself under my breath. I stood there, setting the lifeless carrier on the floor.

"Yes, sir?" he said pushing the button with a questioning look on his dark face. Staring at the crate as if that was what I meant to pawn.

"No, not that," I corrected. "That's my dog Miles."

"Okay, what then?" he said as though he was pre-occupied and didn't really have the time for whatever drama I was bringing into his store. He probably thought I was just another tweeker looking to unload a gold chain or fake diamond earrings swiped off some unsuspecting vacationer.

Then sheer horror took over every ounce of my soul in that very moment.

I fell to my knees. Crippled.

My watch wasn't on my wrist.

It was back at the hotel, next to the bed. A million miles away. And there wasn't a goddamn thing I could do about it.

"What is it?" he asked, seemingly frustrated at what was happening on my side of the bulletproof glass. As if I was an annoyance, like a mosquito or an ingrown toenail.

I knelt there in his lobby doing everything I could to stop the tears from coming. Panic taking over every bit of composure that I still had left.

"Sir!" I pleaded. "I have a Rolex Submariner back at my hotel. It's the two-tone blue face. I'm staying at the Plaza," I told him. "My best friend is dying in here," I explained as I tilted the front of the carrier up so that he could see Miles, who didn't make a peep.

"I've gotta get him his medicine, or he's not gonna make it. Please, please, I'm begging," I said trying to choke back the tears. "Please . . . please just spot me two hundred dollars, and I'll be back within the hour with my watch."

I begged with everything I had, just looking for some sign of compassion. Just one ounce of pity. A semblence of sympathy.

"It looks like he's already gone, my friend," he said calmly through the glass.

I opened the cage and grabbed Miles' furry, little head. He opened his eyes and panted a little bit.

"No! No! He's gonna make it!" I exclaimed. "Please Sir. Please!"

"I don't front money here, my friend. Come back with the watch. Then we can talk."

It sounded like scripted line that he'd long ago memorized. I could see in his eyes that he didn't believe for a moment that I had a Rolex, much less anything at all of value.

"I'm sorry, sir," he went on. "Unless you have something worth pawning, I am afraid that there is nothing else that I can do for you."

I started to bury my face into my hands. I didn't want this guy to see me, but there wasn't a whole lot that I could do. I felt the tears coming. But just like the puke the night before, I knew that I could make it before they came.

Pulling the carrier to my side, I turned around swiftly and headed towards the exit. My throat was in a knot that felt like I'd swallowed a six-foot saguaro cactus. I pushed the door, but it wouldn't budge. The knot tightened. Then I heard the buzz from behind the thick glass, and I pushed my way out. As I did, I heard a comforting voice come through the tiny little speaker.

"It will be all right, sir," he said with a sincerity that left me wide open for his next words. "It's only a dog"

I didn't turn around. I wouldn't turn around. Over my dead body.

By the time I heard that security door close behind me, the tears were pouring down pretty good. My throat had a football wedged in it, and my knees were wobbly. There was a little alleyway just to the side of the pawn shop with a couple of dumpsters that I ducked into. I set Miles down gently and got on my knees to see how he was doing.

When I got eye level with the carrier and opened it, I got a whiff. I could tell that he'd shit himself. So, I took him out thinking that he could finish his business right there in the alley. But as I pulled him by his shoulders, I could see that he didn't have the strength to stand on his own anymore.

And that's when it happened.

"Over my dead body." I said aloud to myself. I kissed him on the forehead and tenderly set him back in his carrier. I latched the gate and set the crate secretly behind the dumpster where it was out of sight from any passer's by.

I got up. "Over my dead body," I said again a little more feverishly as I started running at full speed down that side street.

"Over my dead body!" I yelled as I passed by the crowds that had gathered to see all that Fremont had to offer.

I saw out of the sides of my eyes how everybody was staring at me like I was a mad man. That's what I was right then and there. A goddamn loony with tears streaming down my face and rage in my eyes.

"Over my dead body!!" I protested as I ran through aisle six at the Walgreens, grabbing some stupid snow globe with a monument of the Eiffel Tower in it and tearing back to that two-bit, piece-of-shit pharmacist.

"Over my dead body!!!" I yelled with all my might as I hurled that plastic sphere in the general direction of his cranium. It missed, smashing on the shelves behind him, and I grabbed a wooden cane as I closed the distance between me and the counter.

"Give me the insulin!" I shouted at him as I charged forward with the cane. He looked startled as hell and began to pick up the phone behind the counter.

"Give me the fucking insulin you piece of shit!" I shrieked as I jumped the counter and yanked the phone out of the wall.

I grabbed him by the ear with my bleeding left hand and punched him with my right, sending him to his knees. I held on tight to the side of his head while I labeled him another two or three times in the face with the cane.

He was a puddle of jelly by then, his glasses on the other side of the room and blood spewing from his nose and mouth.

"You want some more, Eric?" I demanded. He just cowered in a ball, covering his head with his lanky arms.

"No?!" I yelled. "You had enough?! Where's the fucking insulin?" I asked as I picked him up by the collar on his shirt.

All the little prick could do was point. He tried to get the words out, but they weren't there. I think that he'd shit himself too.

He pointed to a glass-door refrigerator underneath the register, and I saw the bag there with my name on it. I had no time to lose.

I grabbed the paper bag and looked before I left. Sure enough, everything was there. Insulin, glucose, and syringes.

By then, Eric had crawled himself into a corner, wincing and sobbing like the pussy that he was. A bunch of people had gathered at the commotion, but they kept their distance. I'm sure that they thought I was a junkie or something. I didn't give a rat's ass.

I jumped the counter and ran through the crowd. Nobody tried to stop me. Nobody even made eye contact.

As I passed the cashier, I could tell that she was on the phone with the cops, but that didn't faze me a bit.

I ran out the door and into the mass of people between me and the side street.

By the time I got to the alleyway, I don't think anybody knew where I'd gone. I'd done my best to get the hell away from everything, just like John Dillinger would've done.

"I've got it buddy!" I said as I got to the carrier and hurriedly crouched down and opened the crate. "We're gonna be all right."

I sat cross-legged and pulled him out gently. He looked up at me and seemed so relaxed, so at peace.

I put him on my lap, pulled out the vial of insulin, and ripped open the plastic bag of needles, sending them flying in every direction. I took a deep breath to try and calm myself as best I could.

I grabbed one of the syringes, took off the protective cap, inserted it into the vial, and did my best to stop shaking. It took everything that I had, but I measured as close to twelve units as I could. Once I did, I grabbed the scruff of his neck, gently shoved the needle in and put the hammer down. And with that, it was done.

I held him real close there in my lap, leaning against the military green dumpster that had acted as our camouflage in that moment.

I could vaguely make out the red hue of police cars off the brick walls around us, but I didn't hear any sirens. I was sure that they would be able to tell that Eric was a little prick, and they'd probably recognize that he got what he deserved anyways.

So, we lay there, propped up against that dumpster in some rat-infested alley in downtown Las Vegas. Just the two of us.

And in that moment, I was completely at peace. I really was.

I closed my eyes and imagined that we were back in Chicago again. I forgot that I was sweaty and grubby. My hand wasn't bothering me a bit, and the alley didn't smell all that much like feces anymore either.

Me and Miles were lying on the couch watching TV, and Jenny was busting my chops about one thing or the other. We had doctored up a pizza and were watching the Cubbies lose another heartbreaker. It was springtime, and as usual, the boys just couldn't find their bats.

Jenny and I were talking and joking about nothing at all. Not a goddamn thing.

But we were home again. In that moment, sure as shit, we were there. We really were. Right back in the sweet spot of our lives.

CHAPTER 19

It was probably fifteen minutes or so I'd guess. I awoke to the sound of my phone ringing.

Sure enough, it was Hope. But by the time I could get it out of my pocket, there were two cops standing over me with a flashlight shining right in my mug. I guessed that they heard the ringing too.

It didn't much matter though. Miles was gone by then.

His body had already started to stiffen up, the way that a body will do. I set my phone on that cold, damp concrete so I could pick him up with both hands.

"Come on, man," one cop said. "We've gotta take ya in."

I stood up, carefully cradling Miles in my arms as I rose. I rubbed his head real good. Right behind the ears, just the way that he liked it.

"What about Miles?" I was somehow able to get out. "What about my dog?"

"I'm sorry, pal," the one cop said as he held out a pair of handcuffs. "I think your buddy's already gone."

POSTLUDE

So, that's how I got here today. I told you from the start that I was gonna share my story with you whether you gave a shit or not.

Like I said, you've probably got your own problems and all. I'm sure that you do.

As for me, I don't really have all that many anymore. I went through hell and back over the past year or two, at least it felt that way to me. Shit. Maybe it would've been a cakewalk for you. Heck if I know.

But if you asked if I'd do it all again, I'd have to tell you the truth. Hell yeah, I would. In the blink of an eye.

I lived to tell the story, which is more than a lot of guys can say.

In a way, maybe I'm glad that I landed here. Truth is, I don't know where else I'd have wound up otherwise.

At least I found myself a quiet little corner to write all this crap down. You know, for posterity, just like my mother would've wanted.

I got to tell it the way it happened too. Not how it should've happened or how I think somebody would've wanted it to happen. I didn't sugar coat a goddamn thing for anybody.

I owed it to Jenny. I owed it to my old man. I sure as shit owed it to Miles. And if I've learned anything at all on this rocky ride, it's that I owed it to myself too.

You see, it's just like my old man always used to say: "It all comes out in the wash."

And you know what? He was kinda right.

I mean, by the time you get around to reading my bullcrap story, the Cubbies just may have gone all the way. As for me, I've got my money on it, just like I always have.

Against all odds, I'd throw everything on the line for those loveable losers. Because if they can go all the way, well, that's pretty much proof that anybody can. And I think that we all need to believe that these days.

But in the end, it doesn't much matter. We all wind up in the same place, regardless of what path we take to get there. I've seen firsthand how sometimes the roads with the smoothest pavement turn out to have the sharpest turns and the steepest inclines. But we traverse them nonetheless. Just like those goddamn salmon.

As for me, I'm already gone. I guess you could say that I took the road less traveled.

Do I wish that I'd recognized that black-eyed dog when I saw him? Hell yeah, I do. But even if I had, there wouldn't have been a whole heck of a lot that I could've done about it. And like I told you, I never was much good at spotting stuff like that anyway. If I were, I wouldn't be here in the first place.

You see, there aren't a whole lot of assurances in this life. That much I know. I'd bet that I could count them all on a finger or two.

But one thing that I can promise you beyond a shadow of a doubt is that no matter what route you take, you're gonna wind up there, hiding out in the same backstreet alley, sleeping in the same divey hotel room, slouching on the same old barstool, answering to the same damned mug in the mirror.

We all do. Kicking and screaming. Just like the pussies that we are.

Already GONE